too much left unsaid

too much left unsaid

A NOVEL BY
LEE COLLINS

ISBN: 9780985807757

Published and printed in the United States of America by the Write Place. Cover and interior design by Alexis Thomas, the Write Place. Cover photography by Barb Ashton.

For more information, please contact:

the Write Place
709 Main Street, Suite 2
Pella, Iowa 50219
www.thewriteplace.biz

Scripture verses were taken from the King James Version of the Bible.

To Dan and Barb, our parents and our children.

And we know that all things work together for good to them that love God, to them who are the called according to his purpose.

Romans 8:28

HUMMEL FAMILY TREE

CONNORS FAMILY TREE

McENROE FAMILY TREE

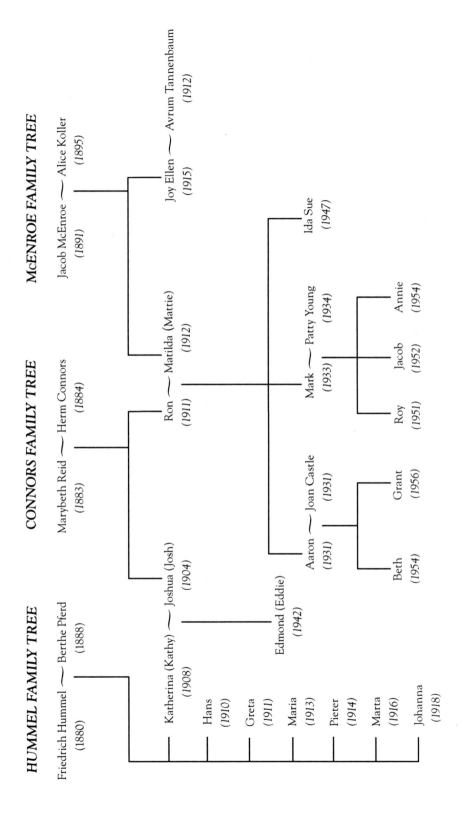

1

Mattie
JULY 21, 1969

*C*an *you believe it? Man walking on the moon! And we've just watched it! Imagine. Right here in my living room. I'm so glad you're here with me to see it. Help yourself to another brownie—or, no, we've been watching over two hours, let's go into the dining room and have something more substantial.*

I made pimento-cheese sandwiches—Ron's favorite—and some Perfection Jell-O salad. Sit right over there while I get the tea.

I can't get over it. "One giant leap for mankind." This will go in my journal, for sure. Commander Armstrong today set foot on the moon.

Yes, you can smile, but I do write in a journal every once in a while. Funny, but if you were to read my journals you wouldn't see much written down there. You'd see notes on the weather and what I fixed for meals. I recorded if we'd taken a drive or I'd gone to a church meeting. There's nothing there about most of the important things that happened in my life—

Oops, sorry I splashed the tea. I didn't burn you, did I? Good. I'm glad I didn't get it on your jacket. Here's another napkin. I don't know why I'm so clumsy today. Maybe I'm just excited because you're here.

Mercy me—my life's been so much more than what you'd see written in my journals, I can tell you. You know I love to tell stories, but the real story is filled with events I've never shared with anyone before. So much has been kept secret for so long.

Seeing history made today reminds me that in my fifty-seven years a lot of water has gone under the bridge, and you must be wondering about everything that has shaped our family. So many broken lives, so many dreams unfulfilled, so many surprises God has revealed. So much left unsaid.

I believed for a long time that everything in my world was as it should be, but so much was missing. So much was missing.

52 years earlier

On my fifth birthday, August 24, 1917, Papa took me aside. He told me, "You're big enough now to help with dishes and feed the chickens. We'll start your allowance today." I knew little two-year-olds like my sister Joy weren't big enough to help, and they didn't get any 'lowance. I was special.

Papa counted out five pennies, one for each year. He told me he would give me this magnificent sum every week from now on.

"I can buy a' ice cream cone," I exclaimed with delight.

"No, Mattie, my dear. Four cents isn't quite enough to buy ice cream."

"One, two, three, four, five," I counted. "There's five here, Papa. I can get a cone at the soda shop for five pennies."

"Yes, but you must always give your thanks to God for your bounty, my sweet. God loveth a cheerful giver. We need to show God how thankful we are. One penny must go into the collection plate tomorrow. You'll need to save your four pennies until next week and then you'll get five more—one for God, and four for you."

"If you say so, Papa," I told him, but I didn't quite understand. "Then next week I will buy my cone. I'll buy candy at the candy shop and I can give some to Joy, too."

Papa called me his sugar plum and gave me a big hug. His hugs scratched my face, but they made me feel safe and they always smelled good, just like the pipe that he smoked.

I spent my four pennies on candy at the candy shop, but the next week I still did not have enough, after I gave my one penny to God, to buy an ice cream cone. It took a few weeks of always being a penny shy for my five-year-old mind to figure out that saving a penny one week would allow me to have five pennies for the ice cream cone the next week, and still have a couple to spend on candy.

The day I figured it out, Papa bounced me on his knee and declared I was the smartest little girl on the planet.

—

Parkersville, Ohio, was my world, a small rural town where Papa and Mama, me and my little sister Joy lived together. We had a little white house at the edge of town with farm land across the road. Only a few blocks from us was the school that Papa took care of as janitor. I was so proud that I would soon be going to school, though I already knew how to read a little.

My papa loved me. I'm told I was a fussy baby, unable to nurse, exasperating to Mama. I didn't understand why at the time, but Mama stayed in bed a lot. Her Aunt Susan, who lived just down the street, often came over to take care of her. I loved Aunt Susan. We'd read books together, and I would make up stories to tell her. When my little sister, Joy Ellen, was born, Mama spent lots of hours with her, rocking and cuddling her. Joy was a sweet, calm baby. Mama doted on her. But Papa loved me.

Sometimes I would hear my parents arguing. Mama would raise her shrill voice and I would stop my play to listen.

"Jacob," she complained, "what am I to do with that child? You fill Matilda's head with stories. I can't get her to do anything."

Papa didn't raise his voice, but he spoke very slowly. "If you'd open your heart to Mattie and appreciate her more, she'd welcome it, Alice. Listen to her amazing gift with words and ideas. She sparkles with imagination. Listen to her tell stories to Joy sometime."

I did love to tell stories. And Joy loved them.

"I have no friends here. Can we go somewhere else? Your friends resent me, call me an outsider. They hate me because you chose me over them."

"You're imagining it. Take the girls out walking. Meet some new people."

"How can I take Matilda anywhere when she is so willful?"

Shortly after that, my papa went off to the war.

—

I was only six years old when my father died in the Spanish influenza epidemic of 1918. I didn't understand what had happened. I only knew he had gone away to make the world safe for democracy. That's what he told me when he gave me his Bible to keep for him while he was gone.

Aunt Susan later told me he went for training to Fort Sherman, Ohio, preparing to go fight in the Great War. The flu swept through the camp in the late summer and early fall. Many soldiers died within a few days. By the time the news came, Papa and many others were just put in a big grave nearby. Mama hurried to Chillicothe, but she was already too late to bring Papa's body back to Parkersville. I never saw my papa again.

—

After papa died they held a memorial service for him at Parkersville Presbyterian Church. Everyone loved my papa. Lots of people came to the church. Ladies from the church would hug me and cry. I cried, too. I wanted Papa to be there with me, and smoke his pipe, and put his arms around me.

Mama complained about her headaches. She'd clean our little house from top to bottom, scrubbing floors and walls. Then she would clean all over again. She would yell at Joy and me if we left anything out of place. Except for the yelling, she pretty much ignored us. I took Joy aside and told her stories I made up. I missed my papa so much.

One day Mama got a letter from her brother in Texas. Uncle Bubba's letter told her to pack up us girls and go down there. When she read the letter she let out a joyful whoop. She smiled at us, the first smile in a long while. She swept Joy up into a hug and headed for our bedroom. Over her shoulder she yelled to me, "Pack your things, Matilda, we're going to Texas where there's money to be made in the oil fields. This is no place for us with your daddy dead."

I rebelled. "No! I don't want to go. You can't make me."

With Papa gone I didn't want to leave Aunt Susan. I bolted out the door and ran down the street to her house.

Mama came storming after me, yelling to Aunt Susan, "Where is she?"

I hid behind Aunt Susan's big dresser and listened. Mama told her aunt about her brother's offer to take us in. She said I was just being stubborn.

"I know this is all hard for you, Alice," Aunt Susan said. "Remember Mattie is also confused." She hugged me as I crept out from my hiding place. "Maybe you should leave her with us until you get settled with your brother. Taking both youngsters would wear you out. I'll work with Mattie. I'll help her understand."

"She's a stubborn child and won't listen to me," Mama said, collapsing onto the porch swing.

"Bob and I will see that Mattie keeps up with her school work. I'll have her write to you."

Mama covered her eyes and shook her head. "Maybe that would be best," Mama said, turning to go. "But only until I can get settled and come back for her."

—

My life with Aunt Susan and Uncle Bob fell into a comfortable routine. I studied my lessons and did well in school. I missed my dear papa. I talked to him in my prayers when I talked to God. I missed my mother and sister, too, wondering where they were and if they might return. Every year as my birthday came around, Aunt Susan had me write a letter to Mama. I always asked her when she was coming back to get me. Mama did not respond to the letters when I wrote at seven years old, or at eight, or nine years old. "Has Mama forgotten all about me?"

I asked my great-aunt.

The year I turned ten, Aunt Susan told me I should stop writing, that Mama had asked her not to send any more letters. That was the year I got a letter containing a single dollar bill and a short message:

Dear Matilda,

I hope you are being good for your aunt Susan. Life is hard here in Texas, and I have had to make do. You should consider yourself lucky that you are there. Your new daddy told me to send you this dollar that you can use any way you want. We will not be able to send you any more for a very long time. Do whatever your uncle and aunt tell you to do and be good.

Alice Wilson

I looked at Aunt Susan. "I'm being good, aren't I?"

"Of course you are, dearie. You're my sweetheart."

"What does she mean—a new daddy? How could I have a new daddy? My papa died." I didn't understand her words. "I know my papa loved me—I know Mama doesn't!"

Aunt Susan opened her arms to me, almost smothering me in her big breasts. "Your mama loves you, too, Mattie. It's just been hard for her. She married Mr. Wilson so he would take care of her and Joy."

Maybe it was my own fault that Mama left me."Why hasn't she come back? She said she would, didn't she?" I'd asked those questions many times before.

"It's best to put her out of your mind, dear. She has another life there and you have a life here with us. You are content here, aren't you? You should think of all the good things you have here with us. You are safe and loved."

As I was holding the letter, the dollar dropped to the floor.

"What do you want to do with your dollar?" Aunt Susan asked.

"I don't want her old dollar. Throw it away."

I saw Aunt Susan pick up the dollar and tuck it into her apron pocket. I guess she put it into the college fund we were building.

I couldn't understand. How could Mama send such a letter and not even sign it "With love"? How could she not even sign it as "Mama"? Would I ever see her, and my sister, Joy, again?

I looked at the letter again. I crumpled it in my hand. Then I threw it down and raced from the room yelling, "So there!"

2

Kathy
1918 – 1938

Summer heat oppressed the plains of North Dakota. An impending storm promised to ease the 1918 drought, but now the lowering clouds felt threatening to the children huddled on the porch of the small cabin. Katherina hunkered down with her young brothers and sisters, telling them some of the folk tales they had heard so often from their mother. Her ears were tuned to the sounds from behind the door: moans and grunts, an English voice soothing the cries, her father's German muttering. The younger children accepted the noises from within as sound effects to the story of Snow White's perils. Only eight-year-old Hans and Katherina herself paid any mind to what they heard. Even at ten years old, the girl knew the sounds were bad.

Mutter's intermittent screams diminished to sighs, then rose again, like Snow White's cries as the huntsman raised his knife to slay her.

The groans quieted. Suddenly a small cry emerged from within.

"Katherina," her father bellowed. *"Kum! Schnell!"* Leaping up, she rushed inside. The shutters were closed. An oil lamp lit the single room. The rank smell of blood, of sickness, turned her stomach, forcing her to swallow her bile. Blinking at the darkness, her eyes focused on the bed where *Mutter* lay silent, blood soaking into the worn sheets under her. A small, squalling form lay naked beside her. *Vater* was yelling German curses at the woman assisting his wife, telling her to leave.

"Take the baby, Kathy. Wrap her up," Mrs. Kingston instructed the girl, as she tried to staunch the flow of blood from the mother. "It's been a hard bearing, and Berthe needs to rest." Kathy took the child and wrapped her in the clean, faded *decke* her mother had already prepared.

The tiny girl's cries quieted. Silence filled the room for an instant, then

Friedrich's curses resumed as he watched his wife's color drain. "*Gott in Himmel. Nein! Nicht tod.*" The other births had not gone like this: six healthy births, six children, from herself down to the eighteen-month-old Marta. *Vater* was claiming that it was the fault of this English woman attending. She must leave them. She must stay away.

Katherina cringed at her father's curses. She knew how quickly his rage could turn physical, especially when he'd been drinking. Mrs. Kingston hovered over Berthe, doing what she could to comfort her. "God bless you, child," she murmured—to the new baby? to Katherina? to Berthe?—what did that matter? The curses filling the room drowned out the blessing. Mrs. Kingston ignored the father's words as she bent over the dying mother, the moans diminishing until they ceased altogether.

At length she turned to Friedrich. "I'm afraid there is nothing more that can be done for her. Should I take the child to care for? I will bring Mr. Kingston and his brother to help you bury your wife."

"*Nein, nein! Gott in Himmel! Geh weg!*" Friedrich shouted. He shoved the woman toward the door as the children cowered in a huddle on the porch. "*Komm nicht zurich!* Don't come back! Go away!" he shouted with another stream of curses.

"Kathy, care for the baby," Mrs. Kingston said as she bent down to hug her. "I'm so sorry about your mother. We'll be back tomorrow to help with things."

Katherina clutched the baby and followed Mrs. Kingston onto the porch where the other five children stood in confusion. "Come in and say goodbye to Mama," Katherina sobbed. "She is sleeping now. She'll wake up in Heaven like *Aschenputtel's* mother did." Her tears fell then, as she tried to picture how life without *Mutter* would be.

—

When Mr. and Mrs. Kingston and other neighbors came the next day, Friedrich drove them away.

"It's your fault. We always healthy babies had before and Berthe did well," Friedrich managed to say in his broken English.

"Now, friend, be reasonable," Mr. Kingston said. "There was nothing Margaret could do for Berthe."

"*Nicht Freund!* She bewitched my Berthe, to seek her help. *Mein Frau* would not have died if she had not let your wife come in."

Friedrich barred the door against them. Stricken with grief, he closeted his family in their small cabin. He refused all offers of help. Friedrich buried Berthe himself in the small plot on their farm. He sent away well-wishers.

After Berthe was in the ground, he called the six older children to the cradle where the small baby *Vater* had named Johanna lay. He told them, "Together we stay. We don't need outsiders. We will make it on our own." To Katherina he said, "You must cook and housekeeper be, Katchen. You are the oldest. You must the *Mutter* now be."

"Please, *Vater*, how can I do that? Mama wanted us to go to school to learn English so we can have a better life."

"*Mutter* is *todt*. I need you with the babies. That is what must be! You will at home stay. We will not with the English mix."

—

Friedrich's determination to avoid his neighbors saved the Hummel family. By the fall of that year, they began to hear tales of many people, including those Friedrich had sent away, succumbing to a deadly flu. Kathy would later learn that hundreds died in the state and thousands throughout the country.

By the following spring, the isolation became too much. Friedrich allowed Katherina to take eight-year-old Hans and six-year-old Greta to the country school at the Crossing. But she had to explain to Miss Smith, who had been her teacher since she started school, why she would be staying home.

"*Vater* says I cannot come any more. He says I am needed with the babies."

"Kathy, I'm sorry. I wish you could be here. You must keep up your learning. Let me give you this book of Grimm's fairy tales written in English. Do you know their stories?"

Kathy loved Miss Smith. She loved being called Kathy instead of Katherina or Katchen. She clutched the book with its woodcuts. She smiled for the first time since her mother's final struggle with childbirth months before. "*Schneewittchen!* I know her with the seven little men. And *Aschenputtel!* How wonderful. Mama told us these stories, that she learned as a girl in the *Schwartzwald* in Germany. I tell them to the *kindern*. Now I can read to them in English, too. *Danke*, thank you, Miss Smith."

"When you need more books to read, dear, I will find you some."

Kathy cradled the book in her arms and raced back home.

Whenever Kathy had a break from the labor of the household or from the demands of the children, she would read. She continued to tell her brothers and sisters tales her mother had told her of the Black Forest. She read them the stories in English from the book Miss Smith had given her. Often when chores were done, the children would join Kathy in playing make-believe based on the tales.

The fairy-tale world made Kathy's childhood tolerable.

But not everyone enjoyed the games. One day, as the children were laughing, pretending to be Snow White and the dwarves, Friedrich came storming into the house from the barn. He ripped the book from Kathy's hands, throwing it to the floor.

"*Stille.* Be still," he hollered, holding his head and stumbling toward the table. "No more of those *kindische Marchen.* There is work to do around here." He grabbed the heavy wooden spoon sitting there. He swung wildly, striking Kathy, sending her reeling. Blood gushed from her cheek. Friedrich continued to strike Kathy as she covered her face and curled up. He struck again and again until he staggered drunkenly to the floor.

Marta started to cry, but Greta hushed her, and hurried the younger children outside. Hans went to Kathy's side to help her. He stared at his father on the floor. "I thought it was supposed to be the stepmother who was mean. Maybe *Vater* needs to hear the stories himself. Next thing he will send us off to the woods to make it on our own."

"I'm sure it's hard for him to hear *Mutter's* stories when she is gone," Kathy replied as she picked up the book and smoothed the pages.

"When *Mutter* was still here, she took the beatings. When we lost her, he turned his anger on us," Hans replied. "Stop saying, 'Tomorrow *Vater* will feel better.' Each day things keep getting worse."

—

As the years passed, things did get worse. The family struggled to cope. The children never knew when Friedrich's mood would swing to violence, but they learned to steer clear of him when they could—which was nearly impossible in the tiny cabin, especially during the winter. Snow had almost buried the small cabin by mid-winter of 1924. Friedrich had done nothing but drink, sleep, and order the children about all winter long. The children were down to eating cold oatmeal made from the meager stores they had put aside in the fall.

One evening Friedrich dragged himself up from a drunken stupor and entered the kitchen calling for his supper. "Where are you, Katherina? Get your nose out of that book. Bring me something to eat."

Kathy scurried to get some cold oatmeal in front of the drunken old man. If she hurried, she might calm his anger and keep him from taking it out on the other children. Friedrich swept the dish to the floor, yelling for something hot.

"I'm out of firewood, *Vater*," Kathy said quietly. Friedrich yanked off his belt and slammed the table, looking about for Hans, by now thirteen and stronger than his sister.

"Why is this so? Hans! Why have you not brought the wood?"

"The snow is two feet deep. The only firewood is deep in the woods. You can go yourself to gather it if you want it so much." Friedrich sobered at the words of defiance. He swung the belt at his son, drawing blood as it lashed across Hans's face. Hans grabbed at the belt and pulled his father off the chair onto the floor, where the older man sat dazed.

Kathy rushed to help her father up, but Friedrich pushed her away and sprawled against the table. "You'll be sorry for that, son." Friedrich shook his fist, and struggled to raise himself.

"Never," Hans yelled, "never as sorry as you will be." Turning to his older sister, Hans stared her down. "Don't you see, Kathy? This life is useless."

Hans bundled up, storming out of the house, plowing through the snow. In a few hours he was back with what wood he found, and he stoked the fire for his sister.

"You're right, Hans," Kathy said as she looked over at her father, now slumped at the table. "We get further behind each year."

"I can't take this any longer. Do what you want, but I'm leaving here for good."

Kathy wept to see her only ally in the house, the only one who could stand up to *Vater*, shuffle out the door, pulling it shut behind him. *Who can I rely on now? Everything is falling on me. Will this ever end?*

It was fourteen years before they saw Hans again.

—

The children grew, and Kathy despaired of things ever changing. When young Will Kingston heard that Hans had left, he came by to see what help he could provide. By then Kathy had reached her full height, only five feet even, but the curve of her breasts and her shapely body showed that she was no longer a child. Will's interest in Kathy was soon cut short when Friedrich threatened him with a shotgun. Word got around that the oldest Hummel daughter was not eligible as long as there were little ones at home.

It scarcely mattered to Kathy. She was trapped there, powerless. If she could ever escape all *Vater's* demands, she'd leave the farm in an eye blink. *Life all on my own! What a blessing that would be. I'll go to a big city. I'll find a good job and live by myself. I'll have nothing to do with any man. I'm sick to death of raising children. Ahead I see nothing but labor on the farm caring for* Vater. *But if I ever have a chance to get away, I'll jump at it.*

—

Early in 1938, Hans came home for a visit, bringing Karl Dietrich. Karl was a builder who had befriended Hans in the years after he had left the family, when he was down on his luck. Hans had told Karl he had sisters back on the North Dakota farm, one of whom might make the perfect wife for a builder. By then Greta had run off with a traveling salesman before she was sixteen. Maria managed to complete enough schooling to begin teaching and moved to Dickenson. Pieter was able to find work in the local lumber mill, and he continued to save money until he could take off for Omaha. Marta served as a maid-of-all-work to the couple who owned the dry-goods store at the Crossing. When that family decided to go West, Marta went along to care for their children. Only Kathy and Johanna remained to work the farm with their father.

A man of action, Karl soon was courting Johanna, the youngest Hummel sister. He asked her to marry him. Kathy and her father would be left on the farm.

Johanna's wedding day of September 25, 1938, should have been joyous.

"Kathy, be happy for me," Johanna begged, as she saw the sadness in her older sister's face. "Karl makes a good living building houses near Omaha. He has a wonderful house built that has an apartment for you and father. We want you two to come stay with us."

"No, no thank you. I've had my fill of cooking and constant cleaning for *Vater*. Nothing I do is good enough to suit him. I'll make my own way now if you will take *Vater*. I'll head for Chicago and independence."

Friedrich overheard Kathy's conversation with Johanna. He thundered into the room, demanding, "How can you desert me? After all I've done for you."

"Yes, you've given me bruises and pain. You've cursed me, abused me, and hurt me. I hope you appreciate Johanna and Karl's willingness to keep you. I certainly do. I plan—" Kathy stopped mid-sentence, shocked at her own sudden boldness.

Friedrich was speechless. She had never talked back to him before. "I only meant to help you learn to be a good *Hausfrau*. I had your best interest in mind," he told her. "I never struck you except to teach you a lesson."

"*Nein, Vater*, no. The lessons you taught were the wrong ones. You have made my life miserable. I'm thirty years old now, and I am done with all that. I will go to Chicago. I won't have to care for you or the children. I'll live my own life at last."

3

Mattie

It's almost forty years ago that I was a senior in the Parkersville High School Class of '30. Someday I want you to tell me what you were busy planning in your senior year of high school. Of course I had a best friend—Ruth Greene, with her blond bobbed hair and blue eyes. All that year she was deep into wedding plans: dresses, flowers, receptions, and all the trimmings, planning her June wedding to John Reed, twenty-six-year-old son (and future owner) of Reed and Son Hardware. She'd have four bridesmaids, including me, of course. "I'll wear a satin, knee-length dress with a flowered cloche with a veil," Ruth told me, "and peach georgette dresses for the bridesmaids handmade by Marie Johnson." I listened to Ruthie's elaborate ideas, but laughed when she said to me, "Mattie, you and Ron should get married, too. We could have a double wedding. It would be such fun."

April 1930

My sweetheart, Ron Connors, was tall and handsome. He was my lab partner in sophomore biology, and we always had such a good time laughing and talking in lab. He asked me out and soon we were going steady. Ron worked part time at the M & P Grocery and was putting aside money to buy a used Model T. We were making plans to marry, but not yet. I loved school. To keep learning as much as I could about the world and life was important to me.

"Ron and I do want to be married," I told Ruth, "but I'm off to the College of Wooster next year if they'll accept me. We'll marry when I graduate."

Ruthie shook her head, and showed me some more magazine pictures of what she wanted for her wedding cake.

The evening of April 9, a Wednesday, the course of my life changed. Ron and I had cooked up a batch of fudge in Aunt Susan's kitchen. We chatted idly about many things—Ruth's wedding plans, his mother's illnesses, A *Tale of Two Cities*, which we were reading for senior English class. We talked about his big brother Josh, who was in the navy. Ron had tried to enlist last fall, but they turned him down because he had rheumatic fever when he was nine and it ruined his heart.

"Ron," I said as we poured the fudge out on wax paper to cool, "I have some special news. Let's go out on the porch so I can tell you."

As we crossed through the living room, Aunt Susan and Uncle Bob were listening to *Amos and Andy* on the radio. Satisfied that they were distracted, we settled down on the front porch swing, laughing and kissing. We could hear the radio in the background accompanied by Uncle Bob's deep laugh. Aunt Susan, tall and substantial, would be quietly smiling no matter how funny the program was, but Uncle Bob, almost as wide as he was tall, laughed loud enough for both of them.

We were waiting for the fudge to cool, but the chocolate fragrance floated in the air. Ron nuzzled my hair. "You smell like fudge, Mattie. I could eat you up!"

I turned my lips to his as he softly kissed my neck. I sighed, but I pulled myself back, breathless. "Be careful, Ron. You know we're waiting. We can't get carried away until we marry, and that's still a long way off."

"Too long! I want you right now. Let's just get married now."

"Ron, I've something I have to tell you. I got my letter from Wooster today. You know I was crossing my fingers that they'd take me—and they did. Ron, I start this fall. All I need to do is sign the letter and send the check." I could hardly contain my excitement. "Uncle Bob and I are going down to the savings and loan tomorrow to draw out my college funds. You know how we've been saving for my college ever since I came to live with Aunt Susan and Uncle Bob."

Ron pulled back, frowning. "I don't know why you want college. Don't go away, Mattie. I really need you to be my wife. Marry me." Ron caressed my breast. I shivered, then pushed away his hand.

"Careful. We're waiting, remember."

"It's hard waiting. Four years is an eternity."

"Don't make this so difficult, love. It'll pass quickly. You know I love you with all my heart. I do want to marry you, but not yet. I'll be your wife, but first I have to go to college. I have so many questions. I want to study psychology and writing and learn to write books for children—or the Great American Novel. Once I have my education, we'll get married. We'll have lots of children. I'll be the best wife and mother that ever lived...not like my mother."

Ron knew about my mother's leaving me when I was six. We had talked about it many times, just like we talked about everything else. He drew me closer. I cuddled up in Ron's arms while we shared a lingering kiss. We sprang apart when we heard Uncle Bob opening the door to the porch, laughing, ready to share the joke he'd just heard.

"I was listening to *Amos and Andy* on the radio. Holy mackerel! They're a riot. They're on their way to Chicago by train with four ham-and-cheese sandwiches. They think they'll make it big there. They're so funny. You ever listen to them, Ron?"

Before Ron could answer, the phone rang inside. We heard Aunt Susan pick it up and say hello. A minute later, we heard her scream, "No, it can't be!" Uncle Bob rushed inside. I clutched Ron's hand and we hurried in. Aunt Susan sat on the steps near the hall table gesturing mutely to the phone. I ran to embrace her, unsure what was going on. Bob picked up the receiver. He said hello, then listened dumbly.

"No! You must be wrong! Chief Lancer been there? The vault was completely empty? I don't believe it! Are you sure? They think Hugan did it? Where is he? Okay, keep me posted." Uncle Bob put the phone down, dazed. He helped Aunt Susan to her feet. Tears streamed down her face as they clung to one another.

"What's going on? Did someone die? Aunt Susan, tell me what's happened." I studied their faces desperately for a clue. "Tell me, please."

At last, Uncle Bob turned to us and spoke. "That was Jim Foster, our neighbor." His voice faltered as he got out the next words. "Jim's downtown and people are converging on the savings and loan. The vault is open and empty. The police are looking for Mr. Hugan, the vice-president. He's disappeared. All the money has disappeared with him!"

"All our savings," Aunt Susan murmured. "And your college fund, Mattie. All gone. What will we do?"

The rest of the evening was a blur. I wept in Ron's arms. He held me and let me cry it out. "I have a little bit saved toward my Tin Lizzie. If that would be any help you're welcome to it."

"Oh, Ron. You are so dear." I burrowed into his arms, crying again. After my tears were spent, I told Ron, "Thank you for thinking of that. I don't think that would be my answer. Let me go back and talk with my aunt and uncle. This loss affects our whole family. I need to find out what it means to all of us." We hugged each other a hasty goodbye.

The first thing Aunt Susan said to me after Ron left was, "Oh, Mattie. I am so sorry. Maybe they will find Mr. Hugan and recover the money."

"Now, Susan," Uncle Bob said, "that seems unlikely. If they catch him, he'll have already spent it. We might as well think of it as gone forever." He put his arm around me to show me he was sorry, though he spoke more to his wife. "We'll get along. We'll manage. We can build our savings again, but it looks like Mattie's college plans are off for a while."

I knew the truth—this wasn't a temporary delay. With the money gone, any thought of starting college had disappeared as surely as Mr. Hugan had.

I went to my room and, as always when I needed comfort, I opened the Bible Papa had left me. *All things work together for good.* That's what Papa would often tell me. I lay in bed, flipping through the Bible, looking for answers and thinking things over. The reasons I had given Ron for delaying our marriage no longer applied. I loved Ron. I meant to marry him after college. If I must put aside college, why not commit to marriage right away? Why wait when the reason for the delay was gone? Perhaps marrying Ron was the window God was opening, even as He closed the door on my college dream.

—

I woke up the next morning with a plan. After talking it over with Ron, I approached Ruth. "Next week is spring break. Go to Wheeling with me on Monday, Ruth. Stand up with me while I marry Ron."

"What? You mean it? It's because of Mr. Hugan and the savings and loan, isn't it? Oh, Mattie! If you wait until June we could have a double wedding. We could share the day."

"I can't delay now, Ruthie. I'm afraid if I don't marry Ron right now, something terrible will destroy this dream, too. I'm taking this as a sign that God wants us to marry now. We won't tell anyone yet. I can still finish the school year and graduate."

Ruth wasn't the only one who'd heard about the embezzlement—judging by the jabbering at school, the news had spread quicker than lightening through the town. Mine wasn't the only life turned upside down. I mourned my lost dream, but I refused to let it destroy me.

On Sunday I told Aunt Susan, "Ruthie and I are taking the train to Wheeling tomorrow to see about the wedding." Aunt Susan smiled her approval. "I'm staying with Ruth overnight afterwards since we're on break. I'll see you Tuesday morning." I put on my best green dress and shoes, the ones I wore to church. I donned hat and gloves, packed a small train case, and kissed Aunt Susan goodbye. I met Ron and Ruth at the B & O station to catch the early train.

On the train, we chattered about the huge step ahead. "Are you sure this is the right thing to do, Mattie? You can change your mind even now," Ruth told me.

"I'm sure. I know this is what God wants for me. Why would He take away my chance for college, if not to lead me here?"

"It's too bad your mother and father aren't here."

"I miss Papa. I wish he were here," I told her. "And I miss my little sister, Joy. I can't really say I miss Mama. Why hasn't she ever come back for me?"

Vendors came down the train aisle hawking sandwiches, drinks, and candy. Ron bought three sandwiches, but I pushed mine aside, too wound up to eat a bite. When the train arrived at the Baltimore and Ohio train station, a magnificent *beaux arts* building with marble floors, we didn't even stop to look around. We crossed to City Hall and bought the license before hurrying to the First Presbyterian Church. Ron was humming, "Yes, sir, that's my baby, now." We asked the kind-looking elderly woman where we could find the minister. She pointed us to his study, where we found him busy reading.

Ron waved the marriage license. "Please marry us, sir. She has finally said yes and I don't want her to change her mind."

The pastor put aside the Bible he had been reading. He studied us, not quite ready to do it. "Are you sure this is what you want?" he asked me.

"Quite, quite sure!" I laughed. *There is no turning back now.*

He led us into the side chapel. He donned his robe and stole. "Dearly beloved," he began, reading the ceremony from the Book of Common Worship.

This is it. We're really doing it. Ron and I as one. Thank you, God. I'll be the best wife that ever lived.

The pastor finished reading the vows. Just as Ron said, "I do," I could feel my face flush. The next thing I knew I was lying on the floor, and Ruth was bending over me.

"Are you okay? I knew you should have eaten something."

I sat up, dazed and embarrassed. "Sorry. I don't know what came over me."

"It happens all the time," the pastor assured us. "Don't worry about it. Mattie, do you take this man to be your lawfully wedded husband?"

I sat up straight on the floor and smiled. "I do."

"Kiss your new bride, Ron. You are man and wife."

Ruth, Ron, and I returned to the B & O station to share our wedding supper, steak and fried potatoes. I'd had nothing to eat all day, and I wolfed it down.

Ruth presented me with a new hankie embroidered with a C, for Connors.

"Good luck, chickadees. Guess you'll soon be making whoopee." Ruth waved, smiling as she boarded the afternoon train back home.

—

That evening, Ron lifted me over the threshold of the tiny room in the Ohio Hotel. We bounced on the bed and cuddled, very ready for our one-night honeymoon. Ron kissed my face and neck. I removed my green dress and hung it carefully in the closet. More kisses and caresses as we sank into the bed, continuing to embrace. The tension that had grown as we held ourselves back waiting for marriage was released at last. The next morning we two sleepy lovers returned to Parkersville. We told no one our secret until the end of the school year.

—

Throughout the next few months, planning for Ruth's June wedding filled all our time. I helped Ruth send out invitations. I had my peach georgette bridesmaid dress fitted. Aunt Susan looked at me with tears in her eyes. She told me, "I know you and Ron want to marry, and you'll be very happy together. I'm just sorry that we can't afford to do for you what the Greenes are doing for Ruth."

"Don't worry, Aunt Susan. I know you would give me the world if you could. I don't envy Ruth. She and John will have a beautiful ceremony, but they won't be any happier than Ron and I." I wanted to share our secret with her, but something held me back. Maybe it was that I was basking in the memory of that day and night in Wheeling. Once I graduated I would be ready to tell the world.

Graduation night I took the wedding ring Ron had bought me, which I had hidden in my jewelry box. The simple gold band looked magnificent on the third finger of my left hand. I took Ron's arm. Together we approached Uncle Bob and Aunt Susan. "We want your blessing, dears. We already have God's blessing, we know."

Aunt Susan's face lit up. She embraced us in a big hug. Tears of joy flowed down her face. "My dears. My dear ones. Here I was thinking about how to afford your wedding, and you have gone and done the deed. You two are a match made in Heaven, Mattie. God bless you! And we do, too."

"Thank you, Aunt Susan, for loving me and caring for me all these years. You've been a wonderful mother to me. Ron and I will try to repay your kindness and love."

Later in June, when Ruth and John Reed had their ornate ceremony in the Methodist Church, Ron and I joined the celebration. It was indeed elaborate and delightful. But as much as I enjoyed Ruth's wedding, my own memories of the day I married Ron glowed brighter.

4

Kathy
1938 – 1941

Kathy looked around her small room in Mrs. Alcott's boarding house on Chicago's North Side. She straightened up her bed and put away the clothes she had rinsed out over the small sink the evening before. Friedrich's move from the farm to live with Johanna and Karl made it possible for Kathy to achieve her independence. She stared out the window at the grey city scene. Working at Travelers Insurance was so much more satisfying than raising children in a crowded, tense cabin. Her siblings were all settled in their lives, and she was, at last, free to be herself—the self she'd never allowed herself to be.

Each morning she could catch a streetcar at the corner and head downtown to the Wrigley Building where she rode the elevator up to the twentieth floor to her job. *I've learned about reinsurance, and the endless hours copying figures into columns is enough to engage me, but not so much it taxes me. Mr. Simpson said I will get a raise with my next paycheck, even.*

As she got off work each evening she was amazed by the scene of people bustling every direction, each with some burning purpose which did not include her. The city was overflowing with people for whom she had no responsibility. She liked that fact. Over the years she had anesthetized herself to her own emotional needs. But in Chicago she was beginning to recognize a desire for friends, so she sought a way to fill that need.

Greta Schlegel, who also lived at Mrs. Alcott's boarding house, invited Kathy to attend a service at the Uptown German Baptist Church not far from their home. Raised more on fairy stories than on Bible tales, she didn't know what to expect, but she was warmly welcomed there.

Greta introduced her to Mrs. Hannah Dondersohn, who ran the Wednesday evening programs at the church. "I think you would enjoy working in our outreach dinners, Kathy. With a second big war in Europe brewing, there's a lot of anti-German feelings around. We serve the free meals to demonstrate that we are true Americans."

Kathy happily joined in helping with the weekly dinners. Often service men in the area found the dinners a welcome refuge. No alcohol was served. Smoking was not permitted. Kathy would greet, cook, or bake as her turn came. Her *apfelkuchen* was featured once a month, always lauded as the best apple cake in town.

One Wednesday night, when she had been working at the kitchen for a little over a year, someone new walked through the door. With his over-six-foot frame and regulation navy crew cut, he turned heads as he walked through the door. Kathy greeted him. She always attempted to look taller than her five-foot frame by wearing her wedge platform shoes and piling her golden hair high on her head, upswept in the Betty Grable style. She was suddenly very conscious of her Germanic features with the slight scar on her cheek, her intense blue eyes behind wire-rim glasses, narrow lips, and slightly crooked teeth. The sailor didn't seem to mind at all when he saw the huge smile on her face. She smelled of the *apfelkuchen* she had been baking, much better than any post food had ever smelled.

"Welcome, sailor," Kathy said, as she had greeted many others.

The man reached out and hugged Kathy, lifting her from the floor in his embrace, swinging her about before setting her down.

Confusion and embarrassment engulfed Kathy, but it was short-lived as other soldiers and sailors came through the door. Kathy, face glowing, continued to greet each new arrival. The guests sat down to turkey dinner. Reverend Linsey asked them all to bow their heads as he returned thanks. Soon Kathy and three other helpers were carrying the filled plates to serve the guests. She tried to avoid the sailor, but he kept his eye on her.

As the meal ended, Reverend Linsey explained a bit of the beliefs of the church and invited everyone to join in some singing. Kathy noticed the sailor stayed to add his fine baritone voice to the chorus. He seemed to take pleasure in the old hymns: "The Old Rugged Cross," "What a Friend We Have in Jesus," "Trust and Obey." Kathy, standing with her friends at the side of the room, sang along in her almost-monotone soprano voice. She continued to watch him from the corner of her eye. She touched the facial scar from her childhood, more obvious when she blushed. When the singing ended, Reverend Linsey encouraged everyone to come on Sunday. As the crowd left the church, the man paused to speak to Kathy. "I want to apologize for my exuberant greeting. I'm sorry I was carried away. I couldn't help myself. I thought you were an angel from Heaven." He winked and added, "I'll see you on Sunday."

Just as he promised, the next Sunday he was there fifteen minutes early. As she sat down he maneuvered to sit next to her to share the hymnal. After church Kathy and several friends headed down the street to the soda shop.

"I'll treat you all to cherry Cokes," he offered as he joined them. To Kathy he said, "My name's Josh Connors. I want to make up for last Wednesday. You are my angel, you know." Kathy blushed, her scar reddening.

Kathy and Josh lingered over the drinks while the others excused themselves, giving Kathy knowing looks. Josh told Kathy he was from Parkersville, Ohio, serving as a trainer at the Great Lakes Naval Station. He had sailed the seas for almost twenty years for the United States Navy. "As the world situation seems to be going from bad to worse, and Adolph Hitler's Nazi storm troopers surged into Poland, Norway, and Denmark, I began to question what life was all about. I'm thirty-eight years old, and I don't find the 'pleasures of youth' so pleasurable any longer.

"I was seeking something more, so I tried visiting churches. I loved the free Wednesday night dinners at the church. But my fourth visit was the best. That was the week you took your turn in the dining room."

Later Josh walked Kathy to her boarding house. He managed to convince her to give him the boarding house phone number. "Don't call too late. Mrs. Alcott retires by nine," Kathy warned.

Monday night, as Kathy came in from work, Mrs. Alcott, the landlady, relayed the message from Josh. "He gave me the exact wording for you: 'I'm picking you up at nine on Saturday so we can explore Chicago. Don't refuse me as I only have a two-day pass.' He sounded like a nice fellow. I told him you would be ready to go."

Much to her surprise, Kathy found herself looking forward to the date.

—

Josh arrived at the boarding house before nine on Saturday morning. They did the town, window shopping in all the stores in the Loop, then riding the "el" to Evanston to walk along the windy beach. The smell of the lake and the pleasant breeze blowing against their bodies made them feel alive. Though it was frigid, they took off their shoes and stockings in order to feel the damp, cold sand between their toes. Soon they couldn't feel their feet at all. Laughing, they ran up the beach to find a place sheltered from the wind where they could brush off the sand and pull their shoes back on. Josh rubbed Kathy's feet to warm them, and they huddled close. All the time they were talking.

"Weren't the Loop windows wonderful? Which windows did you like the best?" Kathy asked. The topic seemed safe. She felt that soon Josh might ask her about her family and her childhood, and she wanted to avoid it as long as possible.

"Marshall Field's without a doubt. It feels like they're rushing Christmas, but it's already Advent. It was fun to see the story of Snow White portrayed. It's my favorite fairy tale."

"Mine, too. I learned it as *Schneewittchen* in North Dakota where I grew up. We spoke always German at home. We learned no English until we started to school." *So much for not talking about my childhood.*

"You're smarter not talking German these days. Hitler's moves in Europe have people stirred up. My buddies call sauerkraut 'liberty cabbage.' "

"Hitler's actions shocked us all. He's *boshaft*, wicked. I can't understand how anyone can trust him. Nazism isn't anything like the Germany my parents left to pioneer in this country."

"He's gobbling up the whole of Europe, for sure. For myself, I'm confident the war in Europe will end soon with Germany's conquest. Then Hitler's belligerence will be toned down. Peace will come."

"Josh, how can you believe that? Adolph Hitler will never be satisfied until he conquers the world. *Krieg*, war, will come sooner or later. I wish we could avoid conflict and keep out of any involvement over there. Still, I sense that we will be in the struggle soon."

"Well, my enlistment is almost up. I expect to get out of the navy and settle down soon. I don't believe that we'll enter any European war. The United States has too many isolationists to allow us to be fighting foreign wars."

Kathy shook her head. "I hope you're right. History will tell. I'd so like to visit the *Schwartzwald*, where my *mutter* and *vater* grew up."

"I'll take you there when this is all over."

Kathy dropped Josh's hand and ran along the beach a short distance. Teasing was fun, but her eyes brimmed over as she thought of the tales of beauty her mother had filled her with as a child.

At the end of the day, they went to see a movie at the Uptown Theater, *Our Town* with William Holden and Martha Scott. As they left the theater and walked up Clark Street to Kathy's boarding house, Josh spoke. "How sad. I guess people don't realize that life's little moments are so important."

Kathy pondered. "Emily and George were so *gemeinsam*, so common."

"So much like us, do you mean?"

"I've lived that ordinary life," Kathy murmured. "I prefer my independence."

"But you need me there to make your life complete. Parkersville, Ohio, is enough like Grover's Corners, New Hampshire, for us to be that couple."

Kathy face burned, the scar prominent on her cheek. "You still owe the navy some time to finish your enlistment, I thought. You can't be making such plans yet."

"Not quite yet. But soon I'll be mustering out. Every day we're apart I'll write you a letter, until we're together for always."

Kathy stopped and looked right into his big brown eyes. "Wait a minute. We weren't talking about you and me. Or were you?"

"Give me a chance, Kathy, and I'll prove what a wonderful life we could have."

They had reached Kathy's boarding house, and she put out her hand. "Write me a letter and I'll see how it works out."

"Let me come in and continue to convince you."

"Mrs. Alcott wouldn't approve. I'll see you in church tomorrow."

—

The entire day had been perfect, and Josh was sure life could be perfect, too, with Kathy. For Josh it was all but settled. He was so sure that Kathy would come around to his way of thinking that he sat down that Saturday evening after their first date to write two letters. The first was to Kathy. The second was to his mother and father, Marybeth and Herm Connors, promising that when he came home on leave he would bring a "wonderful surprise."

—

They did meet in church that Sunday morning, December 7. Kathy agreed to spend the rest of the day together, riding the "el" to Oak Park, strolling the neighborhood where Frank Lloyd Wright homes were plentiful. As the train reached Oak Park Avenue, people were rushing in all directions, some running, some crying, some lining up to use the pay phones, many shouting. Newsboys were yelling, "The Japs have attacked Pearl Harbor," "U.S. surprised. Many killed in Hawaii."

Josh stopped in his tracks, grabbing Kathy's arm. "NO! I was at Pearl. Some of my buddies are still stationed there." He grabbed for a copy of the *Tribune* and shook as he scanned the news. "Kathy, I need to get back to the naval station to see if there's anything I ought to be doing now."

He wheeled her around and they ran for the train headed downtown. On the trip back Josh's mind jumped from present to past to future.

"Now you must marry me! Right now, before I'm sent overseas," Josh declared as they parted downtown.

Kathy stared after him as he headed to the bus that would take him back up north. She boarded the Clark Street streetcar to Mrs. Alcott's, mind reeling. So much was happening at once. *Was Josh proposing or joking? The day before we were talking about the movie and married life and all of a sudden the conversation was about us. When Josh said, "You need me to make your life complete," we both laughed. Was any of that for real? I don't want to get involved with Josh. As much fun as we've had, I'm not buying it. Though I know Josh is a much better man than Vater, I can't risk my independence. I'm too old to change. He probably didn't mean any of it except as pleasant small talk. I may never see him again.*

—

The next day, Kathy received Josh's letter in the afternoon mail. She laughed at his review of every part of their Saturday date.

Dear Kathy, my dear Katherina,

I love you. Marry me. Think about the fun we had today and multiply that by a lifetime of joy we can have together. I love you. Marry me.

You are my angel and when we settle down to our lives together it will be heaven. I know you think I have said "You're my angel" to other girls before you, but you really are sent from Heaven and I know it! I love you. Marry me.

What a foolish man. Proposing marriage after our first date, Kathy thought.

I've never been so happy as I am at this moment. I loved the cold beach walk when we could see clear across Lake Michigan. I could see into our future life together—life in Parkersville. I love you. Marry me.

I'm on leave starting December 28 and plan to take a trip home. You must come with me and meet Ron and Mattie and the boys and my folks. We'll tell them we are engaged and making plans for our wedding. I love you. Marry me.

The world is dark now. Hitler's Germany is itching for a fight, but

I don't think we'll be in it. **I love you. Marry me**. I'll take you to see the world when that conflict is over. We will have a wonderful life together. **I love you. Marry me.**

Remember *Our Town*. Parkersville will be our town if you only say yes and come there with me. **I love you. Marry me.**

I know we are older. That just means we are wiser and we have to make up for the years we wasted not knowing each other. **I love you. Marry me.**

She began to cry as she read over and over, "I love you. Marry me." *How could he even think such a wild, impossible thing? I know what my life will be and it doesn't include marrying a sailor.*

I'll be seeing you in church tomorrow, though you won't have this letter yet. We'll go to church and then ride out to Oak Park. I've heard that the Frank Lloyd Wright houses are everywhere there. We can dream of our house—plan the family we will raise. **I love you. Marry me.**

How about two boys and two girls? We can start as soon as we tie the knot. **I love you. Marry me.**

And by the way, **I love you. Marry me.**

All, all, all my love, Josh.
P. S. **I love you. Marry me.**

As she finished Josh's letter, her reserve faltered. *Marrying Josh would never work for me; it is too crazy—yet, he was so considerate, and he so* wunderbar *is.*

Josh's words stirred the feelings she had long kept under tight control. Could he be a Prince Charming coming into her life—one she never expected to meet? To her great surprise, unexpectedly, amazingly, Josh's letter sealed her fate. There was no way to even respond to him until Mrs. Alcott called her to the phone. "It's that sailor again," she said. "Should I be worried?"

"Not at all," Kathy told her. "I'm going to marry him."

—

With so many hurry-up weddings taking place everywhere, it took a few days for Kathy and Josh to get a license and arrange with Reverend Linsey to perform the ceremony. They were soon married and on the train to Ohio. Even as they watched the fields passing and listened to the rhythm of train wheels, Josh tried to warn his new bride about possible tension when they arrived in Parkersville.

"Life on the farm was hard. Dad and I did all the planting and weeding and harvesting. We battled the elements but always seemed to lose. There's seven years between me and my little brother Ron, and many of those years my mother was carrying one child or another that didn't live. Mother was ill so often, losing babies in a flood of blood before they were born."

Kathy nodded. "I know that hard life. It sounds a lot like living on our North Dakota farm. Except *Mutter's* babies came nearly every year and lived. When she died in 1918 at Johanna's birth, she left seven of us. I was the oldest. At ten, I was expected to raise my brothers and sisters. Life was difficult, but we got by. We often had little to eat in the long cold winters but oat porridge. I loved my *brudern* and *schwestern*, but there were times I would have given anything to get away. I felt obliged to be there."

Josh touched Kathy's hand, and kissed her face. "It's easier for a boy, I think. I needed to leave home, Kathy. I wasn't afraid of hard work, but I wanted adventure. The navy, the 'See the World' call, beckoned me. As soon as I was old enough, I got out. I sent money home each month. Never much. Mom and Dad moved to town, to a little house near the railroad tracks, shortly after I left. Dad does carpentry and odd jobs. They barely manage. It took a long time, but I think Mom and Dad are reconciled to my choice of career."

"At least you could leave. I was to the farm a prisoner. *Vater* insisted I should care for the children, and for him as his health began to fail. As they grew up and married and left, one by one, if I would ever get my chance to leave I wondered."

Josh leaned over to hug his new bride. "I'm so glad you did get away, my love."

"When Johanna was ready to marry Karl and go to live in Omaha, I pictured myself left alone with *Vater*. I feared I must give up my dream of leaving."

"But you did. You came to Chicago, and we met."

"If Johanna and Karl had not convinced *Vater* to leave the farm I might still be there. Finally, freedom. I couldn't get out of there fast enough."

"I know you'll love Parkersville, and they'll love you."

"I hope so. I am giving up my job and my place in the city. I could in Chicago stay while you serve, you know."

"But you need to keep the home fires burning. I want to be able to picture you doing that in the bosom of my family."

I hope I made the right decision, Kathy thought. *The bosom of Josh's family does not sound very welcoming.*

The train rolled on through Illinois and Indiana. Josh told Kathy about Ron. "I know my younger brother Ron looks up to me. He calls me his hero! I wish I could be what he imagines I am."

"Did he want to join the navy, too?"

"After I signed up, Ron couldn't wait until he was old enough to do the same. He put together models of navy ships. He made a scrapbook of all the postcards I sent from various ports of call. He read all the books and magazine articles he could find that had anything to do with the navy. When he was old enough he went down to enlist, but his heart had been damaged by the rheumatic fever he had when he was nine."

Kathy looked into Josh's brown eyes, trying to gauge what her welcome might be. "Do your *Eltern* still think you were wrong to join up?" she asked.

"I don't know. They seem to have mellowed as I've told them about my travels. I've seen a lot of sights. I was serving in Hawaii in 1930 when Ron married his high school sweetheart, Mattie. They have two sons now. Aaron is almost twelve. Mark is nearly ten. You'll meet them soon, and they'll all love you as I do."

"I hope you're right."

"The night after our first date, when I wrote to you, I wrote to them. I told them I would bring 'a wonderful surprise,' and here you are."

5

Mattie

After Ron and I married in secret his mother never welcomed me as a daughter-in-law. Josh must have known his mother wouldn't approve of his marriage to Kathy, but I'm sure he tried to reassure his new bride that she had made the right move to marry him and come away to Ohio. Less than a month before Josh brought Kathy home for the first time, we were shocked by events taking place in the larger world, as we listened to them unfold on the radio in our own living room.

December 1941

On December 7, Ron's mom and dad were at our house for Sunday dinner: chicken fricassee, baked corn, green beans, and peach cobbler for dessert. I was in the kitchen cleaning up and putting away the food when Ron yelled, "Mattie, come here!"

Ron and his folks were listening to the radio. I hurried in as Ron hollered, "We've been attacked! The dirty Japs have bombed our ships in Hawaii. We'll be at war for sure! Thank God Josh isn't there anymore."

I rushed out to listen. I held Ron's hand as we listened to the news. Bowing my head in prayer, I breathed, "What a tragedy. God, be with this country and with this world. Show us thy will."

Herm, Ron's dad, shook his head. "When we go to war, Josh will be in it."

"He's served his twenty years," Mother Connors said, twisting her handkerchief. "That's enough! He should be able to get out before he has to go to Japan."

President Roosevelt addressed Congress the next day in a speech that was broadcast live on the radio.

Yesterday, December 7, 1941—a date which will live in infamy—the United States of America was suddenly and deliberately attacked by naval and air forces of the Empire of Japan...I ask that the Congress declare that since the unprovoked and dastardly attack by Japan on Sunday, December 7, 1941, a state of war has existed between the United States and the Japanese empire.

Within a day Congress declared war on Japan. We all wept and prayed Josh would be able to come home and avoid the battles to come.

A few days later, the letter Josh had written Saturday night after his date with Kathy reached Marybeth. She called Ron and me to read it to us. He would be home on leave at the end of December, bringing a "wonderful surprise," and he knew they would be as happy as he was. I believe my mother-in-law prayed that the "wonderful surprise" would be Josh's mustering out of the navy and promising to return home. My sons, Aaron and Mark, hoped it meant their uncle would bring them some more ship models to build. Ron and I speculated about what the surprise might be. We weren't even close to the right answer.

—

On Monday, December 29, the whole family went down to the station to meet Josh. We watched him step down from the train—then turn to help a short, rather plain-looking girl descend to the platform. She was dressed in a simple gray coat over a white blouse and a wool plaid jumper, blonde hair piled high beneath a grey hat with a small veil.

"Meet my wife Kathy!" Josh beamed. "I've waited all my life for her and here she is. Kathy's minister in Chicago married us. Kathy, this is your family: Mom, Dad, my little brother Ron, his wife Mattie. And these young men are my nephews—our nephews—Aaron and Mark."

Silence. The boys saluted their uncle. Marybeth and Herm stood dumbfounded. Clearly, a new bride was the last thing they expected Josh to bring home.

"Wife? This is your surprise?" spoke Marybeth, in a masterpiece of understatement. "Um...How did this happen?"

"It was at church, where they served meals for service men," Josh offered. "Katherina is a wonderful cook. Her *apfelkuchen* is out of this world. I've been going to the German Baptist Church and they've been so welcoming. With the situation in Germany now, they're doing their best to show what good Americans they can be."

What most surprised my husband Ron, he told me later, was the plain-ness and obvious age of his new sister-in-law, though he admired how stylish she looked. Josh was already thirty-eight. Ron had come to think of his brother as the proverbial sailor with a girl in every port. He had never expected to see Josh settled down, least of all with this short, plain-faced stranger.

At least I had the presence of mind to receive the surprise in the spirit Josh had intended it. I stepped forward to greet my new sister-in-law, who looked apprehensive and a little lost. "Welcome, Katherina," I said, and squeezed her in a huge hug.

"Please, I'm Kathy. *Danke.* Thank you. Josh was telling me all about you as we rode the train here."

"Have you known each other long?" I asked.

Josh answered before Kathy could speak. "Only a few weeks, but we know we belong together." Josh put his arm around his bride. "The attack on Pearl Harbor helped convince Kathy to marry me at once. I planned a longer engage-ment and I expected to bring her here to introduce her as my future bride, but I couldn't wait any longer to get things settled for Kathy. My leave is over in a week. I don't know where they'll send me."

I smiled at Josh. "Bless you. You know God's guidance when you see it. He'll protect you, and we'll take care of Kathy until He brings you back safely."

The boys and I took the lead in walking Josh and Kathy down the platform to where the truck was parked. I was pleased for my beaming brother-in-law, yet I wondered what his parents were thinking. They looked at one another without a word.

It was clear to me that Marybeth would not welcome this stranger any more than she had welcomed me. Josh had brought another person who would distract him from his long-overdue role as the son Marybeth expected to support her. Herm took Marybeth's elbow and led her after us out of the station.

—

Ron and I opened our hearts to Kathy, making up for the coolness of Josh's parents. She was how I imagined my lost sister, Joy, might be—though Kathy was seven years older. In those first years we became close friends. Josh and Kathy found a four-room apartment upstairs in a house on the end of Main Street. I helped Kathy furnish the place with "old attic and early in-law" stuff. Josh prom-ised that soon he would return from the war.

Kathy wanted to return to the work world, and I helped her find a job with Roger Gordon's law firm. Gordon's former girl Friday had joined other young women leaving town to go to the cities to work in the factories for the war effort. I heard about the opening and recommended to Roger that he hire Kathy. After he talked to her about what she had been doing at Travelers Insurance, he asked her to start work as soon as she got settled.

Kathy took to her job amazingly well, picking up her duties at the office so quickly that Roger thanked me for recommending her. She often joined our family for supper, and I was pleased to see her putting on some weight. She shopped for new clothes and looked radiant, if a bit tired.

"Office work much better is for me than housework and childcare," Kathy told me as she returned from her first week at Roger's office. "I fear for bearing children, Mattie. I saw my mother hurt and finally die giving birth. I raised the children. It was enough for me."

Until that moment, I hadn't suspected that their honeymoon enjoyment had resulted in Kathy becoming pregnant. By wearing oversized clothes at work Kathy managed to keep her pregnancy a secret from all of us almost until she went into labor in late August. Josh, assigned to the Pacific fleet, knew nothing of his upcoming fatherhood until at last Kathy wrote him about it. He was delighted.

6

Kathy
1942

Edmond Joshua Connors was born in the newly established hospital on Hanson Hill on August 21, 1942. A long, painful labor, even with anesthesia to ensure a painless birth, left Kathy exhausted.

"Mattie, I can't believe it was so hard," Kathy told her sister-in-law. "My mother had seven, and as the oldest I was there for all the births. Until Johanna's birth she came through with no problems. Yet she died soon after Johanna was born. I trusted Doctor Dunn when he told me that the twilight sleep would take away the pain. Maybe it did for the first couple hours, but I think it also made it hard for Eddie to do his part. The labor was so long."

"Relax, dear. Women have been doing this for millennia. When you've held your sweet baby for a while, you'll forget the pain."

"The nurses whisked him away before I could even see him. They have him on a schedule already." Kathy let out a cry as she felt a new wave of pain. "I hurt so much. I think I am bleeding way more than I should be. *Mutter* lay in a puddle of blood when she died. I'm so afraid this might happen to me now."

Mattie put her hand on Kathy's forehead. She frowned. "You do seem a bit warm, but I'm sure everything will be fine. I'll look for Dr. Dunn and see if anything can be done for you."

When Dr. Dunn came in to examine Kathy, he scowled. "Get the operating room ready. We need to stop the bleeding." Within the hour he performed a hysterectomy. Kathy stayed in the hospital a full ten days, recovering slowly from the trauma of birth and surgery.

On the very day of Eddie's birth, a second baby was born in another part of Parkersville who was to become his good friend. Darwin K Jones (whose middle initial didn't stand for anything) was the first son, second child, born to Brenda (née Johnson) and Brick Jones in their little house in Coaltown, the colored section of town. He joined an eighteen-month-old sister, Sophie. The colored community welcomed him with joy and thanksgiving. Brenda was soon up caring for the toddler and the infant. In a few short weeks she returned to her work as a maid at the Hanson house, bringing the children along.

7

Mattie

Eddie was born just three days before my thirtieth birthday. Kathy was already thirty-four. I had been fooled, kept in the dark, about her carrying the baby. I never saw her suffer morning sickness, and I just didn't expect her to get pregnant so easily. Ron and I were married a whole year before Aaron was born. And little Eddie wasn't full term. He came only eight months after their honeymoon. In any case, Kathy's delivery was hard, and the hysterectomy ensured that Eddie was to be an only child.

August 22, 1942

I stood by Kathy's bedside in the recovery room, trying to comfort her.

As I turned to leave, Kathy touched my arm. "I wish Josh was here. I miss him so. He doesn't even know how Eddie rushed the calendar. Josh expects our baby next month." Kathy grimaced and suppressed the next cry. "I didn't want a baby so soon. I never wanted a baby at all. I want Josh here. I need him."

"Ron called our congressman, Representative Boyle, to try to get Josh a leave to come home for a short time," I said. It was a vain hope. With Josh in the Pacific, he would be unable to get home.

"I don't know how I can care for this baby right now, Mattie. I've done my turn at mothering with my brothers and sisters."

"That'll change when you feel stronger," I assured her. "Aaron and Mark are my life, though as they grow they seem to need me less. After Mark was born I still wanted to have a daughter, but Dr. Dunn warned me that my high blood pressure would make another pregnancy dangerous. I envy you your fine son. For now, don't worry. I'll take care of Eddie for you until you're back on your feet."

"You don't understand. I don't want to spend my life being just a mother! I know there must be more to life than shiny furniture and making *apfelkuchen*."

I didn't think she could be serious about what she said. "Once you're feeling better, if you still want to continue to work at the law office, I can keep Eddie during the week."

Kathy smiled to hear this offer. I was glad to have her here in Parkersville with a baby to care for. I thought she would change her mind about wanting to work.

Yet as soon as Dr. Dunn gave the okay, Kathy called me. I was preparing Sunday supper and answered the phone. "I'll bring Eddie over at 7:30 in the morning, Mattie. Thank you for offering to keep him. Roger wants me back at work tomorrow at 8:00."

That evening, after supper, the boys went off to play and I sat at our dining room table instead of heading in to do the dishes. Ron noticed the break in my routine.

"What's wrong, Mattie?" Ron asked me.

"Nothing—well, something, I guess. Kathy doesn't seem to realize how lucky she is to have this sweet boy. I'm thinking how like my mother Kathy is, abandoning her child to be cared for by someone else. When my mother took Joy to Texas and left me with Aunt Susan, I couldn't understand how she could do such a thing. I still can't. Now I think I'll be another Aunt Susan, keeping Eddie while Kathy does what suits her."

Ron picked up the dirty plates and silver and, in a move he seldom made, started to fill the sink to wash the dishes. "It's hard to understand, but we're all different. Maybe you and Kathy can help each other appreciate both kinds of work—yours and hers."

8

Kathy
1942 – 1945

*L*adies' Home Journal, Woman's Home Companion, McCall's, Redbook—in fact, most of the women's magazines of the day portrayed the coming postwar world as one where a woman would find fulfillment keeping her kitchen floor spotless and her house sparkling. Laundry, food preparation, bed making, dish washing, and childcare were sufficient to make a woman's life complete. Kathy, watching Marybeth and Mattie, and recalling her own mother's life, was certain that she preferred her work in the law office. Much as she loved Eddie, his demands on her life had not been in her plans when she left North Dakota. Living through her husband and children's lives was not at all what Kathy wanted for herself. She wanted so much more.

Josh's letters, when they spoke of their future, echoed the women's magazines. "You and the children will run to greet me when I get home from work. Flowers on the table. A warm supper of beef and potatoes. Yum! And *apfelkuchen,* of course."

She wrote back that if they both were working, there would be enough money to hire domestic help.

In 1945 the war in Europe had been won, but fierce fighting continued in the Pacific. Josh's ship, the USS *Indianapolis,* was crippled in March by a *kamikaze* pilot. They returned to Mare Island, California, for repairs and refitting. Because the process would take several months, Josh wired Kathy: "Stateside unexpectedly. Bring Eddie by train to San Francisco Station. I love you. Josh."

Kathy looked forward to seeing Josh after three years, with nothing in the meantime but his letters. She had no intention of taking Eddie. She wanted to reconnect with her husband. She asked Mr. Gordon for a leave from work. She arranged with Mattie to keep Eddie. Mattie was much more adept at managing a child in his "terrible twos." She packed a small bag with a pretty negligee and a minimum of other clothes and telegraphed Josh when to expect her train. As she took the three-day journey, she thought about the bus trip she had taken half a year before to visit her dying father in Omaha.

—

It still grieved her. She was out of touch with her siblings, but six months before Johanna had telephoned Kathy long distance in the middle of the night to tell her Friedrich had had a stroke. He was not expected to live out the week. Kathy took a Greyhound bus to Omaha, hoping to have a chance to say to her father the words she had rehearsed in her mind. *You drunken fool. You never understood that when* Mutter *died we children were grieving, too. It was only and always about you and what you wanted. We got by with little thanks to you. We grew stronger, but we grew apart. I don't know how to love my own son because you never showed us love.* When she got to Omaha, her speech prepared, she was too late. Friedrich was already in a coma. Still she spoke the words to the dying body of her father in the hospital bed. There was no sign he heard. That night he died.

Saying the words out loud had helped, but because she hadn't had the opportunity to make her father understand how he had destroyed her childhood, Kathy was more determined than ever to be her own person, not an appendage of any man. Josh would have to listen.

—

At San Francisco's Union Station Josh met Kathy's train with a bouquet of flowers, a toy Disney Snow White figure for Eddie (very popular with the recent movie release), and his Kodak. He swept her up, twirled her around, and kissed her hungrily. "I love you, Kathy." He looked around and asked, "Where's Eddie?"

"Josh, I couldn't bring him. He has a bad summer cold. The trip would be so hard on him," Kathy lied.

"I wanted to see him, Kathy. I wanted to hug and hold him."

"I just couldn't travel halfway across the country with a two-year-old on the crowded trains. You and I need some time together to get reacquainted. Aren't you glad to see me?"

Josh grinned and gave her a squeeze. "I can't tell you how glad. Smile for my camera and then we'll go to the room I rented for the next few weeks." Josh's buddy Butch had greased some palms to wangle the place for their reunion, not far from the train station. Josh didn't intend to let his disappointment mar their delayed second honeymoon.

He wrapped his arm about Kathy and escorted her to their temporary home. Kathy looked about the room, not much more than a bed, some folding chairs, and a card table where an electric hot pot and a waxed paper bakery bag sat. Kathy swallowed hard. What could she say?

"It's beautiful, Josh. I love it." She opened her small train case and took out the negligee, smoothing its wrinkles. "Close your eyes and I'll slip out of these traveling clothes."

Josh ogled his wife. "I'm your husband, Kathy. Don't be shy."

"I feel like a newlywed today. Please!"

Josh turned, realized he could see Kathy in the reflection in the window, and grinned. "Okay. Just this once. Maybe we can make Eddie a little sister on this honeymoon," Josh joked.

Soon they were making up for lost time getting to know each other's bodies. Kathy knew, though she hadn't told Josh, that she'd not have any more children. She was able to share sex without fear. It was more wonderful than she remembered.

Later Kathy got up to brew a pot of coffee, and they sat at the little table eating croissants from the bakery down the street. "I'm sorry I couldn't bring Eddie, but I just couldn't manage," Kathy said, apologizing again.

"I'm sorry you didn't, but it's okay. As soon as we can get these Japs under control, I'll be there in Parkersville with you both. You can quit your job and devote yourself full time to Eddie and me. And the other kids," he said, grinning mischievously.

Kathy frowned at her husband. "I don't plan to quit my job, Josh. I tried to tell you that in my letters."

"Nonsense! You may need to work for a little while, until we get settled, but then I intend to support you. You'll be my little 'lady of the house' that keeps our home a welcoming place to return to each evening." With a laugh he continued, "You can have my pipe and slippers waiting along with my supper when I come home from work."

"No, Josh," Kathy's face turned red as she rose from the table. "No, no, no! I did the 'lady of the house' routine with *Vater*, and the *kindern*," she said, reverting to the old German terms from her childhood. She burst into tears.

"Okay, okay, dear. Don't cry. We'll have plenty of time to settle this. Lie down with me and relax," Josh said. "I've two weeks of leave ahead."

Kathy threw on a robe and scurried to the bathroom in the hall. She rinsed her face and spoke to her image in the mirror. "We can put this off. I'll wait for a better time, but Josh has to know that what I want and need is very different from his dream of me. I'm going to enjoy this next few weeks while I can."

But the two weeks were cut short when just three days later, Josh received word that his leave was cancelled. The *Indianapolis* would sail earlier than planned. The lovers parted far sooner than they had expected, before they had a chance to resolve their differences. Josh's parting words to Kathy at the train station were, "Get ready to give your notice to Mr. Gordon when I get back. I love you."

Kathy returned home in a bad mood.

—

Josh's ship sailed with a secret cargo. When the U.S. dropped an atomic bomb, the components of which had been delivered by the *USS Indianapolis*, on Hiroshima, Japan, the war in the Pacific ended sooner than anyone had hoped.

9

Mattie

The end of the war was the beginning of our troubles. As soon as President Truman made the announcement at 7:00 p.m., August 14, 1945, that Japan had surrendered, millions of people worldwide went joyfully crazy with the news. Everywhere people were celebrating. War over! Boys coming home! End of food shortages, gas rationing, news censorship, the blackouts, the scrap and war bond drives! Loved ones stationed far away would soon be home. Gone were the fears of a costly invasion of the Japanese homeland. The war-weary nation exploded in a frenzy of joy and thanksgiving. It was V-J Day.

August 14, 1945

In Parkersville, the police and fire sirens pierced the air. Church bells rang from every steeple. The war was over. Everyone was screaming, squealing, shouting, whooping. Cheering crowds filled the downtown, waving flags, hollering, blowing horns and whistles. Factory steam whistles blew louder, then softer, then louder, for attention. Aaron and Mark and their grade school friends grabbed pots, pans, lids, and wooden spoons and marched up and down the streets. They loaded Eddie, soon to turn three, into their red Flyer wagon and handed him a flag to wave. Firecrackers and shotguns added to the din. I couldn't wait to celebrate with Kathy, so I grabbed Eddie and hurried down the street. No use trying to drive over. The streets were crowded with tractors, cars, and revelers.

When we arrived, Kathy was collapsed on her sofa clutching a yellow envelope. Her eyes were red with tears. Her always neat blonde hair was a complete mess. Her breath came in gasps. I took one look and swallowed hard. "What does it say, Kathy?" I asked, not wanting to know. Kathy thrust the telegram in my hands without a word. She sobbed and hugged her son.

The Navy Department deeply regrets to inform you that your husband, Joshua Herman Connors, is missing in action in the South Pacific.

"Mattie, it can't be!" Kathy cried. "I'm sorry about our last quarrel. When I left him I was in a terrible mood. I told him I can't be the wife he wants. It's not who I think I am. It's not who I want to be." Kathy, anger mixed with sorrow, threw herself in a heap on the sofa, banging the cushions with her fist. "I'm sorry, Josh. I'm so sorry!"

Eddie looked at his mother's disarray and burst into tears himself. I stared at the telegram. I read and reread the words, wanting not to believe. "It only says missing. He's missing," I ventured. "They'll find him, Kathy. You'll see. He'll return to celebrate with us."

With that glimmer of hope she calmed a bit. I packed Eddie an overnight bag so he could "sleep over" with his cousins. For the rest of the day we glued our ears to the radio, dialing up and down for any news that might tell us more. Speeches, celebrations, only an occasional reminder of the great costs to our nation. The next morning we searched for news in all the papers: *The Plain-Dealer*, *Wheeling Times-Leader*, and *New Pittsburgh Constitution*. Ron even went down to the B & O station to buy the *New York Times* when it came in by train. It was there we read the news that we didn't really want to see.

The Times shouted the war's end in four banner headlines:

JAPAN SURRENDERS, END OF WAR!
EMPEROR ACCEPTS ALLIED RULE
M'ARTHUR SUPREME COMMANDER
OUR MANPOWER CURBS VOIDED

In the lower right corner of that August 15 front page was the article that answered our questions:

Cruiser Sunk, 1196 Causalities
Took Atom Bomb Cargo to Guam

Impossible! The *USS Indianapolis*—torpedoed. Two weeks before! How could that be? It was Josh's ship—sunk by a Japanese submarine. Almost 1,200 people on board! For some reason the navy hadn't realized the ship was even missing. Yes, the war was ending, but what excuse could there be for the navy not knowing about it? For 100 hours the crew struggled in the salt water, before 315 survivors were picked up. If they only rescued 315, was Josh one? What happened to the over 800 missing navy men? When and where could we find out more?

"Why, why, why?" Kathy asked over and over. "What happened to Josh? Why haven't we heard? He should be coming home to me! He promised. He promised! How could God let this happen to him—to me?" Kathy rocked back and forth, covering her ears, shutting out this hateful, unfair news. As Kathy grieved, the rest of us prayed and worried.

A few days later another telegram came confirming Josh *was* killed in action. When it arrived there was no comforting Kathy, however we tried.

We held his memorial service with no body to be buried. I shed new tears as I recalled the service I sat through as a six-year-old after my father died a war ago. Like me, Eddie would be growing up without a father.

10

Kathy
SEPTEMBER 1945

Kathy could scarcely get her mind around the tragedy. Josh, who had promised to come home to her, was killed when the war was almost won. Josh, who had spent but a few weeks of the last four years with Kathy, would never return after all. Josh, who she knew more from his letters than from seeing him face to face, with whom she had quarreled at their last meeting, Josh would never hold her again. Even Eddie's embraces, dissolving into puzzled tears to match his mother's, did not snap Kathy out of the deep despair. Eddie continued to stay with Mattie and Ron while Kathy wrapped herself in sorrow.

"Do something, Ron," Mattie implored. "She needs to take her life back. Remind her Eddie needs his mother. Tell her that you miss Josh, too, but she has to come out of mourning and join the world again."

To please Mattie as much as to comfort Kathy, Ron walked across town to Kathy's house. Before he left he picked up the emergency key Mattie kept in the kitchen drawer. Ron knocked. No answer. After several attempts, he hesitantly let himself in. No one in the front of the apartment, so Ron made his way back to Kathy's bedroom. Kathy lay curled up on the single bed facing the cream-colored walls. The room was a mess, clothes tossed atop the small, white dresser, the room's only other furniture. The flowered bed coverlet lay in a heap on the floor. The morning sun was streaming around bright, yellow-flowered drapes.

Ron spoke. "Kathy, I'm so sorry. I miss him, too. We were so ready for him to come back triumphant."

Kathy, eyes red and swollen, turned to face him. "Oh, Ron, I know other lives were lost, too. Josh and I had so little time together. He was so strong, so *wunderbar*. We had so much planned for the future, and now there is no future for us. No future for me."

"Don't think that, Kathy. Think of Eddie. Think of how much Josh loved that you had his son. You have a place here in Parkersville in all our hearts." Ron's words were brave, but he soon found tears running down his face. Unable to control himself, Ron began to sob.

Kathy rose and led him to her bed to sit. Her tears, that she thought she had exhausted, streamed down her cheeks again. Ron put his arms around her. Together they wept. There seemed to be no stopping it. At last, cried out, they lay together. Softly he stroked her hair and she accepted his ministrations. The tension of denial that had paralyzed her began to melt away. She sank into the pillows. She let go of the bitterness that the telegram had mustered in her. They lay together for a long time. Kathy relaxed finally into a much-needed deep sleep.

"You are a beautiful woman," Ron whispered into the air. "No wonder Josh loved you. I didn't understand when he brought you here that January day what attracted him to you. I've come to appreciate your inner beauty as you have grown to be one of us. Please get better. Rejoin the world." He held her close, and she slept in his arms.

Ron, too, unwound, embracing his brother's wife. She moaned in her sleep and turned over so her face was close to his. Gently he kissed her eyes, swollen from the crying. The feel of her soft skin on his lips caused his body to stiffen as he drew her closer. It didn't seem fair that he and Mattie had their family and life together and Josh had been taken away, leaving this woman alone in the world. How vulnerable Josh had left Kathy, bringing her to a strange town and going off to fight a war. Thoughts of his brother loving this dear woman wrenched his heart. She deserved protection and he could provide that, at least. She deserved loving, and he would give her that as well, if she would accept it. With that thought he drifted off to sleep.

Four hours later, Kathy awoke from a dream of Josh's tender embrace. At first she didn't realize that the arms holding her were not Josh's, so she cuddled closer. Ron stirred, and still half-asleep, he kissed her softly. She returned the kiss before she could stop to consider.

—

They lay together for the rest of the afternoon. At last, Ron stirred and looked at the clock on the table. Much as he longed to stay with Kathy, night was falling and he needed to get back to Mattie.

"Will you be all right now, Kathy? I have to get home. Know that you are loved and needed. We all want you to get through these hard times. Things do get better."

"If only Josh and I had the chance for a better parting than we had," she whispered; Ron had to strain to hear. "We quarreled when I went to see him this summer. He expected me to be the full-time wife and mother he envisioned. He didn't know me for who I am, but conjured up a dream wife. Maybe we could have worked things out, but now it's too late."

After Ron left, Kathy recalled the warm pleasure she had just felt in his embrace. *That is the way to heal the hurt,* she thought. *You see, Josh. It's your fault I am here with Ron. You should have come back to me.*

11

~

Mattie

Sometime in April, the year after the war ended, I was at Aunt Susan's house helping her sort and pack what she would take to Wheeling to the old folk's home. Since Ron and I had set up housekeeping, we hadn't spent a lot of time with my aunt and uncle, though we still loved to visit each other. I hated to admit it, but Uncle Bob needed more care than Aunt Susan could provide. If truth be told, she needed help, too—more than I could give her.

Spring and Summer 1946

"Not very much here that we will need there," Aunt Susan said as she surveyed the stuff piled up in the front room. "The pictures of family don't begin to tell our story, do they? The day your mother came to stay with us in 1911, just for the summer, we were already forty, years older than you are now." I packed up the framed family pictures in newspapers. A very few would accompany Aunt Susan. Most would go home to my house to be hung in the back parlor. One, of a young girl in a muslin dress, caught my eye. I studied the picture that had hung in Aunt Susan's hallway for years. "Who is this again, Aunt Susan?"

"That's my sister Matilda, your grandmother, when she was six. She married Caleb Koller, who took her to Texas when she was only twenty. You looked so much like her when you were little. Still look like I remember her."

I glanced in the hall mirror, still to be packed up. I tilted my head, imitating the stance of the little girl. Did I look like my namesake when Papa died and Mama left me? Now Aunt Susan was telling me I looked like Mama's mother. Was that why Mama left me?

"When Matilda was widowed in spring of '11," Aunt Susan continued, "she sent your mother to visit us that summer because she didn't know what to do with her. I guess I wasn't much better at dealing with the Belle of the Ball that was Alice Koller."

"Tell me more about Mother, Aunt Susan. She was sixteen, then, wasn't she?"

Aunt Susan sat back and reminisced, recalling those days.

"At sixteen Alice was too wise in the ways of the world: a little vamp stirring up the local swains. With her twenty-inch waist and her auburn hair swept up onto her head like a proper young woman, she made an immediate stir. The boys her own age vied for her attention, but she paid little attention to them. She set her sights on the twenty-one-year-old, hard-to-get Jacob McEnroe, your father.

"He fell for her charm. Soon she was expecting his baby, you. A hurried wedding brought her into Jacob's circle, but she never felt accepted there. The young women and their families snubbed her. She got all the blame for her condition, your father garnering only sympathy for being 'trapped.' 'She's different. She's common. And she's not from here.'

"Alice complained to me and your father what she sensed. I overheard her tell Jacob more than once that the others hated her. She thought they were jealous that she had landed him. She wanted to move somewhere else. Your father, though, thought that she was imagining things, and that after she had the baby they would have to accept her.

"Alice was uncomfortable with her pregnancy, adding fire to her complaints. With your birth things got worse. You fussed as a baby, not eating or sleeping well. Even while you slept, your mother worried all the time, dreading when you'd wake up to fuss again. She found the simplest tasks too demanding. I stepped in to provide care. We had a special bond between us, you and I.

"Three-and-a-half years later, Alice's pregnancy with your sister was much easier. When little Joy was born, everyone who saw her remarked on her beauty. Your mother delighted in taking Joy out in her carriage to be admired. You knew even then that Joy got all the attention. You clung to your papa. What a pity when he went away to war," Susan finished with a sigh.

"It was a pity!" Mattie said. "I didn't know what to do without him. I'm so glad you were here for me."

"When your father died and your mother took Joy to Texas, we considered ourselves lucky to be able to keep you. Though we thought at first your stay would be temporary, it turned out to be our lifelong pleasure. You were a delight to raise, Mattie. Your father would have loved to see how you turned out."

"I still miss him, Aunt Susan, though I love you and Uncle Bob."

"Do you miss your mother and sister, too?"

"Of course. No. I'm not sure. I'd really like to talk to Mama about how she could desert me. I could never leave Aaron or Mark, even though they are growing up to be their own selves. I do miss my little sister. I'd like to find her to discover how her life turned out."

"Alice was her own worst enemy. She made decisions too quickly and she regretted them just as quickly. I'm sure she regretted that she left you behind. I think the Texas life closed in on her, including meeting Mr. Wilson, and she never got back on track."

"Have you any idea where she and Joy are now?"

"No one knows. In her last letter from Texas begging me not to have you write again she said it made her too sad to read your letters. She had another family. Mr. Wilson had a son already. She hinted that she was carrying another child when she wrote. She told us to keep you and tell you to forget about her altogether."

"I couldn't forget. She left me with so many questions. Do you think my mother is still alive?" I asked her as I wrapped up the last of the pictures.

"I think you should assume that she isn't, dear. She was a frail thing," replied Aunt Susan as she eased her way into her chair. "You might try to find her through the Texas Department of Records or some such."

I considered the idea, but what with the packing and moving my aunt and uncle on top of the normal routines of my busy life, I didn't get the letter written until after Aunt Susan died.

—

My friend Ruth Greene Reed, who'd been the sole witness at my wedding, directed the Girl Scout day camp with me that summer after the war ended. Leading the Brownies and Scouts in activities was a break for me. I had been tied up with worry about Kathy's slow recovery from the news of Josh's death and with daily care of Eddie, not to mention moving Aunt Susan and Uncle Bob. All through July, Ruth and I busily planned and led the Brownies. It was fun, but tiring. One afternoon Ruth encouraged me to stop by her house for some fruit tea.

She seemed nervous as she poured our tea. She cleared her throat and said, "Mattie, how are things at home?"

"Busy, busy, Ruth. Aaron and Mark are off delivering their papers every morning and evening. They are taking all the lawn mowing jobs they can get. They're never around to help with Eddie these days. Ron works long hours at the post office, leaving early, getting home late. He often stops over at Kathy's apartment to check if she has any chores to do."

"I wanted to talk to you about that," Ruth began. Then she reached across the table to take my hand.

I frowned and asked, "About what?"

"Something's going on between Kathy and Ron. I'm almost sure of it. Surely you noticed something peculiar in how he's acting."

I vaulted up, knocking over my glass. Embarrassed, I reached for a kitchen towel and mopped away at the mess. "You're nuts, Ruthie," I said finally. "Nothing is going on. I'm surprised you'd spread such gossip."

"I wish it were gossip, Mattie. I'm almost sure Ron and Kathy are making whoopee."

I wrung out the towel and hung it over the edge of her sink. "You're wrong. I trust Ron." As an afterthought, I added, "I'll just ask Ron." *It's not like Ruthie to spread gossip. Nothing could be further from the truth,* I told myself. But there was that little nagging voice in my mind asking, *Could it be true?*

A few days later, before I'd gotten up the courage to talk to Ron, I got a call from Uncle Bob in Wheeling.

"Mattie, Aunt Susan has had a stroke. I think you need to come right away!"

I called the post office trying to find Ron. I tried several other places and finally reached him at Kathy's house. By that time I was frantic. "Come home right away, Ron. We have to drive to Wheeling to see Aunt Susan. She's ill."

Ron soon arrived and we drove to see my aunt. On our trip to Wheeling, I challenged Ron's prolonged absences from home. "Ron, what's happening with us? You spend more hours with Kathy than you do with me these days. Of course, she's hurting, but she has to get over it sometime. I wonder if you're helping her, or keeping her from healing by making her think more about Josh."

Ron seldom disagreed with me out loud, but he changed the subject. Could Ruth be right? "It's not easy for her. She and Josh had so little time together," Ron said.

"It's not easy for me, either, that you are never home when I need you. You have to decide where your loyalties belong." With those words, I swiveled to stare out the car window before the tears forming in my eyes could betray my despair.

12

~

Ron
AUGUST 1946 – JUNE 1947

Mattie's words as they drove to see her aunt astonished Ron. He should choose where his loyalties lay? He drove along speechless, staring at the road ahead. What? Choose? His being with Kathy was all very innocent. He only meant to comfort her (and himself) and to provide some male parenting for little Eddie. Could he be hurting Kathy, keeping her from healing and accepting the situation—as Mattie suggested?

For the first year after the war ended, it had seemed like a normal thing to be with both Mattie and Kathy. They both needed him, and each of them offered him something he felt he needed. He didn't feel he was hurting Mattie, busy with her church and community work. Neither Kathy nor Mattie suffered from any lack of his attention.

When Aunt Susan had her stroke and Mattie called Ron to drive her to Wheeling to see her, he had been in bed with Kathy. He had dressed quickly, still full of sexual tension, and hurried home. Mattie had already packed up for their travel. The call from her uncle had her worried.

"Do you remember the train ride we took fifteen years ago to Wheeling?" Mattie asked as they drove on. "What's happened to us since then?"

He remembered the secret trip, especially their honeymoon at the Ohio Hotel. He smiled, considering her question. "Nothing happened—we have a wonderful family with our two boys and our busy lives."

"Well, why are you so seldom at home these days? You spend more time with Kathy than you do with me."

"She needs so much, Mattie. Josh brought her to a strange town and then left her forever. He didn't intend to do it, but that's what happened."

"I know she's hurting, but she has to get over it sometime. Where do your loyalties lie?" she repeated.

This time Ron didn't hesitate. "With you," he said. He would break it off with Kathy.

After the Wheeling trip, Ron paid special attention to Mattie, and they had a sort of second honeymoon period. They managed to conceive a child during the fall of 1946, and both were excited about the possibility of a little girl, even though the boys were in their teens. Dr. Dunn had told Mattie it wouldn't be good for her to get pregnant again, but they ignored his advice and wished for a daughter.

Their anticipation was darkened by the fact that Mattie was so ill all during the pregnancy. She began throwing up in her first trimester. She thought the stomach upsets would pass in a couple months as they had for Aaron and Mark. Instead, she continued to be morning, afternoon, and evening sick for most of the pregnancy. Her blood pressure was sky-high on every doctor visit. Dr. Dunn said she had toxemia, a very serious condition. He ordered her to stay in bed to avoid complications. She spent the last three months almost entirely bed bound. Ron, Aaron, and Mark took over the household tasks and cared for her.

Aunt Susan died while Mattie was bed bound waiting for the child's birth. Ron went to Wheeling for the funeral with the boys, for Mattie could not travel. Ron brought back some of Aunt Susan's effects, including the letter from Mattie's mother, which Aunt Susan had picked up after Mattie crumpled it up all those years ago. She had straightened it out and tucked it safely away.

"What should I do, Ron? Do you think there is some way I could find Mama and Joy?"

"I didn't find any envelope with it. Alice Wilson might be anywhere. Do you know that she went to Texas?"

"I'm sure of Texas. I could write to someone there as Aunt Susan suggested." Mattie went over to her typewriter and typed out a letter to the Texas Department of Vital Statistics in Austin asking for information about a marriage between Alice—what last name would she have used?—and someone named Wilson. She had no idea what his first name was. And the date? Between 1918 and 1923, she supposed.

Mattie did not expect much success from the inquiry, but she thought it worth a try.

—

When Mattie's labor started and she needed to go to the hospital, Ron and Mattie told the boys to pray, to pray especially for their new little brother or sister.

Mattie opened her father's Bible and Ron read aloud the verse from John's gospel about Jesus going to prepare room in Heaven.

For a day and a half, Mattie lay in labor. The night of Ida Sue's birth was agonizing. Ron paced the waiting room like a caged lion. Waiting, waiting, waiting! What a sterile place a hospital waiting room is. Twice a nurse had come out to tell other fathers that the labor had been completed. Ron used the pay phone to call home to talk to Kathy, who was staying with the boys.

"Still waiting!" he told her. "Not looking good at all. When will this all be over? I thought when Mark and Aaron were born that waiting was a nightmare of uncertainty. This is much worse. How are the boys doing?"

"They're fine. Worried about Mattie. Eager to hear some news. Remember when Eddie was born we had a long wait. Are you able to get any rest?"

"I'm much too anxious. I wish I'd not put her through this. Dr. Dunn said no more children, but she so wanted a daughter, we thought it was worth a try. Now I'm scared and I feel responsible."

"Don't, Ron. Don't go through that all again. It was God's will, not yours or Mattie's fault."

"I've had six cups of their terrible coffee. I'm a walking zombie. How are you holding up at home?"

"We're all fine. Be sure to call when you hear anything."

Ron looked over and saw a nurse. "Sorry, Kathy, I see the nurse coming out. I'll call you when I have more news." With that, he hung up the phone and walked over to see if she could tell him about Mattie.

"Sorry, Mr. Connors, no news yet about your wife."

He walked over to the worn sofa and sat down to wait some more. The hands on the clock on the wall crawled slowly forward. Despite himself, Ron felt his eyes closing.

———

Suddenly he was startled awake by a light touch on his arm. It was Dr. Dunn, looking sober. "It was a girl, Ron, but she was stillborn. The placenta detached. She didn't get enough oxygen to sustain life. Mattie has had a hard time of it. She is under sedation. If you want to go in and sit by her bed, go ahead. She still doesn't know that the child died."

"Died? Our daughter died? Oh, God." Ron couldn't help himself. He wept. *The longed-for girl born at last and lost so quickly. Mattie put up such a struggle and in the end...*

"I need to see Mattie. How soon do you think she'll be awake?"

"It should be about an hour. Should you be calling someone?"

"I'm not sure I'm up to it yet. But yes, I need to call Kathy and have her tell the boys we won't be bringing a baby home."

After calling Kathy, he went in to sit by Mattie's bedside, holding her hand and wishing he could do more. When she opened her eyes, she saw in his face that all was not well.

"Pray for us, Ron," Mattie murmured. She sunk into unconsciousness again.

At last she awoke. Ron told her about Ida Sue. She buried her head in her pillow, sobbing, "We waited so long. What did I do wrong? I shouldn't have been so prideful. I should have been satisfied with what God gave us in the boys. I wanted a daughter. I wanted her so much."

Ron laid his hand on her forehead and they both cried again.

"Don't blame yourself, dear. Your job is to get well soon. We need you at home." She turned away, but he held her hand. "It will be okay. Get some rest."

Two days later, Ron took the boys to the graveside service for Ida Sue. Mattie was too ill to be there. Pastor Stevens preached to the small crowd at the grave about Jesus's love for the little children. "In God's time all good things will come to pass." He talked to the boys about how Ida Sue had gone to heaven to be with Jesus. Eddie was there as well sitting with Kathy. He looked up at the minister. "Where is my little cousin?" he demanded.

After ten days of lethargy Mattie returned home. Between the physical strains and the sorrow of losing her daughter, she was slow to return to her former self. The months of frail health, joyful anticipation, worry, and enormous disappointment left all of them needing to adjust to another dream not fulfilled.

A couple months later, as everyone was still mourning Ida Sue's passing, Mattie received a form letter from the Texas state government telling her she would need to contact the county where Alice's marriage took place to get any information about the license. Even if she had had more information, Texas had 254 counties listed in the form they sent her. That avenue for finding her lost mother did not seem to be fruitful. "Perhaps God doesn't want me to find out," she told Ron.

Kathy continued to come daily to the house after work for the next few weeks. She paid attention to Mattie, but she barely spoke to Ron. She and Ron had never talked about why he had stopped visiting her. Mattie was devastated over the loss of their daughter, but so was Ron. He and Kathy tried to comfort Mattie, but who would comfort him?

13

Eddie and Dar
1947 – 1959

Five-year-old Eddie was confused by the changes in his life. Aunt Mattie was no longer sick, and Eddie was glad of that. Yet he puzzled about the adults streaming to her house bringing casseroles and cakes and fresh-baked bread. Even if Eddie had been able to express his confusion in words grown-ups would understand, no one seemed to have time to answer the questions of a small child. The baby they had been waiting for was missing—dead, they told him, her body in the box they put into the ground at the cemetery.

The fall after Ida Sue's birth and death, Eddie started kindergarten. There he met Dar Jones. Five years before, Dar had been born across town on the same day as Eddie. Dar, too, had questions about death. The mine where his father worked caved in late in the spring of 1947. Before the debris could be removed Brick Jones was dead. A celebratory funeral was held in the AME church that confused, rather than comforted, Dar. He missed his poppy. Dar heard about Ida Sue's death from his mother Brenda when she came home from her work as Hanson's maid. "Be kind to little Eddie Connors when you see him. He'll be in your class at school."

Both boys were withdrawn when school began, but somehow each found in the other a kindred soul. Dar saw Eddie sitting alone when other children were running and playing. He went over and said shyly, "You're Eddie Connors. Are you sad about your little cousin?"

"Un-huh," Eddie answered. "Preacher told me she gone to be with my daddy and with Jesus. Mama told me my cousin's body was in that box they buried. I wanted to know where her head was. I don't understand why she's not here."

"The body and the head don't matter. What matter is where her soul is!" Dar ventured, repeating words he'd heard at his poppy's funeral. "Her soul gone to be with Jesus, just like my poppy's soul. They in Heaven, with pearly gates and streets of gold. It's a lot better place than Parkersville. My mama told me."

"But, don't dying hurt?"

"A course. Like stubbing your toe, but a lot worst. But you forgets all about it when you see the pearly gates." Eddie considered the idea with some skepticism but was silent, waiting to hear more.

"My poppy's funeral was a big party, but still lots of tears flowing. Everybody came and sung praises 'bout my poppy and about Jesus. Singing and shouting to the sky. Preacher told us to be happy for Poppy 'cause where he is, there's streets of gold and gates of pearl."

"Do you think that's true?"

"Preacher said so. I don't think preachers are 'lowed to lie."

Eddie was having a hard time understanding it all. "Pastor Stevens told me, 'Your little cousin is with Jesus. Your father and many other loved ones are welcoming her right now at the gates of heaven.' You really think those gates are made of pearl?"

"They said so at Poppy's funeral."

"What good's pearly gates? I think Heaven hasta have good things to eat: ripe peaches, and ice cream, and Aunt Mattie's cookies."

"Yah, that'd be good, too. I bet there's golden streets, gates of pearl, and good things to eat in Heaven. Jesus would see to it."

So the two children worked it out to their own satisfaction, and that day the bond of friendship was forged.

—

Dar and Eddie talked about lots of things as they grew that they never considered discussing with their mothers. When Dar got a magnifying glass, the boys talked about the mysteries of things you couldn't see with the naked eye. When Eddie got a telescope to study the heavens for his tenth birthday, they talked about how sailors of the future might reach the stars in starships. Though the boys shared a birthday, family celebrations did not include the best friend in the party.

As they grew up, Dar and Eddie were active in the Boy Scouts of America, starting out in a Cub pack led by Eddie's Aunt Mattie. As second through fifth graders, Dar, Eddie, and five other boys had her as den mother. She made scouting fun, with projects like cooking, exploring and making things with Popsicle sticks, yarn, glue, and objects they found in nature. When they entered sixth grade, they joined Troop 127 led by Ed's Uncle Ron, where they participated in all the activities they could fit into their schedules. By that time, wood craft, merit badge work, camping out in the nearby woods, and going off to Scout camp filled their days.

When they were thirteen an article in *The Saturday Evening Post* about the *USS Indianapolis*, the ship Eddie's father had died on, came out. Kathy tried to hide the story from Eddie. She would not allow any conversation about the tragedy that had ended Josh's life. Dar brought Eddie a copy of the article that the two of them studied together. Impressed by the bravery the sailors had exhibited, Eddie told Dar that he wanted to serve as his father had. "It must have been terrible for those brave men, but I'm proud of my father for serving. I'm going to enlist when we graduate." Dar, who was the better student, longed for opportunities to go to college, and maybe law school, to be able to solve the world's problems.

Both boys went through the ranks clear up to Eagle Scouts. It's hard to say who was most proud of the accomplishment: Scoutmaster Ron and Den Mother Mattie, or the boys' mothers, Brenda Jones and Kathy Connors. One would have thought the two widowed mothers would have a special kinship, but Kathy never could get over the fact that Brenda was colored and a maid. Kathy accepted Dar, right enough, but she considered him somehow different from others of his race, the exception that proved the rule. Brenda accepted that Eddie's mother had very narrow ideas about race. She pitied both the attitude and the woman who held it.

The boys were fortunate to live in a town that, with its majority white population, had never made segregation an issue. Dar and the few other colored children attended public school and participated in all school and community activities. They continued to be buddies throughout their school years. They tried out for high school sports and lettered in football, basketball, and baseball.

In the fall of 1959 their football Coach "Ham" Hamilton took the Parkersville Panthers to Weston, West Virginia, for a non-conference football game. Eddie and Dar were in the starting lineup, excited about the road trip. As the Panthers got off the bus in Weston, there was a small stir. Weston's Coach Masters frowned and ambled over to Coach Hamilton. "I hope you're not expecting to put that Nigger in the game, Ham. My guys won't play if you do."

"What's your problem, Buzz? Never heard of *Brown versus the Board of Education?* Of course Dar will play. He's my best lineman."

"Game's off if you insist on that! We're a private academy, not subject to that Supreme Court nonsense. We have standards here. Niggers don't play in this stadium."

Coach Hamilton called the boys together as they were starting to head for the visitor's locker room. "Here's the deal, boys. Their coach has challenged our putting Dar in the game. Says they won't play us if we do. Seems they claim that only white guys play on their turf. What say, Dar, are you willing to sit out this time?"

Eddie shot a puzzled look at his friend. What was this all about?

Dar shrugged his shoulders. "I don't feel much like playing today, Coach. I can sit on the bench and lead the cheers."

"You won't be able to suit up in their locker room, Dar. Is that still okay?"

Eddie jumped in with questions. "Why can't he just suit up and sit on the sidelines?" Then it dawned on him what was happening. "You know what? I don't feel much like playing today either, Coach. Dar and I can go sit on the bus during the game."

A number of the other team members started to catch on.

"Hey Coach, my stomach feels queasy. Don't think I can play." This from Josh Reed, Parkersville's best kicker.

"Better not put me in, Coach. I got a murderous rage comin' on," said another boy.

Coach Hamilton looked from one player to another. Then a huge smile broke out on his battered face. "Right, I think we might all go on over to the Wimpey's Take Out and grab some burgers. Might as well make the trip worthwhile. I'll tell the officials we accept the forfeit and we'll head on back after some burgers and ice cream. Climb back on the bus, boys. We're outta here."

Riding back, Eddie and Dar talked about the non-game they had just participated in. Stuffed with burgers, fries, Cokes, and ice cream, they were whooping it up as much as if they had just beaten the Weston Warriors by some lopsided score. "I knew that that sort of thing was happening some places. We've talked about it in history class, but I guess I didn't think it would happen to us."

"Get real, Eddie," Dar replied. "I see a lotta this kind of shit down in Mississippi when I visit my aunt Ruby. A lot more folks are ready to claim they're better'n me. Funny thing is, they seem to believe it."

"Dar, do you think this is what we'll be living with in our future?"

"I hope to change it someday. Things are changing too slow, but they're changing. I'll be off to Morehouse College in Atlanta when I graduate next year."

"You're a good student, Dar. You'll make a difference, I know. I wish I was half as good as you. The navy is my future."

"Maybe you'll find some way to help things change, too. It'll take a lot of us working on it to make it happen. But we have to start somewhere. Guys like that

Weston coach can't keep getting away with that stuff. It's been against the law for five years now."

"I wonder how long it will take to open peoples' minds."

14

Mattie

We've finished all the tea I made, dear. Wait while I brew another kettle full and I'll tell you more of the story.

Losing my daughter was too vivid a reminder of so many losses in my life: my parents and little sister, my ambitions for college, Aunt Susan's recent death, and Uncle Bob's illness. I tried to forget my sorrow by keeping busy with volunteer work and church activities. After the blow of Ida Sue's stillbirth, I set my mind on being the best wife and mother possible.

I tried many times to mend fences with my mother-in-law, who stubbornly clung to the resentments she had formed when she saw her sons leaving her. I know Kathy, too, went out of her way to be kind for Josh's sake. It did little good.

Herm tried to keep the peace to make up for his wife's disdain. He used his wood-working skills to craft small treasures each Christmas for us. The cards always said, "Merry Christmas from Mom and Dad." Even so, we both knew the end tables, jewel boxes, and display shelves Herm made for us were peace offerings from him alone.

1950 – 1960

When Marybeth developed cancer in 1955, both Kathy and I tried to make her last days more comfortable. She complained constantly, about the pain, about the unfairness of being ill, and about the "thieving" daughters-in-law who had stolen away her sons' love. She died in the summer of 1958. Herm died of a stroke the next spring.

My boys were growing up over those years. Aaron followed the path all of us expected. He went off to the College of Wooster, as I had not been able to do. He continued on to seminary and a calling as a Presbyterian minister, just as I had always wanted of him. He was a wonderful preacher, very involved in activities to better conditions for the poor and oppressed. He lived his faith.

Mark's career path was a bit rockier. Just two years younger than Aaron, he started off to Hiram College in the fall of 1950 planning to study science. He had a promising future ahead of him. Then Patty Young, Mark's sweetheart, a high school senior, greeted him with news he wasn't ready for.

Patty later told me about their first meeting when he came home on his Christmas break. Before he even could give her the present he'd brought her she told him, "I'm pregnant, Mark. I wasn't sure at first, but it's plain as day now."

"What'll Mom say when she hears? She'll have a fit."

"I guess we have to tell her, don't we?" Patty asked. "That's going to change so many things."

As I later explained it to Ruth, I guess Patty and Mark had gone too far in their August goodbyes. All fall Patty had worried she might be pregnant. By Christmas time there was no further question. When I heard the news, I don't mind telling you, I was shocked. I took no time to regret the circumstances. I set about making things come out okay. I called Pastor Bradley, and took Patty and Mark in tow. We went to his office with a plan. As soon as it could be arranged, Patty and Mark got married, and they set up housekeeping with Ron and me.

I was determined that they not ruin their lives with this turn of events. "I won't have you giving up your dreams of college," I insisted. "I'll care for the baby when it comes while you both get over to the Branch to take classes. Mark can work at the grocery—Patty, you can, too, when you're strong enough. A college degree is your key to a good future. I know, because I was denied one. You can both be teachers and earn a good living."

The baby, Roy Ronald, was born that spring. Just as I had promised, I kept Roy while Mark and Patty continued school. Since Patty had to drop out of her senior class, she studied over the summer, graduated, and began classes in Oxbridge, at the Ohio University Branch campus.

By 1954, Patty had a contract from the Parkersville Elementary School to begin teaching third grade. Their second child, Jacob Young Connors, was born while she was still in school. I also cared for him while Patty taught. Mark's progress through classes, because he worked full time, was a bit slower, but he began teaching the next year, seventh and eighth grade math. Their third child, Annie Lynn, was born in 1954. She was my treasure, and still is. Since I wasn't given a daughter, I took great pleasure in my granddaughters.

15

—

Kathy
LATE 1940s – 1960

Kathy saw that with Mattie wrapped up in her own grieving, Ron didn't know where to turn for comfort as he mourned his daughter's death. Before long he had returned to her bed. They developed a routine which allowed them to steal some time together several times a month. "Do you love me, Ron?" Kathy would ask. Ron would mumble assent, but would not say the words Kathy wanted to hear. *Love doesn't seem to be a part of this relationship,* Kathy thought to herself. *Were Mattie to ask either of us if we are unfaithful to her, we'd both deny it. For Ron, being with me, and for me being with Ron, is nothing but a way to escape our lonely lives.*

—

In the summer of 1960, after Eddie had left for the navy, Kathy got an unexpected visit from Butch Nelson, who had been a shipmate of Josh's on the *USS Indianapolis*. A number of Josh's letters in that last year had mentioned Butch. A career navy man like Josh, Butch had received a "Dear John" letter from his Texas wife just before Kathy's visit to Josh in '45. Josh used Butch and Ellen's story as an argument for Kathy quitting her job to be "just a housewife."

Fifteen years later, Butch's visit to Parkersville took Kathy by surprise. They had met briefly when she visited Josh in California. She never considered whether Butch might be among the 300 survivors or the 800 sailors lost at sea.

"I was in Indianapolis for our ship's reunion, Kathy, and got to thinking about you and Josh. He sure was bonkers about you! Writing letters every day like he did. To hear him tell, you were the perfect find in wives!"

"Far from it, Butch. We struggled the whole time I was out there in California over what sort of wife I should be. We had very different ideas about our future together." Kathy's eyes filled with tears as she recalled those bitter words between them. "And then, to have the visit cut short by his recall to the ship. So much was unresolved."

"Josh told me about the quarrel. He didn't know what you were trying to say. I think I did, what with Ellen leaving me in the midst of our lives."

Kathy asked Butch to say more about how his former wife convinced him that she needed her independence.

"It took me a while," he began. "In the end I realized I couldn't hold her against her will anyway. I met her when I was stationed at Corpus Christi Naval Station. I never knew a lot about her background except she came to town as a small child with her mother. She was mostly raised by her mother's brother and sister-in-law, who had a crowd of children of their own while her mother worked as a waitress in a diner near Corpus Christi. She had an older step-brother and two half-sisters. Her brother was sort of a buddy of mine. He introduced me to Ellen, the popular head cheerleader for the high school football team, the Lake City Lions. She longed to leave the small town, and I was glad to take her away. I got orders to report to San Diego in 1932. Ellen consented to marry me so that she could see the world, especially California. You never saw such a girl for wanting to get to Hollywood. She bought all the silver screen magazines available, for she had the dream of putting her beautiful face in movies. For the next ten years we lived in base housing or small apartments, while I served on short and long cruises.

"In 1942, after the war started, the navy assigned me to the Pacific theater. I knew our life together left her feeling unfulfilled, but I thought we'd make it through until the war ended.

"No Hollywood talent scouts came around, so Ellen went to work in a factory making airplanes, still longing to be discovered as the next June Havoc. Instead she met this rich guy when he came to see about investing in the war effort. His offer to take her away from the humdrum and make her life glamorous and useful came at a juncture in her life when it sounded most attractive. Her letters disturbed me: 'You don't understand me; I need to be me;' that sort of stuff. In the end, she decided that whether or not I understood her need, she would leave our marriage to try out life with Mr. Rich Guy. She just wrote me the 'Dear John' letter and took off with him.

"Ellen's mother had not approved of our marriage, so she was no help in salvaging it. I think she was happy when we broke up, and glad to have a wealthy son-in-law. Not that the marriage did the mother any good. Ellen wasn't really very nice to her mother, either. There was a lot left unsaid between them, too many mysteries in their past that Ellen never understood.

"She broke my heart, but she did manage to convey to me that for her being a woman mattered more than being a wife. I told Josh what Ellen had said. At first he couldn't see it, but as we sailed and talked some more, he began to catch on. He showed me part of the letter he was writing to you as we sailed for Leyte. I guess you never got that letter. He was trying to make it up to you for the quarrel."

By the time Butch finished the story, Kathy was again weeping. The loss from fifteen years ago felt as intense as a brand new wound. Butch reached out to hold her. "He adored you, Kathy. I know you would have worked things out if that torpedo hadn't sunk us."

"How could the navy not realize you were struck? Not even searched for you? I can't understand how that could have happened." Kathy's voice rose hysterically as she screamed her anger—aimed at the Japanese and the U. S. Navy and now at Josh's shipmate. She began to beat at his chest. He stood and received the blows. He considered it the penance he owed for surviving when so many of his shipmates had not.

Anger spent, Kathy collapsed into his arms.

"Josh wasn't among those struggling in the water, Kathy, if that's any consolation," Butch said. "He was on duty in the boiler room on the midnight shift when the torpedo struck. That's the part of the ship it struck."

Kathy sighed. What consolation could that be? Then thinking of the tales she had read of sharks, of burning heat by day and freezing cold by night, of men going mad with thirst, she did feel consoled. "I'm so sorry, Butch. How awful for you! How did you survive?"

"I've suppressed most of it, it was so terrible. We thought we would soon be picked up, but it appeared no one even missed us. Just after midnight the torpedo hit, leaving us in pitch black. Some of us had kapok life jackets, but they get waterlogged in a couple days. My group clung to each other, sharing the jackets between us. As the sun rose, cold was replaced by blazing heat. The sharks swarmed as the sea turned red with their kills. But the worst was the thirst. Men went wild with thirst and starvation. Two of my buddies swam away, sure they saw an island in the distance."

Butch was silent for a long time, while Kathy waited for him to continue. "Not a sign of rescue for four days. Late on the fourth day a seaplane happened to spot us. That night we saw the searchlight of the *USS Cecil Doyle* pointing to the sky. I thought it was another mirage at first. Eventually 315 of us were rescued and transported to the *USS Tranquility* hospital ship."

"Oh, Butch. What an ordeal! So tragic, so sad. It breaks my heart. Perhaps Josh was one of the lucky ones."

Butch and Kathy sat together a long time in silence. Finally Butch rose from his chair and reached for his duffel bag.

"Where are you going?" Kathy asked.

"I should move on. I'm glad I stopped. I wasn't sure I should, but I wanted to tell you that Josh really loved you."

"Don't leave yet. Stay a few days. You can stay here. I have vacation days coming and I'll take some time off. I can show you some of Josh's letters and we can talk more."

Butch agreed and sat again. They stayed up late talking and fell into bed exhausted, holding each other to compensate themselves for the losses of war. The next day Kathy shared with Butch many of Josh's letters, and together they managed to laugh at some of the silly things Josh wrote. They talked more about Butch's wife Ellen as well. For the next three weeks, Butch stayed in Kathy's apartment. They explored each other's minds and bodies, having delicious sex that transformed Kathy's attitudes toward her own body.

"You make me feel like a real woman, Butch. I was a virgin until I married Josh, and after the hard life raising my brothers and sisters I was determined to remain an old maid, a woman independent of men. Then Josh came along, and the war, and he swept me off my feet."

Butch rolled over to give Kathy another kiss. "He was no virgin, I know, but he never loved anyone as he loved you. Consider me his stand-in. If he had returned, you would have been loved like this." Butch demonstrated and Kathy reveled in his attention.

"Josh's brother tried to fill the place Josh vacated. But I'm 'the other woman' with no claim on him. He's a married man, and he loves his wife. He can't say 'I love you' to me."

"You know I'm not the marrying kind any more. What we have is precious but temporary, you understand."

"I do know that. And I am content that you will be moving on in a few weeks. But you are helping me decide that what has been between Ron and me isn't any good any more. It's poisoning the friendship I had with Mattie, Ron's wife. She was a rock for me when Josh first brought me here."

"Does she know about you?" Butch asked.

"I'm not sure. I never spoke to her about it. On some level I think she has known for a while. At least she realized Ron was spending time with me. When she suspected it, I guess she considered her options. People in Parkersville do not divorce! They just don't. When it started, I knew I was only 'borrowing' his life when I was most vulnerable. Nothing permanent could change for me."

"Are you still involved with him?"

"Off and on. When Ron went back to her they had a daughter who was stillborn. Ron told me he had promised Mattie we would not spend any more time together. I agreed that would be best. But we drifted back into old habits."

"You're strong. You know yourself. You can do as you please with your body. I won't forget this time we've spent."

Mattie learned of Butch's visit, and called to invite Kathy and Butch to supper one evening. Kathy tried to refuse, but Mattie insisted it would be good for Ron to talk with one of Josh's buddies. *Yes*, Kathy thought, *it might be good for Ron to see I'm not dependent on him anymore.*

"You'll always be in my heart, dear Kathy," Butch told her after the supper with Ron and Mattie was over. "I really must get on my way." As he embraced her for one last goodbye, he whispered, "I'm not the letter writer Josh was, but I will try to write. I hope you'll reply."

"I won't promise to do that. This time together has been *wunderbar*. Maybe it is just as well to keep to memories."

In the end, for it ended with Butch returning to Texas, Kathy did not regret either his visit or his leaving. A brief fling that reminded her of her womanhood was all it had been. But it gave her the power to stand up to Ron, to tell him to leave her alone. She would not be his back-up wife.

16

~

Mattie

When I heard Butch Nelson, one of Josh's old navy buddies, was staying with Kathy, I was anxious to meet him, to talk to someone who had known Josh in those last terrible days. I called Kathy to invite them to supper with Ron and me. At first she turned me down.

1960

Kathy hemmed and hawed on the phone. "He won't be here very long, Mattie, and it's hard for him to talk about those last days."

"I think it would be good for Ron to hear some stories about his brother's navy days. You know Josh's death affected him deeply, too."

"I know it did. I'll ask Butch whether he wants to meet Ron. But don't count on it."

The next afternoon she called me back and accepted the supper invitation for the two of them for Saturday night. I fixed a ham-and-potato casserole and baked corn because Josh always liked that dish and I wanted to keep things low key. I made my German chocolate layer cake, though. I knew Kathy liked it.

I didn't know what to expect when Kathy and Butch came through the door. I expected Ron to be glad to have a chance to learn more about his brother, but he seemed reluctant to say much. He and I had both read *Abandon Ship* by Richard Newcomb, so we knew quite a bit about the "navy's greatest sea disaster." Truth is, I wasn't sure myself what Butch would be willing to talk about or what we would be willing to listen to.

The evening went well. Butch liked the casserole and raved about the German chocolate cake. Supper conversation was pretty general—navy routines, the ships and duties, difficulties of trying to have a "normal" home life when the service calls. Kathy and Butch seemed very comfortable with one another. It flashed through my mind that maybe they would fall in love and make a life together. Ron called me a romantic for having such thoughts, but then I always did want to see people in couples.

After supper Ron asked Butch about his family. "I guess you have a wife in California now," he said.

Butch answered that his wife had left him (and my hopes for Kathy rose a little). When he started talking about his first wife, Ellen, my heart skipped a beat. I couldn't help thinking as he added more details to the story that maybe, just maybe, Ellen was really my lost sister, Joy Ellen.

I jumped right into the middle of his description when he said she came to Texas as a small child with her mother. "That could be Joy!" I shouted. "I know it's a long shot, but Ellen might be the sister I lost over forty years ago!"

"I hardly think so, Mattie," Kathy told me. "Think how many widows with small children move to a more congenial setting."

"But the timing is right. Butch, do you have any idea when Ellen was born?"

"We celebrated her birthday on Valentine's Day, but she told me once that she didn't think it was her real birthday."

"Can you write to her, Butch? Or give me her address and I'll write. It's a chance, though a small one. The whole story sounds like what Joy's life might have been after she left Parkersville."

"I don't have a current address, but I think I can locate her through some mutual friends. I seriously doubt that she could be your sister." I was ecstatic, though Ron, Kathy, and Butch all told me to calm down. I so wanted to find my sister.

17

~

Kathy
1960

Kathy felt she needed a change in her circumstances after her brief fling with Butch Nelson led her to push Ron out of her life. She had given too much of herself being what men wanted her to be: first her father, then Josh, then even Eddie, had laid their expectations upon her. Kathy understood that Ron's passion was divided between her and Mattie. Though they had enjoyed each other, Ron could never bring himself to say "I love you" to Kathy. It was time to set her own agenda. She would devote herself to her work and her own needs.

Kathy's boss, Roger Gordon, had political ambitions. His handsome features, his beautiful head of coal-black hair, and his dark, serious eyes got people's attention. His smooth talk and deep voice moved people to believe his words. His role in the Washington County Republican Party suited him, for he was able to influence fellow citizens in the voting and governing process. He thought of himself as a big fish in a small pond. He wanted more. Roger began to think bigger about what might be in store for his career.

His firm represented Congressman Boyle of the Ohio Second District. Roger had heard Boyle talk from time to time about leaving his place in Congress, and he began to think that "Representative Roger Gordon" sounded like a good title. His wife Rhonda would make a nice presence in the capital city. She had money. He considered her boring in bed, but there were other places to find pleasure of that sort. Sex was available for sale to a man of his circumstances.

~

As part of her plan to look after her own needs, Kathy began looking around for a house to own. When she asked her boss Roger to look with her, he guided her to homes that, though attractive, were well out of her price range. The two-story colonial at the end of Jefferson Street was perfect, she thought. "If I had the means, this house would be mine in a minute," she told Roger.

"I'll make the down payment as a bonus for your good work in my office," he offered. "Buy this one. I'll help you with the payments."

"How would I repay you?"

"We'll work it out," Roger replied, so Kathy shrugged and signed the mortgage papers.

Once Kathy was moved into her new house, Roger dropped by.

"Great place you have here, Kathy. I like how you've decorated." Roger brought an expensive crystal vase filled with roses as a housewarming gift. He helped himself to a seat on her sofa and studied her as she admired the vase and flowers. "The roses make your face shine. I'd be glad to bring some every week or so."

"Roger, you've done so much. I don't know how to repay you," Kathy said.

"Come sit here by me. We can talk about that."

Roger patted the sofa and as Kathy sat down on the edge of the seat, he pulled her so her head was resting on his shoulder. Kathy frowned, trying to figure out where this was leading. *Watch it, Kathy*, she told herself. *Something's going on in his mind.*

"You know, Kathy, I sense in you a hidden passion. Maybe that sailor brought it out, but you exude an essence that leads me to believe you need someone to care for you." He kissed her roughly on her hair and then moved to plant a kiss on her surprised lips.

"Whoa," Kathy said as she rose. "What was that about?"

"You wanted to know how to repay me. You have something you have kept to yourself too long." Roger stood and grasped her shoulder. He encircled her body with his arms and pressed himself against her.

Kathy tried to break his grip, but he was stronger and more determined.

"I'm sure Rhonda would consider such 'payments' a bad idea," Kathy gasped.

"Forget about Rhonda. She hasn't near the passion you have!" Roger, at five feet ten inches, was more than a match for Kathy's five-foot frame. He carried the protesting woman to the bedroom and began unfastening his trousers. He pushed her down on the bed, pinning her arms with one hand as he fumbled with her skirt. After a brief, fruitless struggle, she yielded as he managed to get her dress aside and thrust himself upon her. In minutes the whole adventure was over. Roger straightened himself up and smoothed his hair.

"I'll pick you up for work tomorrow. I'll stop by the bakery to bring some fresh rolls. Why don't you just wait to dress until we've had 'breakfast,' " Roger smirked as he adjusted his suit coat and walked to the door. "See you around seven."

Kathy watched him leave, aghast at what had just taken place. She balled her hands into fists and hugged herself. Her head ached and her thoughts swirled about. *Here's one more man wanting to take from me. But what can I do about it? Some offer,* Kathy thought to herself. Then she considered the possibilities. *Why not? I've little to lose and lots to gain. I'm a well-paid prostitute, but it pays the mortgage.*

Roger, as a married man, made no promises to Kathy, but it was clear he enjoyed her companionship more than he did Rhonda's. It meant little to Kathy that Roger preferred to be with her rather than his wife. Kathy kept her cool, expecting little, but she explained to Roger that she would set the limit on the amount of sex she would permit. She gauged in her own mind how much she "owed" to Roger, and did not let his desires overwhelm her judgment. Sex with him was perfunctory, nowhere near as satisfactory as the fling she had enjoyed with Butch Nelson. It did not measure up to those few wedded days she spent with Josh, nor with the pleasure she had experienced with Ron. She considered sex with Roger a business arrangement only.

18

~

Mattie

You can imagine how anxious I was to hear from Butch with an address for his former wife. I kept checking the mailbox for the letter while Ron reminded me that it was only the slimmest chance that Butch's ex-wife was my sister. Finally the letter arrived.

September 1960 – January 1961

Once I had Ellen's address, I carefully worded the letter to her and sent it off with a prayer that she would reply with good news. In the middle of January 1961 a letter came in reply.

Dear Mattie,

No, I am not your long-lost sister, though it gave me pause to think of such a possibility. My mother, Mildred Fanner, left her abusive husband in Oklahoma in 1920, taking me with her to live in Texas. We have no roots in Ohio as far as I know. Perhaps I have a clue, however, to your missing sister.

I had a school friend named Joy Wilson who had a mysterious background similar to my own. In fact, the similarity is why we became friends. I think every child imagines that she must be adopted or come from some other place, but Joy and I discovered that we were alike in our histories. Her stepbrother teased her about not being a "true" Wilson, and he often managed to drive her to tears with his torments. Joy and I vowed together to find our "true home," but it was only so much teenage talk, as it turned out. I've not learned any more about my abusive father, not did Joy know *anything about her family when last I heard from her in 1948 or so.*

I ran away with Butch in 1932 at age sixteen to seek adventure, especially hoping that I might break into the movies. I guess every girl in the country wanted to be Bette Davis or Joan Crawford. I thought it would be a cakewalk, once they laid eyes on me, but I was wrong.

Joy finished school before she came to visit me while Butch was on a long cruise. Joy actually got a bit part in a few movies, in large crowd scenes. She married a fellow actor, but that lasted less than a year, I think. The last I heard she had a job in a defense plant welding airplanes. After the war those jobs evaporated.

I've completely lost track of Joy now. Wish I could help you out. I hope you find her.

Sincerely,
Ellen Fanner

She knew Joy. It was good news, bringing me a step closer to my sister. Joy had grown up and gone to Hollywood and worked in the movies. If only Ellen were still in touch with Joy. If only someone knew where she was.

I wrote to thank Ellen for her letter, and to wish her well. I begged that if she should ever hear from Joy to please let her know about me. We exchanged Christmas cards for a number of years afterwards, but there was never any news from her about my missing sister.

There must be a way to find Joy, I thought. Now at least I had a clue that Corpus Christie was where I should direct my inquiries. Maybe a letter to the postmaster there would find Alice Wilson. It was worth a try, so I sat down at the typewriter and typed out another letter.

19
~

Election Fever
1964

September 9, 1964. Mattie and Ron Connors were watching the Monday Night Movie, *David and Bathsheba*, on NBC. It was an old Bible movie from the early 50s, starring Gregory Peck and Susan Hayward. Mattie had finished a dish of ice cream and thought to herself that tomorrow she would start to diet. At fifty-two, the weight seemed harder and harder to lose. Her husband Ron, just a few months older, was still big and strong, straight and tall, though his balding head, sun-caused wrinkles, and slightly sagging jowls betrayed his age. His mustache had a hint of gray among the dark brown hairs. Ron was getting sleepy, almost dozing, when a startling political campaign commercial came on, just before 10:00 p.m.

> *A sweet little girl, long hair and freckles, about the same age as the children in Mattie's kindergarten Sunday school class, stands in a field of flowers pulling petals off a daisy. She counts, "One, two, three, four, five, seven, six, six, nine," and the petals are all gone. The little girl looks sweetly up at the sky while the camera zooms in on her face, blacking out as the screen is filled by her eye. A male voice intones, "nine, eight, seven, six, five, four, three, two, one," then there is the sound of a huge explosion and the flash of a mushroom cloud from a nuclear detonation.*

Mattie gasped. She scarcely heard the voiceover, President Johnson's voice telling the viewers to love one another or die. The words appeared on the screen: "Vote for President Johnson on November 3." An announcer read the words, then added, "The stakes are too high for you to stay home."

Mattie looked over at Ron, a staunch Republican, expecting him to say something. She still hadn't decided about how to vote in November, but she expected him to go ballistic. She shook herself, as if to shake off the impact of the message. "Did you see that, Ron?" she asked.

Ron startled. "What? Sorry. I think I'm ready for bed about now." He rose, then went to the porch to light his pre-bedtime cigarette. He appeared to not even have noticed the commercial.

—

Across town, in the colored section of Parkersville, Brenda Jones sat in her crowded front room watching the same movie. Her son Darwin, dark-skinned, flat-featured, curly hair cropped close to his head, was home for Labor Day weekend, relaxing with his mother before returning to Atlanta, Georgia, for his senior year at Morehouse College. He had hoped his boyhood friend, Eddie Connors, would be in Parkersville over some of the summer, but Ed was in the navy and they had to settle for letters to exchange ideas. Dar imagined that if Eddie were watching this movie, they'd joke about it. Much as they both loved the Biblical stories from the Old Testament, this Darryl F. Zanuck movie, despite its Academy Award recognition, seemed long and boring.

Dar perked up when the *Vote for President Johnson* commercial came on.

"Well, the Democrats aren't holding back anything. That message should get out the vote."

Brenda turned to her son. "Don't you think that was a bit extreme, Dar? We want to support the president, but a large number of Negroes are still not able to vote, especially down South."

"That's what makes this so clever, Mama. It doesn't point out Senator Goldwater's vote against the Civil Rights Act. Even though the Republicans staged a long filibuster last summer, President Johnson got the act through Congress and signed it in July. It's the law of the land, Mama. White folks in the South may not like it, and they'll tend to vote for Goldwater. But this ad should cause them to think twice. They won't want a nuclear world. This ad says the senator from Arizona might well bring it to them."

"Dar, I hope you're right. I still think it's a bit over the top, though."

"Mama, all's fair in love and politics. At least that's one of the things I'm learning at Morehouse."

—

In White Grove, Michigan, Aaron Connors and his wife, Joan, also tuned in to NBC. Aaron, a Presbyterian minister, had been shaking his head over how

Hollywood portrayed the story of Israel's great King David.

Aaron sat up when the commercial came on screen. He slapped his fist on his knee as he watched the little girl and the countdown. "Yes! Take that Senator Goldwater!" This commercial, coming the same day the President had spoken in Detroit at Cadillac Square to open the fall campaign, should be enough to convince people that his opponent was trigger-happy, not to be trusted with the presidency.

"Do you think Senator Goldwater would really drop a nuclear bomb in Vietnam, Aaron?" Joan asked her husband.

"Well, he talks like he would. Remember in his acceptance speech at the Republican Convention this summer. He told his followers, 'Extremism in defense of liberty is no vice.' "

"I wonder what Mom and Dad will have to say about the ad, though. It's pretty scary. I'm glad the kids were in bed and didn't see it."

"And I hope Aunt Kathy wasn't watching," Aaron said. "Her boss at the law firm is having her devote a lot of her work hours to promoting Goldwater's election."

—

As it turned out, Aaron's Aunt Kathy had not watched the Monday Night Movie, but the next day at her office she heard plenty about the commercial. Her boss, Roger Gordon, was rabid. Two months before, Roger had gone as a delegate to the Republican National Convention in San Francisco that nominated Senator Barry Goldwater of Arizona to run for president against Johnson. Roger had told Kathy of the excitement at the Cow Palace and the struggle Goldwater's followers had to win him the nomination. Roger reported to Kathy how keyed up he was to hear Senator Goldwater's acceptance speech. "He declared Communism as the principal disturber of the peace in the world today. He said, 'I would remind you that extremism in the defense of liberty is no vice' and 'that moderation in the pursuit of justice is no virtue.' "

That summer and fall, much of the work of his law office was promoting the conservative agenda Goldwater stood for, doing everything they could to get Goldwater elected. Mailings and meetings took up much of their time.

"How dare they!" he fumed in response to the commercial. "I went to the convention. Senator Goldwater is nothing like they're saying. He's the voice of the conservative movement. He'll keep taxes low, keep government small! Put conscience back in government! I know, I know, I sound like a political advertisement. Now the damn Democrats—sorry, Kathy, I should watch my language—the

Democrats are trying to demonize a good man."

"I know you're right, Roger. I'm glad I didn't see that terrible commercial. Johnson's ad sounds desperate. Maybe this will blow over so we can get our message out." Kathy had no faith in Johnson after he had upset the applecart with his civil rights efforts. Government was intruding where it had no business being. "People need a real choice for a conservative president. In my heart I know Senator Goldwater is right." Kathy laughed as she realized she, too, was repeating a campaign slogan.

—

Rather than blow over, the uproar increased. ABC and CBS replayed the commercial as part of their evening newscasts each night that week. All told, it was viewed by 40 to 50 million people in the United States. It resonated deeply with a nation that saw the "end of the world" as a real possibility. The battle for the hearts and minds of the entire world was being waged in a United States election and in the jungles of Indochina.

20

~

Mattie

Election fever was in the air. But we had our minds on other things, as we prepared for a vacation trip to see Aaron and Joan and the kids in Michigan that October. It seemed the very day I was trying to get things done, the phone wouldn't stop ringing. Ignoring the few extra pounds I was always promising to shed, I bustled from one task to another.

October 16, 1964

At 9:00 a.m. on Friday morning, I already had brownies—granddaughter Beth's favorites—in the oven. The delicious aroma filled the house. Cookie dough was in the refrigerator ready to slice and bake, and I had laid out the makings of several mac-and-cheese casseroles, waiting for Ron to bring the milk when he came home from work. The phone rang again.

"Morning, Mattie. Joan from Hanson Funeral Home. You know Deb Sanders's funeral is Tuesday. The family asked me to pass on the arrangements so you can get them in the papers."

I jotted down the details, adding them to the pile of information I had accumulated to type up to mail to the Wheeling and New Pittsburgh daily papers. As a "stringer" for the Parkersville news, I earned pocket money by reporting the local news to the *Times-Leader* in Wheeling or the *Constitution* in New Pittsburgh. I phoned in the funeral information to the copywriters at the newspapers since it would be another week until the *Parkersville Weekly* came out next Friday. That task completed, I sliced some cookie dough, put in a pan of cookies to bake, and returned to my phone and typewriter set up in the dining room.

I needed to call Mary at the hospital about who was there and call the police station for their report. I hadn't heard about the Twig meetings or the Altar Guild plans either. I'd make some calls to get that into today's report. I hurried to the kitchen to take out the first pan of cookies, put in a second. I grabbed one to eat. Ron would have a couple when he got home. I used the old Toll House recipe as my standard, but I formed them into rolls and refrigerated them to slice, which made them taste more chocolaty. I made a few more phone calls and finished typing up the news I had gathered. (Hilda Graves had company from Florida this week; Dr. Ingram attended a medical conference in Pittsburgh; five-year-old Jacob Smitt was hospitalized to have his tonsils removed.) I carried the envelopes to the mailbox on the porch.

I got the last tray of cookies into the oven—more delicious smells. I started some yeast dough as the phone rang again.

"Mattie, it's Carol. Can you prepare the ham loaf for Deb's funeral lunch on Tuesday? You make the best ham loaf in Parkersville, bar none."

"Thank you for the compliment, Carol," I said. I knew Carol, the minister's wife, was right about that. No one knows pineapple juice is the secret ingredient. "I would, but we're on our way up to visit Aaron and Joan and the children tomorrow and I won't be around. I'll provide some of my Parker House rolls. I've already started the dough rising. I can bake them this afternoon and drop them off at your house. Maybe Mary Barnes will do the meat."

"How is Aaron doing in Michigan? Is he liking the new church?"

"I think so. He's only been there a few months. We haven't been to see them yet." I'd have liked to talk longer, but I knew I had more to do. "Carol, I have to run and see to the rolls. I'm making a macaroni-and-cheese casserole to take over to the Sanders' house this evening. Sorry I can't help with the dinner any more than that."

"I'm sorry, too, but we'll have to manage without you. Have a good trip and be safe."

I shaped the rolls and set them to rise. I tidied up the front parlor a bit and then went upstairs to begin the packing.

I opened the bedroom window to take in the glorious day. Blue skies sparkled, with the temperature in the 60s. Wispy white clouds drifted past and the faint odor of wood smoke came from someone's burning brush. All over the rolling hills around Parkersville, trees flashed gold and orange and red. The maple in our yard, one of the first ones to turn, was a stunning mix of colors, yellow and golden and flame. I needed to pack for the trip, or I would have been out in the garden to bring in the last of the squashes. The leaves outside the window cast a golden glow on the floor of the room.

I had laid out the clothes I was taking. I folded them and put them into the serviceable old suitcase I had pulled from the back of my closet. I packed the blue cotton dress, folding it carefully. I packed the cream-colored cotton dress and the peach cotton dress as well. All my dresses were ones I had sewn from the same pattern with a few minor variations in appearance. The light blue one had a matching sweater I knit last spring while watching *The Guiding Light* on TV. I liked the way this particular pattern fit me. Lane Bryant in nearby Wheeling, West Virginia, catered to larger-sized women, but they were expensive. Growing up in a frugal household made me cautious about spending money. One Lane Bryant purchase, the navy blue two-piece suit I bought on sale last spring, did go into the suitcase. I'd wear the suit to Aaron's church, so he'd be proud of his mother as he looked out from the pulpit. I didn't want my daughter-in-law to be embarrassed by the poor relatives from Parkersville. My girdle and stockings were lying on the bed next to my sensible, but quite nice, shoes. I put them in.

When I glanced up at the dressing table mirror and studied my face, I was glad I'd got my permanent a week ago. The first week after Florence did my hair, it was always too frizzy. Those home permanents were especially bad, and I did want to look my best, so I had splurged at Florence's shop for a perm and then a cut. Touches of gray in my hair didn't look too bad. Florence had suggested a rinse to cover the gray—"Washes out in a couple of weeks"— but I'd noticed Kathy's choice of the rinse and a perm made the color a little too uniform to look natural.

Packing the suitcase was a labor of love. Soon I'd be seeing my ten-year-old granddaughter, Bethie, and eight-year-old Grant. We missed seeing them very often, for they lived nine hours away in White Grove, Michigan. Ron's vacation would be our chance to drive up and visit. When Beth was younger, she'd spent some summer vacation time with us. She hadn't come last summer though, because Aaron's family was just getting settled in his new parish.

I glanced at the clock. *Where was Ron?* I'd take a little break from packing to make coffee and lay out a plate of chocolate chip cookies for him, but he was late. He'd been getting slower and slower these days. I'd asked him to stop at M & P and get some milk to go into my cheese sauce.

Ron's job was driving a mail route to deliver to rural customers—RFD. Before that he had driven truck for the M & P store, going every week to Tennessee to pick up produce. Driving for the post office required a reliable car; that suited Ron, who loved cars. The excuse to buy a new one every couple years was another perk of the job. The current model was a 1963 Chevy Impala, gray with black interior. He had extended the steering and pedals so that he could sit on the right-hand seat to put the mail into the boxes along his route.

When I heard Ron pull into the drive, I left my packing and went downstairs slowly, feeling the arthritis in my joints. I entered the kitchen and laid out red gingham place mats and coordinated napkins. I put out a china plate with a few chocolate chip cookies. I poured a large brown mug of coffee for Ron and a smaller flowered one for me.

Ron came in, hung his coat by the door, and stood there looking at me. He had a puzzled look on his face and asked me why I was sitting at the table with a snack laid out.

I looked up at my husband, once again thanking God for the life we had. "Did you bring the milk?"

"What?"

"The milk. I asked you to pick up a quart so I could make the macaroni-and-cheese casseroles. I have one for Mark and Patty and the kids and one to go over to the Sanders' house. Deb's funeral will be on Tuesday."

"Milk?" Ron repeated. "Milk? That's what I forgot. I thought there was something I was supposed to get. Didn't Marv deliver milk this morning?"

"Ron, you know perfectly well Marv gave up the milk route two years ago. We buy it at the minimart or at M & P. Well, don't bother. I'll use powdered milk in the cheese sauce. It tastes almost as good when I use the Amish cheddar cheese. Sit down and drink your coffee." I pushed the plate of cookies closer. Ron reached for one and dunked it in his coffee mug.

"I'd like some milk to put in this."

"Ron, you don't use milk in your coffee. You gave that up when they started bottling homogenized milk and you couldn't skim off the cream from the top of the bottle to float in your coffee. Are you feeling okay, dear?"

"What? Oh, sure, just distracted about some things. Um…Biggs called me into his office before I went out on my route and told me to be extra careful about packages. I only had a couple to deliver today."

"Maybe that's why you forgot the milk. Don't worry." I finished my coffee and cookie, but Ron sat neither eating nor drinking.

I started to gather the cups. "You haven't drunk any of your coffee and it's getting cold. Shall I add some more to warm it up?"

Ron absently sipped from the brown mug. "It doesn't taste right in this glass," he declared, thumping the mug down on the table and spilling coffee in all directions.

I pushed back my chair and grabbed my napkin to begin mopping up. "For Heaven's sake! Get the dishcloth and bring it over here!"

Ron looked around. He shook his head and shrugged his shoulders. Then he rose and ambled out the kitchen door where he lit up a Lucky Strike.

I managed to sop up the mess with the napkins and the place mats. *Oh, Ron,* I thought to myself. *You really do need a vacation. I'm glad we're going to get away.* I got up and went to the sink to get the dishcloth.

Later, returning to my packing, I opened the precious Bible that was my one legacy from Papa. *I still miss you, Papa. I wish you hadn't left me.* I closed my eyes to breathe a prayer: *This is the day the Lord has made. I will rejoice and be glad in it. I thank thee, Lord, for all the many blessings thou hast given me. Be with Ron and me as we travel tomorrow. Grant us traveling mercies and keep us in thy watchful care. Amen.*

I closed my father's Bible, which I kept on the bedside table. I wouldn't take that Bible, my prized possession. Instead I packed the newer Revised Standard Version of the New Testament. Its more modern language made some passages clearer, more understandable. I used it perhaps more often than the King James translation which had been Papa's. I packed it in the suitcase, along with my *Today* meditation guide.

I packed my makeup (just a lipstick, a bit of rouge, and powder) in the suitcase. I tucked extra underwear and another pair of stockings into the knitting bag I'd carry everywhere along with my purse. One never knew if the car might be broken into and the suitcase stolen.

Next, I started to put in clothes for Ron. He preferred store-bought shirts for work, blue cotton with a pocket for his pens and note cards. One or two of those should go along for the trip. I had planned to ask Ron whether to pack the red plaid shirt or the green plaid one I'd made, but decided to put in both. It might be cold in Michigan in October.

A few years before I would have called Kathy to report that we were going away. We'd been like sisters in those early days when Josh first brought home his bride. When Kathy had Josh's baby prematurely, I was there offering comfort and childcare. I loved Eddie as much as my own sons. But ever since Josh's death, the friendship between us had been strained. When I promised Josh to look after Kathy until he returned safely—well, it didn't work out, did it? I felt I had broken a promise. I had no way to relieve Kathy's despair when the telegram came or even later. Ron had been able to assuage Kathy's grief, but I seemed unable to reach my friend. I never quite understood what had happened to damage our close friendship. I was a touch jealous that Ron could comfort Kathy and I, myself, was unable to do so. I felt Ron's closeness with Kathy detracted from the friendship Kathy and I had developed when we first met at the Parkersville train station.

I'd been a bit guilty when I was pregnant with Ida Sue to be having a child when Kathy was still mourning Josh. Maybe it was my guilty joy that cursed the pregnancy. I tried to express this idea to Kathy during my weeks of bed rest and afterwards, but Kathy would not hear it. "Nonsense," she told me. "I won't listen to that." It was one more thing that caused our friendship to cool.

Politics was another issue. I had strong feelings about the unfair prejudices affecting the few Negroes in Parkersville. In my view, President Johnson's efforts to enact civil rights legislation was a positive thing, to extend justice to all people. Housing for blacks was sub-standard in Parkersville and around the country. I knew Brenda Jones's family couldn't get a mortgage in her neighborhood because the banks wouldn't approve it. I thought it a shame that Dar and Eddie, when they were youngsters, had to cross the tracks to spend time together.

I admired the work of Rev. Dr. Martin Luther King, Jr., when I read about him in the news. It was high time that human rights be protected.

Kathy's views were different. She lamented, "Niggers don't know their place." She followed Goldwater's line on legislation. She told me a private person should have the right to do business, or not, with whomever they choose. Like Goldwater, Kathy opposed the Civil Rights Act. Also, over the years Kathy had gotten involved with the Full Gospel Baptist Church and become very fundamental in her beliefs about the Bible. More than once, Kathy had told me Presbyterians were headed for Hell.

When Eddie said he wanted to join the navy, against his mother's wishes, I encouraged him to go, but my encouragement added another layer of stress between his mother and me.

So this October morning in 1964, preparing for our trip, I did not call to say we were going away. Kathy probably knew anyway.

—

I snapped the suitcase closed and called for Ron to come up to carry it downstairs. I called a couple of times, then painfully went to find him. He was sitting on the front porch swing, smoking and looking at the changing leaves.

"Ron, the suitcase is ready for you to bring down," I told him.

"Suitcase?"

"Upstairs on the bed. Don't worry. I tried not to make it too heavy. We'll carry your suit and our good coats on hangers. We'll lay them in the back of the car."

Ron put out his cigarette and mounted the stairs to enter the bedroom. I expected him to come right down, but I guess he was exhausted and fell asleep.

When I called him down to supper an hour or so later, he rose and came down to eat. The suitcase stood by the dresser, waiting.

It was still there when we went upstairs to bed, and still there the next morning when I went down to fix breakfast and coffee. When I called Ron to breakfast, I yelled, "Bring down that suitcase when you come and hurry up. Our vacation trip to see Aaron is starting."

Within the hour we had everything packed into the car and were on our way to Michigan. As Ron steered the Chevy out of Parkersville, I relished the changing scenery. What profusion, what extravagance, God sent each fall to please our senses: the delectable aroma of wood smoke and the scent of the apples ripening on the trees, the sound of the gentle breeze moving the branches and the honk of geese migrating north, the sight of row upon row of crops ready for harvest, and the gorgeous display of red, yellow-gold, brown, and orange trees.

"How blessed we are to live here, to have this joy," I murmured.

21

~

Eddie, Dar, and Kathy

On the same October day Mattie prepared for her trip to White Grove, *The New York Times* headlined an article from Oslo, Norway, announcing the 1964 winner of the Nobel Peace Prize. The Rev. Dr. Martin Luther King, Jr., thirty-five-year-old civil rights leader from Atlanta, Georgia, was honored "for the furtherance of brotherhood among men and to the abolishment or reduction of standing armies and the extension of these purposes." Dr. King called the honor a tribute to millions of Americans who followed the precepts of nonviolence.

Mattie and Ron did not focus on this world news, busy as they were getting ready to travel. Their nephew, Edmond Connors, by this time a skinny, tall sailor, *did* pay attention. He was at the naval base at Newport, Rhode Island, awaiting assignment to the Seventh Fleet operations in the South Pacific. He expected orders within a few weeks, though he hoped the Vietnam conflict would end soon if President Johnson were reelected. He made it a point to read the *Times* whenever he could pick up a used copy in the post exchange. "Hooray!" he cheered aloud as he read the article. He and Dar had been watching Dr. King for years.

Eddie folded up the *Times* and gathered all the dimes and quarters he could find to use the pay phone to call his friend. Busy signals, tied up lines, people waiting for their turn at the phone; it was always a challenge at Eddie's end. Then there was the likelihood Dar wouldn't be reachable in the dorm. Generally, however, Friday nights provided a good chance to reach Dar, who would likely be studying in his room. Lots to learn in college, apparently. When Dar was called to the phone, he was the first to holler, "Did you read the news? My guy, Dr. King, gets the Peace Prize in Norway this December!"

"I know! That's why I'm calling. I wanted to celebrate with someone. Lots of guys here have no idea what this means. You and me talked so many times about him. Remember when we were seventh graders, he led that bus boycott in Montgomery for a whole year."

"Yeah, after Rosa Parks wouldn't give up her bus seat to a white guy. Who would've thought in those days that a black man from Georgia would be given such an honor?"

"The award comes with a big money prize. According to the article, Dr. King will donate it all to civil rights causes."

"I bet we'll be hearing the news replaying parts of the speech from last summer. At the Lincoln Memorial, remember?"

Dar nodded his head, even though he knew Eddie could not see the gesture. Dar had joined a large contingent of fellow Morehouse students to travel to D.C. last year in August to be a part of the March on Washington for Jobs and Freedom. Eddie had watched the rally on television from his base.

"I was there! Remember? It was awesome! I've practically memorized the speech. 'I have a dream that one day this nation will rise up and live out the true meaning of its creed: We hold these truths to be self-evident, that all men are created equal.' That's what he said, quoting the founding fathers. Powerful stuff. 'Now is the Time!...Let freedom ring from every village and every hamlet, from every state and every city...until we all can join hands and sing in the words of the old Negro spiritual, Free at last! free at last! thank God Almighty, we are free at last!'"

Eddie spoke the last words in unison with Dar, " 'Thank God Almighty; we are free at last!' Wish I'd been in Washington then."

"Last summer when I taught in the Freedom School in Mississippi, my eyes opened to the enormous job ahead," Dar told his friend. "White and black volunteers were teaching. But you'd find a lot of closed minds down there."

"So I've seen. The Democratic convention made the news refusing to seat Negro delegates from Mississippi!"

"It's a long story, Ed. I'll tell you more when I see you."

"I'm hoping to get to Ohio for Christmas, Dar. See you then?" Eddie turned around as one of his shipmates tapped him on the shoulder. The line of guys wanting to get their chance at the phone snaked across the room, and he was getting some dirty looks. "Got to go, Dar. Keep the faith! I miss you, buddy."

Eddie expected to be sent to Vietnam the next year unless Johnson was elected and put an end to the fighting over there. Eddie sat on his bunk remembering his buddy, Dar, and the old high school gang.

The boys and their friends had never made any distinction between who was colored or who was white, not even when they reached their teens and had school dances. Parties pretty much included everyone, with most of the kids circulating, not pairing up. Dar and Eddie went to dances and parties as part of a mixed group that included Dar's older sister, Sophie, an attractive brown-skinned girl with processed hair, straightened with heat and lye to take out the kinks. Her regular features, with a slightly broadened nose and full lips, defined a lovely young lady. At the "dress-up" dances, Sophie's dance card was always full, and Eddie's name always appeared on a couple lines.

Eddie smiled again at the thought that the Nobel Peace Prize was going to Dr. King. He considered calling his mother, but he decided not to, as he was well aware that her attitude toward Dr. King was not at all like his own. He decided to go to his barracks to write a couple letters instead.

—

Eddie's mother, as he suspected she would, had quite a different reaction to the news about Dr. King's receipt of the Nobel Peace Prize. Kathy brought home the *New York Times* from the office when Mr. Gordon finished with it. That evening as she read the offending article, she groaned. She threw the paper down on the floor, disturbing Heather, her calico cat, who meowed loudly, jumping into her lap. She pushed Heather to the floor and spoke out loud. "Giving the Nobel Peace Prize to that agitator. Disgusting!"

She grabbed the paper to carry it to the trash where she stuffed it in with determination. To Heather she mumbled, "I've nothing against Negroes as long as they know their place. Our Eddie has been best friends since kindergarten with that colored boy Dar from Coaltown. When Eddie wanted to bring his new friend over to the apartment, I even got some special dishes for Dar to use. I always washed those dishes separately, but then when the two boys joined Mattie's Cub Scout pack, I stopped worrying. It got to be too much trouble to keep the dishes separate. Dar was very respectful and Eddie loved him so, that I almost forgot how dark his skin was."

Calming down a bit, Kathy sat back in the rocker, allowing Heather to find a comfortable spot on her lap. She continued her musing. *Dar's an exception. Better in school than Eddie, I have to admit.* Eddie never applied himself, though she had tried everything to get him more motivated. Dar seemed to thrive on reading. He always had a book in his hand.

Kathy's mood darkened as her thoughts turned to Dar's sister Sophie. She was part of that gang the Eddie hung around with, a group of about six to eight kids, though she was a couple years older. Around sixth grade, the age when boys hate girls and girls loiter nearby to gossip about the boys, the gang sort of drifted apart. Dar still came over, but Kathy didn't see much of Sophie.

I think she left town for a year or two to live with her aunt in Mississippi, and missed a couple years of school. I remember the day Sophie tagged along with her brother, back in town, back in high school, in Eddie's grade then. The kids were about fifteen or so. Sophie was all made up, wearing a tight skirt and a blue twin sweater set that emphasized her breasts. I heard her talking to Eddie about the winter formal, asking whether he was going to take a date. It was brazen. I thought she should know her place better than that, and I "happened" to interrupt the conversation to ask more about it. She was on the dance committee. Imagine! Well, Eddie and Dar explained that they would attend stag. I relaxed a bit, but I know Eddie signed her dance card a number of times.

Kathy sat while Heather snoozed, her soft purr almost mesmerizing. Dreamily, Kathy spoke aloud to Heather again. "When Sophie finished high school, she left town again. She ran off with some black guy she met down in Mississippi during the summer. They went to Chicago. Had a baby. I'm not sure, but I think I heard she's back with her mother, with the child in school in Annie's class. Could he be Annie's age already? I should ask Annie about him next time she's around."

Kathy rocked back and forth, her thoughts turning back to the article she just read. *Instead of all this agitation, everyone should just cool it. Things will get better over time. Senator Goldwater's right. The federal government shouldn't decide who a person does business with.* Kathy brushed the old brown and gold calico to the floor. She tromped to the kitchen and opened a can of food for Heather, raising her voice as she slammed the food down on the floor. "Why can't they just leave things alone? There's enough trouble in the country without black people stirring up more. President Johnson and that King fellow stirred up a hornet's nest with their civil rights law. I know what it's like to struggle to make a living. On our farm in North Dakota, some years we had so many mouths to feed and the crops failing." Not surprisingly, Heather did not answer, but hurried to gulp down the food.

"I know you don't care, Heather, but sometimes it riles me up. No government stepped in to help us. Our neighbors and we struggled together. We made it on our own. The ambitious ones like Eddie's friend Dar can get to college to make something of themselves. The others are just lazy. Senator Goldwater knows. He'll show them when he's elected. The government should keep its nose out of private citizens' business."

With her rant exhausted, she smiled at the cat and picked her up for a smooch. "You are so handsome, Heather. I'm glad Eddie brought you home to keep me company. You never seem to disagree with my ideas."

22

~

Mattie

That trip to see Aaron and his family was our last to Michigan, but we didn't know it then.

October 1964

Just a few miles from home we drove through Little Egypt, a section of Ron's rural route. I was thinking about another children's story I could write to send to the *Times-Leader* to publish. They sometimes printed my tales of Billy Bunny and Susie Squirrel and sent me a few dollars for them.

Ron suddenly swerved the car and cried out. "What the Devil—," he yelled, almost driving the Chevy off the road.

I yelled, "Watch out!" and grabbed the steering wheel to guide the car back into its lane. I pulled us over, waiting for my heartbeat to slow to normal as I let out my held breath.

"Ron, what's wrong?"

He ignored me, glaring at the landscape. Where once there had been a beautiful forested hillside, now we saw nothing but stumps and branches. It was as though a giant barber had swept in and denuded the hillside. With the trees gone, nothing would be left to hold back the spring rains or snow melt. The soil would wash into the creek bottoms. Worst of all, there in the valley sat the massive machinery deck of the soon-to-be-assembled GEM of Egypt, the largest earth-moving machine ever constructed. A pick-up truck sitting nearby looked like one of the children's matchbox cars. The deck stood there empty, but the papers had published artist's drawings of what was to come. The entire completed earthmover would be 200 feet tall, and the bucket would be able to move 12,000 cubic meters of land in an hour. The platform took up the entire valley.

I had been talking about this with my friend Ruth a few days before, bemoaning ruined scenery. During the next summer season the machine would be fitted with motors and hoist drums, and a huge gantry to hold a giant dipper. The GEM would lift off mountain tops and expose the coal veins for quick removal.

As the pounding of my heart subsided, I said to Ron, "I don't blame you for your anger, Ron. It's awful what the coal company is doing to the land: destroying the whole mountain to get to the coal. Can they be stopped? Does the government have any control?"

Ron didn't reply. He frowned and returned his attention to the road. We continued on our way, lost in thought. I was considering who I might contact to protest the strip mining, or at least to ensure reclamation of land would follow. The children's story I had been imagining was lost. Ron was quiet. His thoughts must have been a hundred miles away.

As we drove through Columbus, I remembered something Ron said yesterday. "What did Mr. Biggs have to say when he called you into his office?"

"What on earth are you talking about? I don't think Biggs was even in yesterday."

"I thought you said something about packages...never mind, we're on vacation now. I wonder how Aaron's new congregation is doing since they started the fall routines."

I continued to chatter with little interruption from Ron. The trip was long and tiring.

23

~

Michigan Family
OCTOBER 16, 1964

Meanwhile, everything in Michigan stood ready for Ron and Mattie's visit. In the Presbyterian manse, where Aaron and his family lived, soup was bubbling on the back of the stove: chicken, onions, carrots, and celery cooking gave off a comforting odor. A fresh loaf of whole wheat bread sat on the counter. A salad of greens sat waiting for the dressing to be applied. Everyone there was waiting, waiting, waiting. Bethie, a curly-haired ten-year-old with tortoise shell glasses magnifying the effect of her hazel eyes, sat with her brother Grant trying to be patient. Grant, the over-active eight-year-old, bounced up every few minutes to look out the window. The children had made "Welcome to White Grove" signs. They had laid out two or three of their favorite books for Gram to read before bedtime. But bedtime was fast approaching and still no sign of the grandparents or word from them about why they were late.

Aaron pulled at his new blonde beard, wondering what his parents would say about it. Aaron felt the beard would compensate for the lack of hair on his head. At thirty-three, Aaron still had the round face and features of a much younger man, despite his beard. Though he was over six feet tall, many in his congregation thought of him as just out of college. He had completed his sermon for the coming Sunday early, in anticipation of his parent's arrival, because he wanted to be able to spend time with Dad. He ticked off the topics of conversation that would be appropriate. Funny how one had to *plan* conversations with parents instead of just letting them happen. Joan had reminded Aaron not to discuss politics this close to the election, for Ron was a staunch Republican and Aaron and Joan were supporters of President Johnson. It'd been a month since the little daisy girl commercial. Except for coverage on the nightly news, it had not been shown again. Aaron was quite sure that mentioning it would start a huge argument with his father, something he did not want to do. Ron served with pleasure on the city council in Parkersville. He believed government should serve the citizens when necessary, but the citizens should take care of whatever they could on their own. Mattie never ventured a political opinion, but Aaron and Joan suspected she was a closet Democrat and Johnson would get her vote when she entered the voting booth. No use getting Mom and Dad into an argument—so, as Joan had reminded him, no talk of politics.

Aaron planned to ask about the scouting. Both parents had been honored by the Parkersville Council for the work they did with Troop 127 and the Cubs. Mattie had led a Cub pack for each of her sons and her two grandsons who live in Parkersville, Mark's boys. In the years between, she had mentored other boys, too, of course, including Aaron's cousin Eddie and his friend Dar Jones. Aaron recalled his scouting days with pleasure, and he knew his parents did as well.

Baseball would be a safe subject, for both father and son hated the N.Y. Yankees. He knew his father would be as thrilled as he was by the 7-5 Cardinal victory yesterday at Sportsman's Park that made the Cards world champions. All this interior dialogue was intended to distract Aaron from the moving clock and the missing grandparents.

"When will Grandmother be here?" Grant asked for the twentieth time that evening. "I can't wait for her to tell us another Billy Bunny story. She makes up the best stories!" Joan didn't even answer the question anymore, but Bethie explained once again that no one knew when they might drive into the yard.

"Gramps probably had to run an errand before they could leave. Maybe the post office needed him to take care of something. Let's have some popcorn and play Go Fish again."

"I wish they'd get here. I am tired of playing cards."

"Sounds to me like you're tired altogether," commented his mother. "Get your pajamas on and I'll pop some popcorn in the kettle."

While the children left the room to get their night-clothes on, Joan turned to Aaron. She took her print apron from the hook by the back door and put in on over her navy skirt, tucking in the flowered blouse for the fifth time in the last hour. Her dark hair was pulled back into a bun, but escaping wisps curled around her ears. "I wonder what did happen to them. They said they'd be here by suppertime. It's near 9:30 now."

"Bethie's right," Aaron replied. "I imagine Dad had to get something or deliver something for the post office and they got a late start. Still, I wish they'd call. I'm sure they'll drive up any minute."

Joan popped the corn and poured small glasses of Kool-Aid for the children. She added a little more water to the soup as she stirred it to be sure it wouldn't burn.

When the children had finished their snack, Aaron declared that, grandparents or no, the children needed to get to bed. Frowning, they kissed their father and went off to brush their teeth. Joan replaced her apron and went up to tuck them in.

Joan sat by Grant's bed for a few minutes, listening to his breathing and remembering.

—

She had met the Connors her freshman year in the fall of 1950 when they came up to Parents Weekend at the College of Wooster. Aaron brought them into the Student Union at about 10:00 in the morning where a coffee pot sat for students to help themselves. (Free coffee, all you could drink, but the pastries cost fifteen cents each, so the Union made out from the appetites of the crowd.)

"Meet my folks, everyone. This is my dad, Ron, the scout leader! And this is my mom, Mattie, who keeps him in line."

"Good day, sir. Mrs. C. Nice to meet you." Aaron's roommate jumped up. "You're responsible for the delicious brownies that come back with Aaron's clean laundry each week. We love you already."

Mattie smiled and accepted the compliment. Ron laughed. "You boys know a good thing when you taste it, I see. Mattie, you need to leave some of the cookies in the kitchen, not send them all to school."

"They never go to waste here, Mr. Connors. Aaron shares them, even if we have to wrestle him to the floor to get them."

"My dad is about the best scout leader anywhere around," Aaron broke in, before his buddies could carry on much more. "He works for the post office, too, but last summer he took five of us to Philmont Scout Ranch on a wilderness survival trip. It was almost non-survival, wasn't it, Dad?"

"Time to change the subject, Aaron," Ron laughed.

Joan and Aaron weren't yet dating at that time, but she was impressed with how Aaron had proudly introduced his folks to all the students sitting there. Joan thought then that such a warm relationship would be a good trait in a husband and father. It was all academic, for Aaron was dating her roommate. Adele and Aaron didn't quite click, so it was Adele's idea for Aaron to ask Joan on a date. She dated Aaron and several other guys, but Aaron was the one she settled on. The fact he was preparing to be a minister had nothing to do with it, but they had some wonderful talks about God and the world and what they ought to do with their lives. Marrying Aaron had been a good choice.

Joan whispered to her sleepy son. "Say a special prayer for Gram and Gramps on the road. I hope they haven't had a breakdown. By the time you wake up they'll be settled in the guest room. I don't want you making a lot of noise in the morning. They'll be tired because they got in so late."

—

Just after midnight, seated in the living room, Aaron looked out at the flashing lights of Sheriff Smedl's patrol car slowing to a stop in front of the house. Joan and Aaron rushed to the door. The sight of the sheriff's car intensified the concern that had been building all evening. Then Ron's grey Chevy pulled into the drive. A very tired Ron climbed out, while Mattie gathered the things from the front seat that always seemed to accumulate with a long car ride.

"Thank you, officer," Ron called with a wave of his hand and a wide, but tired, smile.

"Dad, what's going on?" Aaron exclaimed while Joan hurried to give Ron a big hug, and then walked around the car to help her mother-in-law out.

"Nothing. I just wasn't sure where the manse was, so I looked around for someone to ask. This kind officer was having coffee in the diner down the road and he knew where to find you. Nice fellow. He guided me right into town and down the right street."

Aaron turned to Sheriff Smedl, a member of his congregation, for confirmation.

"He was driving a bit erratically, likely just tired after a long drive. I was glad to help out. Have a good visit, sir. Pastor Aaron will take good care of you, I'm sure."

Mattie struggled to rise from the passenger seat, her arms loaded with stuff she handed to Joan. "Whew, I thought we'd never make it. Have we missed the children? I told you we'd miss them, Ron. You took the wrong turn outside of Toledo and, of course, you wouldn't ask directions. I'm glad I finally made you ask."

"Mom, I bet you're tired," Joan said. "Bethie and Grant waited as long as we let them, but with church and Sunday school tomorrow they needed to get to bed. Come on in. If you're hungry, I still have soup on. I made fresh bread, too. If you'd rather just lie down, the guest room is ready."

"Just a cup of coffee, I think, dear," Mattie replied.

Joan bustled about the kitchen. She poured coffee, while the men unloaded the car. She took the soup off the stove and refrigerated it for the next evening's supper. Then she and Mattie sat down to talk. Clearly, Mattie was exhausted from the trip.

"Church is at 11:00 tomorrow. Aaron needs to go over by 9:00, but we can slip over right before the service. The children will want to spend some time with you. They've picked out some of their favorite books."

They turned as Ron and Aaron entered loaded down with luggage. Ron was still puzzling, almost to himself, about what had caused the delay in arrival. "I thought Aaron said a right turn coming off Route 30. The road signs all seemed to be pointing in the same direction."

"Sorry you missed the kids, Dad. You'll see them in the morning. Did you get a late start?" Aaron asked as Ron put down his keys on the table. Aaron's question was intended to relax his father as they settled in.

Instead, Ron turned on him, yelling, "Stop it! We're here! I've heard plenty of nagging the last few hours from that old hag. I don't want to hear any more!"

Joan, who had been pouring coffee, jumped at her father-in-law's harsh tone. She looked at Mattie questioningly.

"We're here now, Joan. Don't worry," Mattie whispered.

Aaron shook his head and looked hard at his father. Not the sort of response he expected, nor was it typical of Ron. "Mom? What's going on? Is everything okay?"

Again Mattie spoke in a soft voice. "We're tired, dear. It was a long trip. We'll talk in the morning."

—

The next morning at 11:00 the whole family sat in church. Aaron Connors's powerful sermons aimed to explain scripture. For him preaching involved informing and educating, telling the twentieth century Michiganders what God meant by the words first heard by ancient Hebrews and by the first followers of Jesus the Christ. Aaron knew, from his study of Greek and Hebrew and from his study of Biblical history, that changing times and God's Spirit required translation. Aaron was confident that his preaching could open ears and eyes to what God intended for His people today. God's purpose was to be carried out by the hands and feet of church members, healing, giving, serving, righting wrongs, and bringing the gospel message of love through doing.

Aaron introduced his parents to the congregation before he began the service. The topic of Aaron's sermon was "The Company of Strangers," based on the story in Luke of Jesus preaching to his hometown congregation in Nazareth. "Our enemies are God's friends, as much as we are," Aaron preached. "We cannot expect God to respect *our* boundaries. We are invited to follow Him, or get out of the way."

—

Mattie had to stifle the temptation to applaud at the close of her son's sermon. The smile on her face would have to convey the pride she felt. Her plan for Aaron was perfectly in line with God's will, she was sure.

Many kind comments were made by the parishioners as they left the church.

"Fine sermon, pastor. It made me think."

"Welcome, folks. Glad to have you here."

"Hope you enjoy your stay. Thanks, Pastor Aaron. Good sermon."

Mattie commented as they crossed the street to the manse, "I never wondered before why the people in Jesus's hometown were so reluctant to accept him, Aaron." She gave him a hug and added, "I'm so proud of you!"

24

~

Mattie

We had a wonderful visit with family, once we arrived. We walked around the community taking in the stores and scenery. Joan worked as a substitute teacher, but she had taken the week of our visit off. After Bethie got home from school I helped her gather the colorful fall leaves. I showed her how to press them between sheets of waxed paper to put them up in the windows. Grant and his grandfather played catch. Ron showed Grant how to improve his batting by gripping the bat higher. Toward the end of the week's visit in White Grove, Bethie and Grant had a two-day break from school while their teachers had teacher workshops.

1964

That Friday Joan put a beef roast, some onions, potatoes, and carrots into a Dutch oven and put it in the oven to cook slowly while we left for a trip Aaron had planned. While she fixed the dinner, I prepared a lunch to eat on the road and Aaron packed up the station wagon to go to the zoo in Lansing. Outside the zoo we spotted some picnic tables where Joan spread out a table cloth and opened the wax-paper-wrapped peanut butter and jelly sandwiches. Both children claimed to be too excited to eat, but Aaron gave them a "father" look, and they sat down docilely. Soon Grant bounced up again with excitement.

"I can't wait to show you Herman, the Mexican burro, Gram. He used to be in the circus. Have you ever seen a circus?"

I laughed. "Yes, a time or two, Grant. We had a traveling circus come close to home at least once every summer."

"Last year in first grade we had our own circus. I dressed up like a monkey. I haven't seen the monkeys here in this zoo, yet."

"You'll see them soon enough, son," Aaron told him, as we walked from the picnic area to the zoo entrance.

The children stamped their feet with impatience as Aaron paid admission. They hurried us all to look at Herman, a not-too-exciting burro. Grant wanted to go everywhere at once. Joan and Ron followed the children's lead, but I lingered with Aaron at Monkey Island, looking at one female monkey nursing a small baby. We watched for a while in silence.

"Remember in 1947 when Ida Sue was born?" Aaron asked me, thinking back to that August night. "It was right after my sixteenth birthday, and you weren't feeling well."

The scene flooded back into my memory. "I remember. Celebrating your birthday was important for you. Dad took you boys to Wheeling to see Joel McCrea in *Buffalo Bill* and then out for Wimpey burgers. I wanted to go along but, frankly, I was too sick. I was so worried, too. Dr. Dunn made me stay in bed that last couple months because of my high blood pressure. He said I had life-threatening toxemia. Aunt Kathy had to come to help out, remember?"

"I remember you came into our room that night before you went to the hospital. You told us to pray for our new little brother or sister. You read from Grandpa Jake's Bible, the verse from John's gospel about Jesus going to prepare us room in Heaven. Mark and I were scared. We wondered what you were trying to tell us."

"When I kissed you boys goodnight I kissed you goodbye in my mind. I wasn't sure I would ever see you again."

"I remember you didn't come home with a baby. And you stayed in the hospital for a long time, a couple weeks, as I recall."

Aaron's words brought tears to my eyes once again. The daughter we wanted so much was born dead. "You boys, my wonderful sons, are my consolation, and now your children add joy to my life," I told him.

There was no more time to chat, because Bethie and Grant came running up to grab my hands to lead me into the reptile house, begging their father to show them the salamanders.

25

Ron
OCTOBER 1964

When Mattie and the children ran off with Aaron, Ron settled down on the closest bench. He felt so tired. He needed to rest. "How are you doing, Dad?" a woman asked him while they watched the lions roam the yard. She looked very familiar, but he couldn't quite remember her name, or how he was supposed to know her.

Is this right? Ron thought. *There's something I should be remembering. Yesterday Mr. Biggs had to remind me it was time to go home and start my vacation. And today I'm here at a zoo. I've been forgetting things now and then all my life, but now it seems much worse. I watch Mattie for clues. She hasn't noticed my forgetting much. She remembers for both of us. She's always had a wonderful memory. I think she sometimes remembers things that never happened. I learned long ago not to doubt her. Why am I here with this woman? Who is she? Why is she asking how I am?*

"The navy wouldn't take me. They took Josh," Ron said.

The woman stared at him, a puzzled look on her face. She asked, "Josh was your brother, Aunt Kathy's husband, wasn't he? Aaron doesn't talk much about him."

Ron was even more confused about how this woman seemed to know so much about his family. But he smiled at the mention of Kathy, remembering Josh's letter in 1941 promising a wonderful surprise. *Josh had indeed surprised all of us. It turned out to be, as Josh had promised, as wonderful as it was surprising. He brought home such a pretty, young bride.*

26

~

White Grove

Watching her father-in-law, Joan knew her question about Josh had evoked some strong feeling. *What is behind that smile?* Joan wondered. *I wish I could see what is going on inside his mind.* "We need to get going, Dad. Everyone else is meeting us by the entrance at three. We have a bit of a drive ahead."

~

As they entered the manse, the delectable aroma of beef and potatoes greeted them. "Yum," Grant yelled. "Smell that, Grampa?"

Ron nodded, though he didn't seem to have much sense of smell. Joan directed Bethie and Grant to set the table as she dished up her oven supper. For dessert Joan served the last of Mattie's brownies and cookies (she would make more before they left White Grove) and some ice cream from the store. Soon after cleanup, Mattie, Ron, and the two kids were all weary enough to head off to bed.

"Your mother looks pretty tired, I think," Joan said to her husband as they settled into bed themselves. "She's worked hard, raising you two boys and now looking after Mark's kids. It's funny how different your life and Mark's turned out."

~

The next morning Joan awakened still thinking about Mark. As breakfast ended, and after family devotions, the men walked over to the church. Aaron had asked Ron to make a few minor repairs on an electric outlet. Grant settled down with his comic books in his room. Joan and Mattie took coffee out into the backyard to sit at the picnic table while Bethie did up the few breakfast dishes. In a few minutes she joined her mother and grandmother in the yard and begged Grandma to tell her a story about Aaron as a little boy.

"He was a good student. You are too, your mom tells me. He used to line up all the other kids in the neighborhood and preach to them from behind an orange crate he called his pulpit. We all knew he'd turn out to be a preacher! He worked hard all through school, except in third grade when he tried to convince his teacher he was dumb so he wouldn't be assigned to Mrs. Bates's fourth grade class. He had heard she was a tough teacher. She always took the smarter kids, and your dad thought he could get out of her class if he acted a little stupid. It didn't work, though. I think he would admit that the year with Mrs. Bates was the best one he spent in Parkersville schools."

"It sounds like Billy Bunny and his teacher in the story you made up for us. He tried to fool her into thinking he wasn't smart."

"Yes, it does a little." Mattie beamed as she recalled the young Aaron. "Your dad worked hard from then on to graduate at the top of his class. He won scholarships and took work-study jobs at the college to go straight on through college and seminary."

Joan brought out her mending basket, and both she and Mattie set to work sewing on buttons and patching torn knees in the children's clothes.

"How is Mark's family?" Joan asked. "Wish we got to see them more often."

"They're all well. Jake and Annie still come over to my house after school until their mom or dad can pick them up to go out to their place outside of town. I guess they could ride the school bus, but I like having them come to see me. I do wish you were closer, Bethie. It's fun when you come for the summers."

"What is Roy planning to do after high school?" Joan asked Mattie. "He must be thinking of his future."

"I think he wants to be the next sailor with the Connors name. The navy recruiters are knocking at his door. He has to register for the draft when he is eighteen. Patty is trying to convince him to join ROTC at Ohio State and put off any military service until he has college behind him. With this war in Vietnam going on, I think that would be much preferred. We sure hope the war will be over soon and Roy won't be dragged into battle."

"How is Aunt Kathy doing with Eddie being in the navy?"

Mattie was quiet for a minute. Then she said thoughtfully, "Ron wanted to join the navy, you know, because of his big brother Josh. He had models and pictures of navy ships and a big scrapbook of 'Join the Navy and See the World' stuff. While Eddie stayed with me, he used to study the scrapbook and make up stories of his own. So, between Ron's ship models and the tales of adventure he heard about his father, most of Eddie's growing up was navy, navy, navy all the time."

"So Eddie never got it out of his system?"

"Just about. Aunt Kathy had mixed feelings about his service. She wanted him to be brave like his father, but....You know the navy wasn't straight with her about Josh's ship. Richard Newcomb recently wrote a book about the USS *Indianapolis* called *Abandon Ship*. It was terrible to read about the navy's negligence." Mattie's voice trailed off as she pictured for the ten-thousandth time sailors struggling in the Pacific as the war was ending.

The two women sat in silence for a few moments longer. Bethie seemed to sense their contemplative mood, and was quiet as well. Finally Joan gathered up the coffee cups and sewing supplies. Mattie went inside to pack for the return trip.

27

~

Ron

The visit in White Grove ended the next day. The morning after their long drive back to Parkersville was clear and cold. Ron wanted to get started early on the route, so he arrived at the post office before 7:00. The post office was quiet at that hour. The windows didn't open until 8:30. Postmaster Biggs greeted him at the rear door as he parked the Chevy. "Come on into my office, Ron. I need to talk to you about something."

Mr. Biggs sat at his desk. Ron stood in front of him, slightly bemused at having to break his routine.

"Elmer Drake has been delivering your route the last week. Some of the patrons have been concerned that their mail hasn't been arriving as it should," Mr. Biggs stated.

Ron smiled. "Elmer isn't as familiar with the route. It's no wonder he makes a few mistakes."

"No, these are your mistakes, Ron. The people along Majestic Road say you've not delivered their mail in the last month. You left packages for the Howells at the Howards' house and skipped some mailboxes at the start of your route altogether."

Ron didn't understand everything Mr. Biggs said. He waited, saying nothing, hoping it would clear itself up. He recognized his memory was slipping, but what was this about?

"I talked to you about this before you left on vacation."

"I don't understand," Ron told him. "Majestic Road is Route #2, isn't it?"

"It was five years ago, before we rearranged the routes. We changed the route because of the coal company digging in Egypt Valley. But you've been delivering there the last two years. Until two weeks ago, apparently."

Why didn't they tell me they changed it? They're trying to confuse me. Majestic Road is part of Lansing's route. Ron shrugged his shoulders and said, "Well…I don't know what's wrong. Someone is trying to mess me up."

"Ron, I hate to take away your route, but I can't let this continue. Elmer will deliver this week again. You can case the incoming mail. You need to talk to your doctor, Ron, to find out what's going on."

Ron shook his head, hoping to clear up the confusion he was feeling. Then he rose and walked out the door. He didn't want to do the more menial task of sorting letters into cases. That's how he started. Driving a route was his job. He also didn't want to go home to explain it to Mattie.

Ron left through the back door. Once outside he looked around. He stared across the street at the M & P grocery store. *I know I parked my Chevy in the P.O. lot, but it's not here. Great! Now someone stole my car! What's next? As if things weren't bad enough.*

He walked to Main Street, turned, and began to amble west to get away from there. He continued to wander, not sure where to head. He ended up at Kathy's house.

28

~

Kathy

Kathy that morning was planning ahead to the work awaiting her at the office. The mailing to Republicans around Ohio needed to be sent that day, reminding them President Johnson was too dangerous to serve another term. She finished breakfast and began her cleanup chores, thinking about her sailor son Eddie and how the upcoming election might affect him. What would the election results mean to the continuance or stopping of the military action in Vietnam? Standing at the sink doing up the breakfast dishes before heading out, she was surprised to see Ron walk in her back door and sink into a chair at her kitchen table. One glimpse of Ron's stooped shoulders told her something was awry.

"Ron! What are you doing here? Are you still on vacation?"

"Vacation? Oh, yes, we went on a trip. It was fun. Do you have coffee on?"

"I have tea in this pot. I'm not drinking coffee any more. I can brew some up in no time though. Are you okay? Shouldn't you be back at work?"

"Biggs gave me today off. He said I looked tired after the trip. Elmer Drake is carrying the route today."

"Well, that's good. Relax a bit. I leave for work soon, but tell me, how are Aaron and the family? I haven't heard much about their new church."

"They're fine, I think. They haven't written in a long while. I guess they're pretty busy."

Kathy was puzzled. "Didn't you just visit them last week?"

"Oh, sure! I meant they didn't write before we went up there. Beth and Grant are doing great. We all went to visit the zoo in Columbus."

"Columbus Zoo? Don't you mean the one in Michigan?"

"Oh, yes. I meant in Lansing. I was thinking about Josh while I watched the lions."

Kathy sighed. "I miss him so much. I somehow thought he'd get through the war and come back to me. The day I got the telegram I thought my life was over."

Ron looked around with a confused expression, as if he didn't know where he was. "I remember. We were all stunned." Ron's mind wandered back to the terrible days in August 1945. For a long while, neither Kathy nor Ron spoke. Then Kathy turned from her sink and studied Ron's face. Ron, sitting in Kathy's kitchen, looked so devastated. Kathy broke his reverie with a question.

"You're a hundred miles away in your thoughts, Ron. Do you want to talk?"

Ron looked around, wondering where he was. Kathy poured him a cup of the fresh-brewed coffee. He reached for his coffee cup and drained it. Kathy, frowning a little, refilled the cup. "Would you like something to eat? All I have is graham crackers, unless you'd like a sandwich. I haven't made *apfelkuchen* in a long time."

Kathy looked at her watch, then at Ron's vacant stare. She realized she must be at work soon. She went into her bedroom to gather up her purse and jacket and heard Ron's voice. "We miss you, Josh."

She entered the kitchen with her coat on. "Ron, I need to get over to the office. We aren't all on vacation, you know. Elections are in two weeks and my boss has a lot of things to arrange. I need to see that the Goldwater volunteers are lined up for phone calling. You are welcome to stay and finish your coffee. Please turn off the lights when you leave."

"I think I'll use your bathroom. Then I'll get on home. Don't worry about me."

Kathy puzzled over what might be going on as she adjusted her hat and picked up her purse. The conversation had seemed odd. Before walking out the door, Kathy remembered that she needed her checkbook. She walked back to her bedroom to pick it up. There was Ron lying fully clothed on her bed, sound asleep.

"Well, I guess he needs the sleep," she thought to herself. She let herself out the front door and climbed into her old Ford rattletrap to drive to work.

—

Four hours later Ron woke up and looked around. The sunlight flooded through the window. Where was he? Feeling like Rip Van Winkle, Ron found his way to the bathroom and turned on the water. He splashed cold water on his face a few times. He glanced at a weary, wrinkled countenance staring back at him. "Is that me?" he asked himself aloud. He walked out to the kitchen and studied the Goldwater for President poster Kathy had put up. He studied the calendar where

Kathy crossed off each day as it passed—October 1964. He peered at the clock on the wall but could make little sense of the hands and numbers.

"Wow, I'm late to work."

He hurried up the street to the post office where Mr. Biggs met him at the door.

"So you're back. Did you see your doctor?"

"Doctor? Is someone sick?"

Mr. Biggs shrugged. "You need to talk to Doc Dunn about things. Are you ready to work at putting letters into the case for Elmer to deliver on the route tomorrow?"

"Okay. I expect I need a change of pace. I've been so tired."

29

Election
NOVEMBER 3, 1964

Roger was at Kathy's house, lying in her bed, when the election results were announced on her TV. It turned out to be a landslide for Johnson, who won over sixty-one percent of the popular vote. Goldwater won his native state of Arizona and five deep South states that had been alienated by Democratic civil rights policies. Kathy rose to turn off the television. "Well, that's it then. Only Arizona and the South. How can voters be so blind?"

"This country is on the road to socialism. They don't understand how the 'Great Society' will unleash all kinds of trouble." Roger picked up his clothes and began dressing. "At least Boyle was reelected. He is getting pretty old and I don't think he will continue to run for many more years."

"It was a mistake to allow the Negro people to register and vote," Kathy said. "Eddie's friend Dar has been getting involved in protests and such. I haven't seen him around for a while."

Roger ignored Kathy's line of thinking, for he was speculating on his own future. "Don't you think 'Representative Roger Gordon' has a nice ring to it?"

"What? Roger? Will you run for Congress?"

"Why not? I've already had experience with some of the Republican bigwigs in San Francisco last summer. I think Boyle would support me if he decides to retire."

Not waiting for Kathy's response, Roger was already in the bathroom cleaning up for his ride home. *It would be possible, if I could garner the support I need*, he thought. From that moment on, Roger began to plan for his future in politics. He set his sights on running in 1968 for Boyle's seat.

⁓

By the time of the election, Eddie Connors was in his fourth year of service in the navy. He held the rank of Radio Mate First Class, skilled in all sorts of radio and radar operations. He rejoiced over the election outcome, for it meant that the trigger-happy Senator Goldwater was defeated and the escalation of the situation in Vietnam would stop.

Eddie's relief was too soon and too shortsighted. Despite Goldwater's defeat, President Johnson escalated the war. Before the 1964 election President Johnson, to demonstrate his Commander-in-Chief credentials and his determination to be tough in the Cold War, had ordered air strikes on North Vietnam. Eddie and his navy buddies knew that the encounter between North Vietnamese submarines and two American destroyers deployed in Vietnamese waters the previous August had raised the stakes. Johnson had convinced Congress to pass the Gulf of Tonkin Resolution, which authorized the president to "take all necessary measures" to resist aggression.

With the Gulf of Tonkin Resolution as his authority to expand military might, President Johnson appointed General William Westmoreland to command troops and increased the military advisors to 23,000. The strategy put gradual pressure on the North Vietnamese to support sabotage and guerilla fighting.

Early in November, with no sign that the election had quieted war rumors, Eddie received orders to join the *USS Hammer*, a destroyer in the waters by the Republic of South Vietnam. He was ordered to report for transport on January 1, 1965. He had a one-week leave over Christmas. He called his mother at the end of November when he got his orders.

"Good news and bad news, Mom," Eddie told her. "I have a one-week leave over Christmas. That's the good."

"Don't give me too much bad, Eddie. With the election results, I'm upset enough. Your uncle Ron is not well either."

"Sorry to hear that, Mom. I know you liked Goldwater, but I was glad he lost. Thought it would cool down the aggressive military stance. I still have hope. What's up with Uncle Ron?"

"I don't know, *Liebchen*. Something strange in the way he behaves. He stopped by here after his trip to Michigan to visit Aaron. He sounded *verrucht*, weird. I can't decide whether to talk to Aunt Mattie." She paused, then asked, "What's up with you? I'm glad you'll be home for Christmas."

"I ship out to Vietnam after the first of the year. I signed up to defend our way of life, but going to the jungles of Vietnam makes me feel like one of your fairy tale characters exiled to a foreign land."

Eddie heard his mother catch her breath. "Your dad would be proud of you. He died defending our freedom for you. Don't take any unnecessary chances...." She sounded about to cry. After a quick goodbye, she hung up the phone, and Eddie was left hoping he had not upset her too much.

—

After hanging up abruptly, Kathy sat for a moment while Heather leaped up to her lap. "I'm afraid for him, Heather. I don't want to lose him as I lost his father. I miss Josh, and I'm so afraid for Eddie." She shuddered as the fear sunk in. "Scoot, Heather, I want to look at my letters."

She pushed the cat aside and went to the closet where she kept her treasures in a hat box from Marshall Fields. In the box were two piles of letters, those from Eddie, and those precious ones from Josh, all the letters she had received from him over the few years they had together. The stack began with the December 1941 note proposing to her, which had broken down her resistance and led her to say yes.

Kathy smiled as she read Josh's first letter for the millionth time. Then with tears close to falling she looked at the others that followed: just after he left Parkersville, there was praise for her bravery in taking up the new life; he assured her everyone in Parkersville (even Mom and Dad) welcomed her and wanted her to succeed there; he told tales of the ribbing he had taken from his buddies over "the old man" settling down so suddenly. She laughed when she read how they threw him overboard ("in shallow water, dear, don't worry") to celebrate the marriage. "You are lucky you aren't here, dearest, or they'd shower you with flowers and rice."

Kathy looked at the later letters, v-forms which the government encouraged everyone to use, to save shipping costs to support the war effort. Many of those bore heavy censorship, but he managed to get in a few "I love you's" and even a joking "marry me" that the censors left uncut. There was one last letter that Josh had written and left at the Fleet Post Office in Guam as the *Indianapolis* departed for its final journey. The letter, delivered eighteen months after the notification from the navy that Josh's ship had been torpedoed, she had read over and over when she got it. Now she set it down in the pile unread. It was too difficult to hear his excitement that his last mission would deliver a package that might soon end the war so he could be with her to continue their life together.

At the bottom of the stack were the two telegrams from the navy department, MIA and Killed in Action. Next to the letters lay the medal awarded to Josh after his death. Such a loss, she thought—to us, to Eddie, and to the world.

—

As Kathy stared at the pile of letters, she thought again of the strange morning encounter with a befuddled Ron a few weeks before. Since her torrid but brief affair with Butch Nelson, Kathy had told Ron to stay out of her life. She had moved and begun her "business" relationship with Roger. She had avoided seeing Ron altogether. Then he just showed up that morning after his trip, and they had that bizarre conversation. She hadn't seen Mattie for a while, either. Did Mattie know how Ron seemed to have lost his focus?

Still, it wasn't Kathy's business any longer. She was reluctant to approach her sister-in-law, as Mattie seemed to resent the bond that had grown between Kathy and Ron after Josh died in the war. That period of mourning, though almost twenty years before, might have been yesterday for the vividness of the feelings Kathy still suffered. She had lived in a fantasy half-world of physical comfort found in her brother-in-law's arms. After they had spent the day, first in sorrow, then in loving embrace, she dreamed, wished even, that Ron would say he loved her, but he would never say those words. Realizing that Ron was Mattie's alone had been the final motivation to send him away.

Now that Lyndon Johnson had won the election, Kathy had another reason to be reluctant to approach Mattie with her qualms about Ron's well-being. In her heart, Kathy was convinced Goldwater should have been elected for the good of the whole country.

I'm so fearful of this country's attitude, she mused. *We are not walking, but running pell-mell, headlong into socialism. People are so anxious for security that they are selling their freedom for it. I know I should say something to Mattie about Ron, but she will be so caught up in her sense of "victory" that she won't be easy to talk to.*

30

~

Mattie

I hadn't seen Kathy since our trip to Michigan, though I had thought about her often. I debated with myself about calling her. I even picked up the phone to invite her for Thanksgiving, but I got a busy signal and didn't feel brave enough to try again after that. I wanted to talk to her about the election results, but I was afraid she would think I was gloating. So it pleased me when she stopped by the house the Monday after Thanksgiving.

Thanksgiving – Christmas 1964

Kathy knocked lightly on the front door before sticking in her head. "Anybody home?" she hollered.

"Welcome, stranger," I greeted her, looking up from my typewriter. I glanced around the room, glad I had taken the time earlier to straighten up a little. I rose a bit stiffly—my arthritis again. I started to guide Kathy to the sitting room, the room reserved for formal company, but I changed my mind and invited her into the kitchen instead where I put on the kettle for tea. "Come sit a while. How have you been?"

"*Sehr gut.* I'm good. I wondered how your trip to Aaron's house went."

I got down a plate, filled it with cookies, and put it in front of Kathy. "We had fun," I told her. "We got hopelessly lost on the way, but we did enjoy the drive. Fall leaves were wonderful everywhere. Bethie and Grant were such fun. We all went to the zoo together. Aaron's church was wonderful…" I stopped myself midsentence. I knew Kathy's opinion about Presbyterians on their road to hell. The tea kettle whistled, and I jumped up to grab it. I brewed a pot of tea. While it steeped there was an awkward silence.

I searched my brain for what might be a safe thing to say about Aaron.

"About Ron..." Kathy began at the same moment that I said, "Oh, the tea must be ready by now."

I went to the cupboard and took down two of my best tea cups. I filled them and got out the milk for my guest.

"About Ron..." Kathy began again. "Um...do you think he's feeling okay?"

"As far as I know," I said. "He seems to have picked up a cold on the trip. He took a couple extra days off work, but he has some sick leave coming. Have you talked to him since we got back? I haven't seen you in a coon's age. How have you been feeling?"

"Um...fine." Kathy did not answer my question about seeing Ron. Instead she asked, "Have you noticed anything funny about how Ron is behaving? He seems not to be as focused as he used to be."

"He was tired from the drive. As I said, he's had a cold that he must have caught up in Michigan. We were outdoors at the zoo for quite a while."

"Ron started to tell me that you went to the *Columbus* Zoo."

"That's silly. We went to the Potter Park Zoo in Lansing."

"Don't you think it seems a bit funny—that he would make that mistake?"

"I'm sure you've made the same kind of mistake yourself. Saying one city when you mean another. He's just tired and was coming down with a cold when we got home."

"Still, I am worried about him. His eyes aren't full of life like they used to be."

I bridled. Kathy hadn't even been around for a long while. What made her think she had a right to say anything? "Well, it isn't your worry, in any case. As it happens, Ron has a checkup scheduled with Dr. Dunn right after Christmas. I'll ask his opinion. I'm sure he's going to give Ron a clean bill of health."

I thought perhaps I sounded a bit short with my sister-in-law, so I lowered my tone, took a deep breath, and asked, "Would you like to come for Christmas dinner? It's been quite a while since you joined us for Christmas. Mark and Patty and their three are coming over. Roy is bringing his girlfriend, though I don't think they're serious. Although I wasn't sure Mark and Patty were serious and they were. I'm sure Aaron and Joan will call. They'll want to talk to Aunt Kathy."

"Thanks, Mattie, but Eddie will be home for the week. He'll be shipping out soon after."

"So he told me in his last note. Why don't you and Eddie both come for dinner?"

"We'll have to see. I plan to ask him to take me to Pittsburgh the day before Christmas. I'm going to see Kathryn Kuhlman, the faith healer, in the Carnegie Auditorium. You've seen her on TV, Mattie. Her program is *I Believe in Miracles*.

It's amazing how she can heal people just by touching them. People in the audience can request healing prayers. I'll fill out a request for her to pray for Ron for healing."

"He doesn't need to be healed, Kathy. He's fine." There was an uneasy silence as we both stared into our cups. I knew I sounded angry this time. When I finally looked up, Kathy was gazing at me intensely, with what looked like pity. After a moment, she stood up abruptly and began to gather the tea cups. I rose to finish the task. "Ron is fine, Kathy," I repeated, stacking the dishes in the sink without saying anything more.

"I need to get going. I have a lot of errands to run. Glad you had a good visit in Michigan." Kathy put on her coat and hastened out the door.

"Remember, you're invited for Christmas dinner," I called after her. I thought to myself: *She won't come, I know, but I hope we get to see Eddie.*

—

As Christmas approached, Ron seemed distant. It was the busiest time of the year at the post office, so I assumed that this explained his distraction.

According to family tradition, I put up the Christmas tree by myself. When Aaron and Mark were little they always helped. When they left home, my nephew Eddie and his gang came over to help me put up the tree. Now, they were all grown and away, so the task fell to me. I loved each ornament, and every one reminded me of some Christmas past. I hummed Christmas carols. *If Eddie and his friend Dar get here before Christmas, maybe they'll string popcorn and cranberries to drape on the tree. I'll hang the strings outside after Christmas for the birds. If Dar and Eddie don't come, I'll ask Annie and Jake.*

Ron brought in the tree. I hung the lights and chains and placed each ornament with care. The tinsel strands must be hung one by one, you know, and it takes a while. I saved the placing of the star for Ron. That was always his part. When he came in, I handed the star to him. He looked at it and said aloud, "What should I do with this?"

I laughed at the joke, pointing out where it should go.

31

~

Ron

Ron put the star on the tree as Mattie told him to. He went out to the back-yard to sit at the snow-covered picnic table. Ron knew it was Christmas, but he couldn't figure out how it had snuck up on him. He usually liked Christmas, with its decorations and good things to eat, but somehow it was different that year.

He'd not told Mattie about the post office—how he rode only as a helper to Elmer—on the route which had been his before they went on the visit to Michigan. He pondered, *When we drove to—someplace—to see Aaron, I think—we got a little lost on the road. Mattie kept nagging me. I hate her nagging. I ignore it when I can. We got there okay.*

Ron fretted that he couldn't seem to remember what to call things. *We'll go see Dr. Whatshisname after Christmas. He'll give me a pill to help me remember. He'll give me a note-thing to tell Biggs at work to let me drive my route again. If I think real hard, I can do it. I know I can.*

32

Family Celebrations
CHRISTMAS DAY, 1964

Christmas morning Mattie scurried about the kitchen preparing the dinner. They had gone to the Christmas Eve service and come home late. Mattie encouraged Ron to sleep in, though he usually rose by six in the morning. Patty and Mark and the children came to dinner along with Roy's current flame, Mimi. Turkey with all the trimmings is a quick description of the Christmas dinner, but doesn't do justice to the spread. The turkey was roasted to perfection, a golden-brown bird, eighteen pounds, because everyone loved turkey leftovers for the next week. Some would be packed up to go home with Mark's family. Delicious gravy, two bowls, one with the giblets included and one without, sat on the table like a royal couple on their thrones. Mounds of buttery mashed potatoes, stuffing both in the turkey and in an extra casserole, and a pan of squash, apples, and brown sugar were side dishes worthy of a king. Mattie could not serve a holiday meal without her homemade Parker House rolls. Creamed onions, green bean casserole with white sauce, and two kinds of homemade cranberry sauce had to be passed, then carried back to the kitchen, for there was no room for them on the table. When the main meal finished, the pumpkin pie with whipped cream and the apple pie with cheese had to wait for a two to three hour intermission until the participants could stuff down another bite. Patty brought the pies, but every other dish had been prepared by Mattie over the two days previous.

—

At Eddie's house, Dar and his sister Sophie dropped by to bring holiday greetings. Brett, a ten-year-old the color of black coffee, with closely cropped curly hair and a slight limp, accompanied his mother. Dar had told Eddie in confidence that the time Sophie stayed in Mississippi, missing her eighth grade year, it was to bear this son, who she then left in Mississippi with her Aunt Ruby. Eddie never let on he knew this fact. When after graduation Sophie had returned to Mississippi, Eddie regretted her leaving. She had wanted to be with her son and try to put her life together down there, even taking some classes toward a practical nurse's certification.

Finally, after Brett's father threatened and abused them, Sophie had decided Parkersville, with all its restrictions, was still a better place to raise her son. Last August she gathered him up and left the abuse to return to Parkersville to her mother's home. Sophie worked cleaning houses but was looking for a different job. So much was still closed to her if she didn't "know her place." Brett was in Mrs. Bates's fourth grade class along with Annie Connors, Mark's daughter.

Kathy had served a simple dinner, topped off with *apfelkuchen* and whipped cream. "Join us," Eddie shouted to his friends as they entered. "It's the apple cake you love, Dar."

Kathy served up three more plates and then left the kitchen. She liked Dar well enough, but she put a limit to her hospitality when she felt "outnumbered" by the young people.

"So what's up, buddy?" Eddie asked, between large bites of his favorite treat.

"Ever since the March on Washington, I've been keeping up the fight for our rights, despite the arrests and beatings, even murders," Dar began. He'd already told Eddie about the summer he'd spent in Jackson, Mississippi, teaching basic literacy, arithmetic, black history, civil rights, and the freedom movement at one of the freedom schools. Eddie had also seen newsreels of the violence and the ugly images on TV and worried about his friend's safety.

"I returned to Morehouse this fall, but I kept informed about the work of the guy who recruited me for the freedom school. He was a Howard University student named Stokely Carmichael I met at the March on Washington when a bunch of us went to hear Dr. King give that Dream Speech. Stokely stayed in Mississippi to help organize the Mississippi Freedom Democratic Party (MFDP) as an alternative to the very white, very segregated Democratic Party establishment," Dar continued. "The MFDP managed to elect a slate of delegates to the 1964 Democratic convention in Atlantic City that nominated Johnson for reelection. But the all-white, segregationist Mississippi Democrats who had gone through their own series of party conventions insisted their delegates were the 'official' ones. They offered a compromise to seat the MFDP as 'observers.' When the credentials committee, after some deliberation, ruled not to seat the MFDP delegation, black activists were incensed."

Dar concluded his answer to Eddie's question with a question of his own.

"What was the use of the summer freedom schools and all the efforts to raise consciousness and encourage voter registration if this was the outcome?"

Dar leaned over and lifted his shirt and sweater. He showed Eddie the scars remaining on his back. "A bunch of bigots did this last summer before they arrested me."

Eddie winced, "Ouch! That must've hurt like hell. How can those rednecks be so stupid? I wish I'd been there to return the favor!"

Dar nodded and shrugged, digging into the *apfelkuchen* with relish. "I think we may finally be getting somewhere. President Johnson's going to speak at the Howard University commencement in May. He's celebrating the Civil Rights Act and pushing for a voting rights bill. Equality is a right that has to become a fact!"

Eddie turned the subject to Martin Luther King's speech when he accepted the Nobel Prize in December. "Awesome. He told it like it is. 'We will return good for evil. Christ showed us the way. Mahatma Gandhi showed us nonviolence could work.' He's a believer in the nonviolence stuff! Somehow, though, we're the nonviolent ones and end up getting beaten."

Dar muttered, "I hope I'm right that we're making progress. Martin's words sound good, but I just don't know whether nonviolence is enough."

Eddie turned and smiled at Sophie. "Welcome back to you, girl. Good to see you." To Brett he asked, "How you liking your mama's home town, Brett?"

"It's okay. I liked Mississippi better."

"Brett, don't talk like that," Sophie interrupted. "He has his head in books all the time anyway. And magazines. Thinks he'll grow up to be an astronaut."

By now all the *apfelkuchen* was gone, but Eddie was still hungry. "Let's mosey over to Aunt Mattie's house. She'll have plenty of good stuff to eat." He yelled into the next room to tell Kathy where they were headed. "Want to come along, Mom?"

"Tell them Merry Christmas from me, *liebchen*. See if you notice any changes in your uncle."

As they piled into his mom's car, Eddie opened the door for Sophie and Brett. After they'd settled into the car and Eddie started driving to Aunt Mattie's, Sophie asked Eddie what 1965 held in store for him.

"I'm assigned to the Seventh Fleet in the Pacific. I report right after the new year. We're going to shell bridges, rail lines, artillery batteries, to try to destroy the supply line from the Viet Cong to their armies in the south. We'll be aiming only at military targets, according to the orders I've seen."

They parked at the Washington Street house and clambered out of the car. They knocked on the door, then pushed it open, yelling, "Merry Christmas."

"Come in, come in. 'Home is the sailor, home from the sea.' It's wonderful to see you, to see all of you!" Mattie yelled.

"Haven't had our share of popcorn stringing, Aunt Mattie," Eddie laughed. "Your beautiful tree needs one more touch."

"Lead us to the popcorn, Aunt Mattie," Sophie echoed. "We were over at Eddie's house and kidnapped him away from his mom."

"Annie, look who's here: your friend from school, Brett. Show him your new albums. Do you like the Beatles, Brett?"

"Yes, ma'am," Brett mumbled and hurried out with Annie. Mattie offered pie all around, and soon everyone was stuffing their mouths again and chattering at once. When Mattie went to the kitchen to pop some corn, Eddie followed her in and told her about his new assignment. As she warned him to be safe, Eddie snuck a look at Uncle Ron, trying to spot what his mother noticed. *He looks tired, but that's not so unusual by Christmas Day. I sure hope Mom is wrong about his being ill.*

33

~

Mattie

The visit to Dr. Dunn on January 10, 1965, was a routine checkup. I knew Ron had been acting a bit distracted over the past year, but I hoped some vitamins or antibiotics might make him feel his old self again.

January 1965

Snow fell in beautiful big flakes the day Ron was due to see Dr. Dunn. Ron asked me to drive, saying he'd not slept too well the night before. I found out later Ron had misplaced his car keys and was too sheepish to say so.

After the usual taking of vital signs, knee thumping, and having Ron pee in a cup, Dr. Dunn examined his chest and tonsils. "Looking good, Ron. How are you feeling? I think that your blood pressure is a little high, but that's a part of aging."

"I feel fine, Doc. I seem to be a little slower, a bit more forgetful. Sometimes my eyesight is a bit blurry, but most of the time I feel fine."

I spoke up then, as I had more or less promised Kathy I would. "Ron's eyes are looking sort of dull, I think. He seems more depressed than he used to be."

"Let me look again. Yep, I don't see the old Connors sparkle. Is there some reason for you to be depressed, Ron?"

"Mr. Biggs is not letting me drive my route alone. Can you write something on a doctor's pad to tell him I'm in good health?"

"Sure, no problem," Dr. Dunn replied. "Biggs seems to want to throw his weight around a little too much."

I looked at Ron in surprise. "You didn't tell me you aren't driving your route alone. Is Elmer still going out with you after the holiday rush?"

"Doc's note will straighten it out. Don't you think so, doc?"

"You might be suffering from some hardening of the arteries. You are a little young for that to be happening, but it's nothing to worry about. We all get a bit forgetful in old age," he laughed. "I'll write you a prescription to show Biggs you're in fine physical shape." Dr. Dunn proceeded to do just that. He showed us to the door and told us to come back next year or in between if we had questions.

—

The next morning, I settled into my daily and weekly routines: reports to the Wheeling and New Pittsburgh papers with the Parkersville news notes, calling in funeral details when they arose, Twig meetings for the hospital auxiliary. I wrote letters to the editors of papers around the region and to county supervisors urging that something be done about the GEM, the Giant Earth Mover, and the unfettered strip mining ruining the hills around Washington County. My friend Ruthie Reed came over to help me with the letter writing to congressmen and senators seeking federal action. Ruth's husband John owned Reed Hardware. He was also Parkersville's mayor. He had phoned Ron yesterday evening, in his role as mayor, to check into a citizen complaint about the traffic light on Washington and Main.

While we worked Ruth told me John was concerned. "When he hung up the phone he turned to me and said, 'Well, that was strange. Ron didn't seem to know what I was talking about.'"

"I don't think Ron did connect, Ruth. I'm worried about him," I said.

"Didn't you see Dr. Dunn yesterday? What did he say?"

"Dr. Dunn reassured me, Ruthie, but sometimes I wonder if Dr. Dunn is up to date with the latest ideas in medicine. Maybe something is going on with Ron that is outside Dr. Dunn's expertise. I'll keep a closer eye on Ron and watch for problems."

For several weeks after that I pondered the appointment with Dr. Dunn. It should have reassured me about Ron's health, but it didn't. At the back of my mind I continued to wonder if there was something wrong. He hadn't told me he'd not been driving the route alone.

—

My usual activities distracted me enough so I didn't follow up right away as I now know I should have. Two weeks later as I sat at my ironing board doing up my dresses and Ron's shirts, I wondered what was happening with Ron, and how soon I could get some answers. I watched the snow settling like feathers outside. Annie and Jacob would arrive as soon as school was over. Mark and Patty had an after-school teacher's meeting. Patty would pick up the kids here.

The front door opened and Jake and Annie burst in bringing a blast of cold air.

"Shut the door," I called out. "Were you raised in a barn?"

They shook the snow off their coats, hung them on the banister, and kicked off their boots on the hall rug. "Hi, Gram," they chorused.

I turned off my iron and put it on the back of the stove to cool. Jake helped me store the ironing board, as he often did when they came in from school. Annie went to the fridge to get out a drink. "Could we drink hot chocolate today, instead of Kool-Aid?" she called out.

"Get the small pan from the cupboard and pour in the milk. The Nestle's Quik is on the shelf. Do you need my help, or can you do it yourself?" I replied.

"I think I can do it. I've watched you lots of times. I'm a fourth grader, you know."

"Go to it, sweetie. I need to hang these dresses in the back closet and then I'll be in."

Jake reached into the cookie jar for a handful of brownies, putting some on the plate he took down from the shelf. "I think these brownies are spoiling, Gram. We can help eat them up."

Jake was quoting from a Billy Bunny story I had told him many times. It was an old joke, but, as usual, I played along. "Thank you, Jacob, for preventing the brownies from getting stale."

Wolfing down two or three brownies and gulping down his hot chocolate, Jake grabbed up his coat again. "I'm going down to Jeff's house to work on our snow fort. Unless you need me to help with anything."

The twelve-year-olds had been working on a super fort since the snow began last Saturday. "No, go ahead. I don't think Mom will be here to pick you up until close to five. Did you have any homewo—," but Jake had already fled out the door.

"What about you, Annie? Are you going over to Sarah's house?"

"No, Gram. I wanted to talk to you. Mrs. Bates gave us homework, but it should be fun. She wants us to find something special from our grandparents for a class display. She told me Uncle Aaron was one of her favorite students. I didn't let on I knew the story about how he tried to get out of her class. Do you have any keepsakes from long ago I could take to school?"

"Long ago, indeed!" I laughed. "I didn't grow up in the dark ages, you know. I'm not a colonial maiden. Keepsake? Hmm. My most precious one is my father's Bible. I'm not sure I want to send that to school. Maybe if we wrap it carefully…"

"That's swell. Why is the Bible so special?"

"Well, it belonged to your great-grandfather Jacob. Jake is named for him, you remember. But it is special because of the stories it tells. Bring it down from my bedroom and I'll show you."

Annie ran upstairs and down again in an instant. I knew she liked to go up there, and she'd not have any trouble finding Papa's Bible on my bedside table.

"Here, Gram. I was extra careful. If you let me take it to school I will take wonderful care of it." She set it down on the kitchen table. "My, there's lots of things tucked into it. You must have lots of passages you want to remember."

"Yes, I do. Look here in Second Corinthians: *for God loveth a cheerful giver.* This is the one my dear papa read to me when he gave me my first allowance. Papa was very special, you see."

"Mom told me your father died when you were very young."

"Yes…before he died we used to sit out on the old porch and he would tell me Bible stories and stories about when he was little."

"I'm glad I have my papa."

"You're very lucky. After Papa died, my mama left me with Aunt Susan while she went to Texas with my little sister."

"That must've been hard on you and on your mama."

Still these many years later my face flushed at the memory. My eyes filled with tears. I needed to swallow hard to keep my outward composure. I remembered the birthday letter from Mama—in fact, the letter was tucked inside the cover of Grandpa Jake's Bible. I took out the letter, studied it a moment, considering whether to tell Annie about it. I decided Annie was still too young to hear the whole story. What would she say to make things any better? I wished I myself better understood Mama's decision to leave. I wished again that Mama had been able to explain.

Annie reached out and took my hand. She could see thinking about those events upset me. When I found my voice again, I said, "I thought at the time it was only hard on me. I was very angry and resented it when she went away. She never has been back here to see me or any of you."

"Have you ever tried to find out how your mama and sister are these days?"

I had made an effort to find my mother and sister, but wasn't ready yet to share that with my ten-year-old granddaughter. The letter I had written to the postmaster in Corpus Christie had come back with a notice that Alice Wilson was not living there. If she had been a former resident, there was no one by that name currently residing there.

Thinking about my dead end, I decided it was too much to tell Annie. Instead I said, "You know that just before I was to start college someone stole all the savings and loan deposits and left town."

"Yes, Mom told me that story and said that's why you married Grandpa."

"Well, it was one of the reasons. We were madly in love, but before the money disappeared I thought we would wait until after I went to college. When it was gone, we decided we might as well marry, and the sooner the better. I guess God wanted us to live the life we lived. If we hadn't, there might not be an Annie sitting here talking to me."

I hadn't distracted Annie from her thoughts about what I had told her.

"Still," she said. "I don't see how your mom could have left you and gone away."

"I can't explain. How could she give up a child? It still puzzles me."

Just then a small station wagon pulled into the driveway. "Goodness, here's your mother in the Ford waiting for you to get ready to go home. What do you think we should do about your taking Great-Grandfather Jacob's Bible for your class display?"

"Mrs. Bates is going to invite parents and grandparents to school on April 14, right before our spring break, to see what everyone brought to share. I know! I'll make a sign explaining why the Bible is important. You can come that day and bring it yourself to show."

"Now you're thinking! Great-Grandfather Jacob would be proud of you."

34

Alice Koller McEnroe Wilson
1965

After Alice Wilson abandoned her eldest daughter in Parkersville, her life continued to hand her one disappointment after another. Her second husband, Gene, died at age fifty while working as a lineman installing electricity to farms around Corpus Christie. His son, Gene Jr., left home soon after the funeral, and Alice's daughter, Joy, ran off to check out Hollywood when she was seventeen. All her life Alice had told Joy what a pretty young thing she was, and the siren call of movies drew Joy to leave. The two little girls born of Gene and Alice's marriage, Faith and Hope, struggled with their mother and ended up being raised as Joy had been by their Uncle Bubba and Aunt Maysie.

As Alice entered her seventies, her thoughts returned more and more to the days in Parkersville, Ohio, where life with two daughters, a life that had seemed hard at the time, took on a glow of nostalgia as a simpler, more serene time. When Alice learned she had cancer she realized if she was ever going to tell Joy about Parkersville and her sister Matilda she needed to do it soon. Suffering from the pain and hurrying to get down the story before she died, she wrote out some of the facts she had never shared before.

February 28, 1965

Dear Joy Ellen,

I'm dying—I never thought the time would come. The doctors say they can't do anything for my stomach cancer except give me morphine to deaden the pain. Morphine makes my stomach ache less but aggravates my headaches—what can I say? I'm dying.

But that is not why I started this letter to you. I need to tell you so much—things I've sometimes tried to tell you before, but you—with your Hollywood, rich lady, big city ways—weren't ready to hear. You've been a neglectful daughter and I think you know you hurt me, but I'm dying and I need to forgive you before I go to meet my Maker.

The reason I wanted to—needed to—write to you now is to tell you about yourself and your family—things you always were too self-absorbed to hear. You were a beautiful baby. How did you turn into such a neglectful daughter as you grew? But that is neither here nor there. It is how you are. I hope when you hear this whole story you will be more understanding of the circumstances that forced me to make the decisions I made.

You had a sister back in Parkersville. Matilda was born the first year after I married your father. I'm sure it was punishment for the trick I played on him to get him to marry me that she was such a fussy baby, and exhausting and willful and sassy. Your father spoiled her and so did my aunt Susan. No one ever welcomed me in Parkersville. I was too good for the likes of them—a stuck-up crowd, jealous that I snagged the most eligible bachelor so quickly while visiting Aunt Susan and Uncle Bob for the summer. I showed them all by becoming Mrs. Jacob McEnroe.

When your father enlisted in the army in 1918, I begged him not to go, but he wouldn't listen. "Have to make the world safe for Democracy," he told me. What good came of all the patriotism when the Spanish Influenza swept through the army camp? Your father died so suddenly, with so many others, I never even had his body to bury.

Well, I wasn't going to stay in that hateful town, so I took my maiden name back and packed you up to move to Texas. Matilda refused to come—stubborn child that she was—only six years old, too. Aunt Susan offered to keep her. It seemed the best choice—for all of us.

I think your sister was lucky to be left, as things turned out. Aunt Susan had her send letters from time to time until I wrote and asked her to stop sending them. I am including these three letters that your sister sent to me. Aunt Susan made her write them every year.

Now that I am dying, I leave it all to you. Maybe it would have been better to have taken her and left you behind. Think about that.

Alice did not even sign the letter, but put it in an envelope directed to Joy, along with the three letters from Mattie, written in a childish hand telling her that the daughter left behind missed her sister and mother but was "being good" as she had been told to do. Alice shook her head. *Was it really better for Mattie with Aunt Susan? Was it really better for Joy to be with me? I guess I'll never know, but it might have been better for me to have left them both behind!*

Alice put the letter aside, telling her nurse to give it to Joy only after her death. That death came in January 1967, at age seventy-one.

Alice's stepson, Gene Jr., found the letter among Alice's papers and set it aside until after the funeral. It got mixed in with the sympathy cards and was put away undelivered and unread.

35

~

Parkersville Post Office
MARCH 1965

March 8, 1965, Elmer Drake and Ron drove into the post office parking lot with Elmer hot under the collar. He stormed into the postmaster's office. "I can't take it anymore!" he declared.

"Calm down, Elmer. What's going on?" Mr. Biggs inquired.

"I can't take Ron on the route. He—can't control his bladder. He peed all over my car seat today."

Behind Elmer, Ron, in soggy pants, entered with a confused look on his face. "We needed to stop at that place for me to…I don't…"

"I'll call Mattie to have her come get him. Unless you want to deliver him over to his house. We'll pay for the clean-up on your car, Elmer," Mr. Biggs offered.

"I could take him home, I'm glad to do it," Elmer replied, somewhat mollified, "but what am I supposed to tell Mattie?"

"Good question. And what am I to do about Ron? You go on out and take care of the day's mail. I'll deal with Ron and Mattie."

Mr. Biggs turned to Ron, who was still looking shaken. "Ron, I think something is seriously wrong with you. We can't keep you on here. I'll put you on administrative leave starting right now and I'm calling Mattie. We'll see what we can work out."

~

Mattie was surprised to hear Cliff Biggs's voice when she answered the phone.

"You'll need to come to drive Ron home, Mattie, and bring a change of pants."

"What's happening? Is Ron all right?"

"Come down. I'll explain in person. Can you come right away?"

"I'm expecting the children from school, but I can leave a note. I'll be right over."

Mattie scribbled a note to Jake and Annie, grabbed a pair of Ron's work pants, threw on her jacket, and hurried out the door. *What could be happening? Please, God, don't let him be injured. Let him be okay.*

Ten minutes later, out of breath from half running, half walking fast, Mattie dashed up to the back entrance to the post office.

"Ron, are you okay? Cliff, what happened?"

Neither Ron nor Mr. Biggs was able to answer the two-pronged question Mattie spit out, Ron because he couldn't immediately find the words, and Cliff Biggs because he wasn't sure how to frame the delicate situation. Mattie looked from one to the other as she noted Ron's wet pants. "Here, Ron, go put these on, and be quick about it."

Ron went into the bathroom but couldn't decide what he needed to do. He pulled down the wet pants, but they wouldn't come off over his work shoes. He sat on the toilet, urinated, and then...what next?

Meanwhile, Mr. Biggs led Mattie into his office and began to tell her everything that had happened at the post office since late summer. "I told Ron he should see a doctor," Mr. Biggs said.

"We went to Dr. Dunn in January and he said nothing was wrong," Mattie began. Then she paused. "He said nothing was wrong and even sent you a note to say Ron could drive the route without Elmer's help."

"Yes, I know what Dr. Dunn said," Mr. Biggs spoke with hesitancy in his voice. "I couldn't let Ron do it. He was casing the incoming mail in preparation for going out, and he didn't seem to know what he was reading on the envelopes. If he is this confused here in the office, I didn't know what he would do on the road."

Mattie remembered the confusion on the trip to Michigan, and everything she'd thought since the appointment with Dr. Dunn. She felt embarrassed, angry, and frustrated. Kathy had recognized a problem. *Why have I been so slow to notice what others were seeing? What's wrong with me?*

"What can we do to help him? What can I do to help him?"

"Let's have him come in and talk about the possibilities," Cliff Biggs suggested. "Ron, come on out and let's talk."

No answer from the bathroom, so Mattie opened the door and looked in. Ron had fallen asleep with his trousers around his ankles, sitting on the toilet. She went in, closed the door, touched his shoulder to wake him. With tears streaming down her cheeks, she helped remove his shoes and his wet trousers. Still crying softly, she slipped the dry pants over his feet and helped him into them. Carrying the shoes into Mr. Biggs's office so that there would be a little more room, she knelt on the floor to help Ron put them on.

"I think we need to go home, Ron. Cliff, we'll talk later."

36

~

Mattie

After the incident at the post office, I drove Ron home in silence. What to do now? Ron was okay, no injury to himself or anyone else; but he was also not okay. Dr. Dunn, obviously, would be no help. I'd need to find out more from a different doctor. I'd call Aaron and see what he thought about things.

March 8 and 9, 1965

That evening, after Ron and I ate a light supper and settled in the living room, I decided we needed to talk.

"What do you think is going on with you, honey? How long have you been having problems?"

"I'm so sorry, Mattie. I just don't know what's wrong. I knew something was off, but I don't know what. It's like I'm in slow motion and the rest of the world is in normal speed."

I thought that over. It sounded as though Ron were sleepwalking. "And today?"

"I knew I had to go to the bathroom. I tried to tell Elmer, but the words wouldn't come. He was so angry at me for not saying what I couldn't think how to say. I just couldn't hold it any more. It wasn't like the kids when they were little, not knowing when they had to go. I knew. I just couldn't say the words."

I listened, remembering how I had to listen with the boys when they didn't know a word. I thought about the suitcase Ron had ignored when we were getting ready for our trip to Aaron's house.

"Sometimes I don't know where I am," Ron told me. "I wander down the street between here and the post office and the houses look strange. Or they might look as they always do. When someone on the street says something to me, I think, 'Do I know that person?' "

Mattie shook her head, trying to imagine his confusion.

Ron spoke first. "I'm scared. Am I getting old when I'm still so young?"

"I don't know. We'll call Aaron to ask him what he thinks."

"No, not yet. He doesn't need to know. Let's ask Dr. Dunn about seeing another doctor."

"That sounds like a good idea, dear. But I will talk to Aaron, when we hear what another doctor tells us."

Ron and I talked long into the night. Sometimes Ron lost the train of thought, but I tried to listen.

—

The next morning, as Ron still lay sleeping, I began my devotions. I read the story of the sisters Mary and Martha when Jesus came to visit them in Bethany. Mary was sitting at Jesus's feet listening to him while Martha bustled about getting things ready. Then Martha asked Jesus to tell Mary she needed to help. Jesus replied, "Martha, Martha, you are anxious and troubled about many things; one thing is needful. Mary has chosen the good portion, which shall not be taken away from her."

Mary's portion? To sit and listen? I guess that was God's message to me as well. "Show me the way," I whispered. Listen to Ron even when he cannot say what he wants. *Listen to him as you try to listen to God's voice. Listen. Listening is the way. Listening. Such a simple thing. Such a challenging thing.* I realized I had done that last evening as Ron made an effort to explain actions, thoughts, and feelings he did not himself understand. I also realized that too often I had not taken time to listen. "Thank you, God," I breathed. "I can do all things through Christ who strengthens me."

As I read I heard Ron stirring, so I went to tell him that I intended to be a better listener and a better wife. I watched him as he came down the stairs, half dressed, with an old cardigan open over his pajama tops. "I can't get this thing to stay shut," Ron complained.

I rose to help him, and led him to a chair by the kitchen table. I had laid out the usual silver and his bowl was sitting empty waiting for me to fill it with oatmeal from the stove. He reached for his fork and began to stir his coffee cup. "This doesn't smell right," Ron murmured. "It needs more..." and he looked around. I dished up the cereal, and Ron used his fork to move a glob of the oatmeal into his coffee cup.

"No, Ron. The cereal…" I was about to stop him, to remind him it was not done that way, when I remembered what I had resolved that morning. I watched Ron drink the thickened coffee and kept silent.

"Ron, I think we should make an appointment with a specialist in Cleveland. I'll call Dr. Dunn to ask him for a referral. I'm glad we talked last night."

"What did we talk about? Are you sick, Mattie?"

"Ron, you…I love you, Ron. Finish your breakfast and we'll go into the sitting room and relax."

Later that morning I called Dr. Dunn to ask for a referral. Dr. Dunn again assured me Ron was fine, just getting older, but I insisted. With the phone number of the Cleveland Clinic, I called. I could not get an appointment until April.

April, I thought. *By then, I might need some help. I hate to worry the boys. I'll not call them yet, but soon.* I entered the sitting room to tell Ron of the appointment.

"Ron, we will go to the specialist on April 23."

Ron looked at me and asked me to repeat what I had said. "We'll drive up to Cleveland Clinic on April 23."

"When will that be? What day is it?"

"Today is March 9, a Tuesday."

"Tuesday? I should be at work," Ron exclaimed, and rose to head upstairs and dress.

"Not today, Ron. It's a holiday."

"What day is it?"

I considered whether I should explain again, about the day and about the doctor's visit. "You have today off, Ron. What would you like to do?"

"Let's walk to town," Ron decided, and started to get his coat.

"Let's go upstairs and put on some warmer clothes first."

The weather was warming up, so we had a pleasant walk to town. We stopped off in the five-and-dime store to pick up a new notebook, for I had decided I would write down everything I knew or could find out about Ron's strange behavior. And I would make a note about my new resolve to listen.

37

Mark
SPRING 1965

The first week of March 1965 brought cold and snow. Time for spring quarter night classes at the Branch to begin once again, and Mark was sick and tired of school *all* the time. His job was teaching seventh and eighth graders in Parkersville about fractions and percents, interest rates, and business applications. His job included switching them over to the "new math," which was part of the big push in math and science since the Soviet Sputnik surprise in 1957. He found it quite interesting, but it made the parents and students hostile. Of course, mastering the new math required Mark's return to school. The U.S. government urged teachers to take workshops and summer courses to "help the U.S. catch up in the space race."

All well and good, but attending classes every summer and evening classes year round was getting to be too much. Mark's three children were past the "cute and wonderful" stage. Mark's mom kept the younger two after school and Roy had a part-time job at the same grocery store that had been Mark's employer in the past.

Mark's real interest always had been agriculture, earth science, growing things. He had been fascinated by Rachel Carson's *Silent Spring*. Mark and Patty owned an acreage about ten miles out of Parkersville, and Mark farmed it, trying to follow Rachel Carson's ideas and raise his garden without the use of pesticides.

The whole emphasis of the "new science" was on engineering and space, not earth science and ecology, which most interested Mark. So, on the cold afternoon in March 1965 when the spring quarter began, Mark decided not to attend his first session of Space Science 328 and instead walked into Mulligan's Bar and Grill and ordered a boilermaker. He drank the beer and whiskey, then ordered up a refill. He went to sit at the back booth. Frank Andrews, a pot-bellied young man with long hair and a scruffy beard, drifted over to talk to Mark.

"How's it going, buddy? You look like you lost your last friend."

Mark turned his face away and cast his eyes down, wishing to avoid conversation, but Frank persisted. "Life's a shit, but that's no reason to drink alone. I can offer you something stronger if you want to come out to my truck."

What the hell. In for a penny, in for a buck, Mark thought. "Let's see what you got!" Mark stumbled to his feet and straightened up. *I'm a bit tight,* he told himself. Frank led him to the back, where an old Volkswagen sat in the shade. Before long, they'd exchanged Mark's money for Frank's stash of MJ and sat together smoking. After a cough of surprise, Mark took a strong drag. His mind mellowed, relaxing the tensions the alcohol hadn't touched. "Good stuff," Mark mused. "Beats school all to hell."

"More where that came from, good buddy. Come back tomorrow and I'll take you out to my place."

—

Frank's place was a 200-acre farm near Egypt Valley. Nothing much growing there, except a small marijuana patch Frank cultivated. The Ohio Coal Company had been negotiating to purchase the land and strip it for the coal seams lying beneath the top soil. "Dad's holding out for a better price than they're offering now," Frank told Mark the next day when Mark asked about why it wasn't productive.

"It's my dream farm, Frank. You could grow organic vegetables here. People are looking for pesticide-free veggies. They would pay a premium. I could make a mint here with that market and my green thumb."

"Coal company wants it. What's the use of putting in the work? Let it go. Here's some good weed I've been drying."

After a while Frank's sister Julie joined them in the barn.

"Hey, Frankman. Who's your cute friend?"

"Farmer wannabe, I think, Sis. Whyn't you join us for a drag?"

Julie sat down and the three shared a toke for a while. Julie turned her attention to Mark. Frank perceived himself to be a third wheel. He left the two alone, as Julie began stroking and caressing Mark. Mark responded with kisses and caresses of his own. Mark was high, from the smoking and from the physical sensations Julie aroused. He raised her peasant blouse and covered her body with kisses. Their bodies melded as tension rose and released. Sex with his wife Patty was so ordinary; sex with Julie, at seventeen, with her waist-length brown hair and lithe body, was extraordinary. Mark began to think of how he might exchange the ordinary for the extraordinary. Afterwards they shared another joint, and Mark mentioned his idea about growing pesticide-free produce. She rolled over and looked him in the eye. "Really? Could you really do it? What would it take?"

As Mark began to explain his idea she distracted him with kisses and fondling. With this diversion it was a while until they returned to conversation.

"Patty wouldn't understand…" Mark began to say, but Julie cut him off. "What does she have to do with this? It's my farm. Dad's and Frank's and mine. Come live here and we can do it."

—

For the next few months, Mark sought to spend all the time he could at the Andrews farm. At home he yelled at Patty and at the children. He continued teaching until the end of the school year, not ready to let Patty know what was happening—but she noticed that something had changed.

38

Mattie

As I brooded about the upcoming trip to the Cleveland Clinic, I wondered if I ought to tell my sons and their families about what was going on. The thought of facing the trip to Cleveland alone was too overwhelming. I'd invite Mark and Patty to go with me.

March 24, 1965

After school, Annie bounced in, eyes wide and glowing. That morning Mrs. Bates had dragged a TV into her classroom, and they watched a fifteen minute live broadcast from the moon as Ranger 9 sent back pictures before landing.

"Did you see it, Gram?"

"I'm sorry I missed it. I expect the news this evening will broadcast the landing, and I'll see it then," I told her. "How exciting for you to get to see it live, honey."

"And just yesterday Gus Grissom and John Young orbited the earth in the Gemini 3," Jake told me. Both the kids were crazy about space stuff. I was proud of them for being so involved in the news.

I still had some news to get ready for the mail, so I told them, "Why don't the two of you check whether Gramps can help you with your homework while you wait for your mother?"

Jake, a sixth grader, was studying Ohio geography. Ron told him about how the glaciers had formed the rolling hills of southern Ohio they enjoyed riding through when they accompanied him on his route. "We're on vacation in five weeks, Grampa. Can I go on your route then?"

"Of course you may. You're a good helper," Ron replied.

I looked over at them, thought a minute, and added, "We'll see, Jake. We'll have to see."

Jake ran out to visit at Jeff's house, and Annie went over to Ron with her math papers. Her school was using the "new math," which was supposed to help children understand the meaning behind the numeration system when they did problems. Ron studied what she had written and shook his head. "You should do it yourself, Annie. That's how you learn."

When Patty came to pick up the children, I asked her whether she and Mark would drive to Cleveland on Friday, April 23, with us. "I think you're on Easter break then. Or maybe you could take a day off if you're back in school. It's for a doctor's appointment."

"I can go, Mom, but I don't know about Mark. He says he wants to drive over to Pittsburgh 'for some relaxation.' What doctor are you seeing? Are you feeling okay?"

"It's for Dad. Dr. Dunn says his forgetfulness is natural, but I'm not sure. It seems to be worse than I realized."

"I'm sorry. I did notice he was distracted. But I guess I have been a little bit, too. What can I do to help you out?"

"We might take the kids to the Cleveland Museum while we visit the specialist."

"I like that idea. Might as well have some fun. Come on, Annie, we need to be getting home. I'll pick up Jake over at Jeff's. I saw them playing outside."

39

Aaron
MARCH 1965

Aaron Connors at his pastorate followed the ins and outs of civil rights struggles as they unfolded. He participated whenever he got a chance. He augmented his powerful Sunday messages by working in the community to promote equal housing, assisting laid-off workers in finding jobs, writing letters to legislators encouraging them to change the laws that discriminated against blacks and the poor. Aaron believed in God and country, in equal rights for all citizens, regardless of skin color, to vote and live and work where they pleased. Aaron's congregation, on the other hand, didn't always appreciate his challenging words from the pulpit. They preferred sermons of comfort, reassurance, and solace. If they were sinners, didn't Jesus love sinners and come to save them? If God had recognized their worth by rewarding them with material goods, why must the preacher disturb the status quo? These good people attended church twice on Sunday and again on Wednesdays, studied their Bibles at home and in Sunday school. Negro churchgoers had a different style of worship. They wouldn't be happy in this church anyway. As for all of the preacher's do-gooding, he should be attending his own flock. From time to time the Board of Elders, ordained to oversee the spiritual life of the congregation, listened to complaints about Aaron's activities in promoting Negro rights.

Aaron was aware of the unrest in his congregation, but he still felt it was his responsibility to preach and act as he believed God wanted. He paid special attention to what was happening in Selma, Alabama. On Sunday, March 7, 1965, John Lewis, chairman of SNCC, and Hosea Williams from the Southern Christian Leadership Council scheduled a peaceful march from Selma to the state capital in Montgomery to petition for protection of blacks who were being attacked when they tried to register to vote. Governor George Wallace vowed to halt the marchers. He called out the state troopers to stop them.

The evening of the march, Aaron and his wife Joan sat in their manse watching network television. A little earlier, the high school had called Joan asking her to substitute in social studies for the next week, so she watched the news with an eye toward seeing what might fit into possible discussions liable come up in class. What was shown on television shocked them. The marchers moved peacefully until Alabama state troopers assaulted them with flailing billy clubs, stampeding horses, tear gas, and bull whips. People fell and were dragged along, turning the peaceful protest bloody. By the end of the night sixteen marchers were hospitalized.

Immediately after "Bloody Sunday," as it became known, Dr. King, along with the SNCC and the SCLC, issued a call to action. They asked clergy and laypeople from across the country to come to Selma for a second attempt to march to Montgomery on Tuesday, March 9. Many hundreds of people accepted the call. One of them was Dar Jones, by then a Law One student at Howard University.

—

Because of his many responsibilities during the Lenten season, Aaron felt he had to settle for being part of a regional protest rally in Detroit, Michigan. With hundreds of people from around Detroit, he marched down Michigan Avenue singing protest songs and talking.

"Hello, I'm Aaron Connors," he introduced himself to the woman next to him.

"Viola Liuzzo. Glad you're here," she replied. Viola, he learned, was a mother of five, and the wife of a Teamsters union leader. As they marched together they talked about how unfair life treated Negroes in the South. They agreed that while it was important to be marching in Detroit, participation in this regional march was a weak witness. Both wished they had gone south when the call came.

—

For those who did go to Selma, the trip was frustrating, as Aaron learned from watching the news later. Federal District Court Judge Johnson issued a restraining order to prevent Tuesday's march. Two thousand, five hundred marchers assembled, determined to march despite the court order. Dr. King and Reverend Lewis held a short prayer session and led the group as far as the Edmund Pettus Bridge. They then turned the marchers back in obedience to the restraining order.

Many of the younger marchers felt cheated at not being able to complete the march. White racists, disturbed seeing the northerners butting into their way of life, felt just as frustrated. Many fights broke out. Later that evening three white ministers were beaten, and one, James Reeb from Boston, died from his injuries two days later.

When Aaron heard the news of a fellow minister's death he wept. "It's unacceptable for me to watch from this far away," he muttered. With repeated coverage of the violence on his television screen, Aaron paced the floor, alternately angry and sorrowful. "Next time," he vowed when the news reported Reverend Reeb's murder, "I will be there."

The next Sunday, March 14, he announced to his congregation, "As soon as the injunction against the Selma march is lifted, I will be going to Alabama to take part. I'll miss at least two Sundays, maybe more. I'm sure the elders can fill in during my absence."

Joan was proud to hear his words. It was just what she expected after the week's news. She was frightened, too. There was no telling what might happen there.

"I would welcome anyone from this congregation or the community to join me. I'll be driving down in my Chevy." During the next week Judge Johnson in Alabama ruled the right to march to redress grievances was guaranteed under the U.S. Constitution, so Dr. King and the other organizers set a new date to assemble for a five-day walk from Selma to Montgomery.

No one in Aaron's congregation volunteered to accompany him, so he drove down alone.

Some 8,000 other people gathered in Selma when the third Selma to Montgomery march began on Sunday, March 21, including Aaron, Dar, and Viola. On the third day of the march, when the highway narrowed, only a limited number of marchers were permitted to walk the narrowed road. Aaron and Dar spotted each other and the two marched together the rest of the time. When the highway widened again, still more people joined in. On Thursday, March 25, 25,000 people reached the State Capitol where Dr. King delivered an address. He spoke of "a society at peace with itself, a society that can live with its conscience…" He concluded by promising, "I know you are asking today, How long will it take? I come to say to you this afternoon however difficult the moment, however frustrating the hour, it will not be long."

Twenty-five thousand people do not disperse in a hurry. Some marched back along the way they had come or away in various directions, satisfied with the outcome. Others hitched rides or rode in cars provided by volunteers like Viola Liuzzo back to Selma. Dar and Aaron returned to the campus at the St. Jude

Educational Institute, a private Roman Catholic high school on the outskirts of Montgomery where they had camped on the final evening of the march. Aaron found a pay phone to call Joan, reporting their elation, but also their bone-tired fatigue. He told her he would start back in the morning.

Later on, while Aaron sat listening to his portable radio, Dar called Parkersville to talk to his sister, Sophie. "You should've been there, Soph! People were screaming and laughing and dancing in the street. Dr. King speaks the hopes of our generation. Last night Eddie's Uncle Aaron and I camped at this Catholic church and school and Harry Belafonte and Sammy Davis Jr. sang for us. Peter, Paul, and Mary, and Frankie Laine, and Tony Bennett. Today we finished the march and listened to Dr. King speak. After the beatings and arrests and strain, it actually does feel like we shall overcome at last."

Sophie was watching on television some of the footage of the day's events as she talked to her brother. "Dar! Wait! There's a news flash coming on now. Oh my God! Listen! Here's what they are saying: *Viola Liuzzo, a Detroit mother of five who was assisting with the march, was murdered by four members of the Ku Klux Klan. More news to come…*"

"Viola? Murdered? No-oo! That's awful! I met her, Soph! She was at the hospitality desk in Brown Chapel. We talked together. She was at the first aid station yesterday and today. She drove back and forth taking people where they needed to be. Eddie's Uncle Aaron knew her. Are you sure what you heard?"

"More news to come is all they're saying now. Mama's frantic that you're down there. Do you think it was worth the struggle?"

Dar left the question unanswered as he turned around and looked at Aaron. Aaron sat with his head in his hand, having just heard the same news from the radio.

"Got to go, Soph. Tell Mama I'm safe. I'll get back to school as soon as I can. I'll call from D.C."

Aaron looked up when Dar tapped his shoulder. Tears streamed down his face. Dar scowled, too angry to be sad yet.

"Is it worth it, Reverend Connors? No one seemed to care when only black people died. Now we have people's attention, what's next?"

Aaron drew a deep breath. "I can't answer your question, Dar. I wish I could. What I would want is for the nation to be upset when anybody is killed. If God is carrying his purpose out, it seems too many lives are being wasted in the process."

Dar shook his head. He cleared his throat and muttered, "Some of my classmates think we should take violence to Whitey. But Viola was white, and the honkies have taken their violence out on her. Some of the guys in SNCC are pushing for us to be more aggressive. I'm beginning to wonder if they aren't right.

I don't know."

"We can't do much here and now, but we have to keep working for justice. I need to get back. I'll get over to Detroit when they have services for Viola. Let me take you and your classmates out of here before there's more violence. You need to get back to school. Return to your studies. Finish the year. With your education, you'll be in a better position to help when change comes. This summer is going to bring more trouble, I fear."

"I'm afraid you're right!"

"President Johnson's National Voting Rights Act will put some teeth into the Fourteenth and Fifteenth Amendments. If it forces the South to open the polls to all, things will improve."

—

Aaron drove Dar and three other law students back to Ohio to catch a bus back to school. On his way back to White Grove, Aaron stopped in Detroit to attend the memorial service for Viola. Because of the way she died, the papers declared her a martyr. Two memorial services were held: one at the People's Community Church and one the next day at the Immaculate Heart of Mary Roman Catholic Church. Aaron stayed on in Detroit and spent the rest of the day talking to mourners about Viola and about the cause she died for.

When Aaron drove wearily into his driveway, Joan, who had worried about his safety most of the time he was gone, hurried to greet him. The children were already in bed. She had been bustling around straightening the house, baking a batch of brownies to cover up her anxiety and to welcome him. "Aaron, I'm so glad you're home," she said, hugging him for dear life as he got out of the car. "I was worried you'd end up like that Boston minister, or the woman, Viola, that you knew. The news broadcasts are so full of violence, beatings. I'm so relieved!"

A deep exhaustion was clear in his face and his movements. "I'm fine, just tired," Aaron reassured her, as he returned the bear hug. He set down the duffel and sleeping bag inside the door and collapsed onto his chair. "There's so much to tell you, Joan. So much. We were so elated, and then so disheartened. But I'm bushed now. Wake me in a week."

Then he noticed lights in the church building across the street. He asked her, "What's going on over there?"

"There seems to be a bunch of session members meeting at the church. Do you know anything about it?"

Aaron shook his head. "I don't know of any scheduled meetings. I'm not going over at any rate. I'm worn out."

"Just rest. Why don't you go on to bed? We can talk in the morning." But he was almost asleep in the chair. Joan sat down too, relieved that he was home so she could stop worrying about him.

Not ten minutes later a loud knock on the front door startled them both. Joan went to answer.

Five of the church elders stood on the porch. "We need to speak to the pastor," Otto Smedl, the local sheriff, chair of the church board, said firmly.

"He only got back a few minutes ago and he's exhausted. Can it wait until tomorrow, Otto?"

He frowned. "I think it shouldn't wait, Mrs. Connors." She was startled that he was addressing her in such a formal manner.

"Aaron, Otto and some of the session members are here," she called, just as Aaron entered through the office and opened the porch door.

"Come in, come in." Curious, but feeling the need to be busy, Joan went to the kitchen to prepare some iced tea and a tray of brownies.

The men's voices were strong, drowning out the clatter of putting glasses on the tray. A few minutes later, Aaron's voice boomed: "Don't bother with your committee. I resign as of this minute!" Joan stopped in the act of pouring. She put the pitcher down. What now?

Aaron stormed into the kitchen, cursing. "Damn them. What a bunch of..."

"Aaron, they'll hear you. What is it?"

"The very idea! Do you know what they wanted, Joan? They wanted to form a committee to ask Presbytery to see about having me removed from their church! *Their* church! The idea! MY church! I resigned, right then and there!"

But he was just winding up. "A wicked and perverse generation! 'Seeing they do not see, and hearing they do not hear, nor do they understand,' " he thundered. "People are laying down their lives."

Joan stared at Aaron's reddening face. She felt her color rising as well.

"What have they heard as they sat in church all these Sundays and listened to me explain the Gospel message?" Aaron asked.

It was a rhetorical question, of course, one Joan had heard him ask her from time to time as the frustrations of life and ministry wore on them.

Joan, the perfect minister's wife, always patient and kind, always ready to do as Aaron wished, shook her head. "Aaron, you have a wife and two children. Did you even think about us when you resigned? Can we live on my substitute teacher's salary? Next week is Holy Week. Couldn't you have waited to see how widespread the opposition is?"

Aaron looked at Joan and frowned. "Don't you see, Joan? Could I still work with them if they don't want me? If they don't understand what's at stake? You should have heard Smedl and Bill Harris. And the others just sat there like sticks and went along with them. 'Quit stirring up trouble,' they told me. 'No use letting Negroes'—they used a different word—'vote. They're too ignorant to know who to vote for.' I'm sure they didn't want women to vote either. The founding fathers decided that you had to be a land owner to vote. Half our congregation wouldn't be voters if we still followed that idea."

Joan listened to her husband, knowing that the rant would soon wear itself out. But she thought about how Aaron's hasty words threw their lives into disarray. She expected they could manage for a while on money she made subbing. But the immediate concern for her was that they lived in church housing. Would they need to move again? Where would they go? Joan had worked and gone to night school for her teaching certification while Aaron was in seminary, then taught several years. She had teaching to fall back on but had not expected to need to do so after Bethie's birth. Now the question of how they would live was wide open. Aaron had just thrown all their plans out the window.

While Joan considered, Aaron's exhaustion was catching up with him. Joan moved to where Aaron sat and began to rub his shoulders. She didn't want to add to his burden with her questions. She was proud of him for going to Selma. He lived the gospel he preached. She had vowed to love him in sickness and in health, in good times and bad. Who knew what kind of times would face them now? He was being true to his faith when he stood up to the board. Never mind that he had turned their lives upside-down. They would face what happened next. Anger and disappointment would be part of whatever was to come. So would love and faith and hope. *Nothing else to do now*, she thought as she massaged his back.

—

The next morning, Aaron received two phone calls: the first from John Cahill, clerk of Session. "Pastor, we met again after we left your office. We think it would be good if you stay out the month to preach the holy season. We need you then. After that, we'd accept your resignation and you would no longer pastor at First Presbyterian. But you're still welcome to live in the manse until school is out. Not good for kids to be moved in the school year. Think about it and let us know."

Aaron and Joan had sat up half the night talking things over and praying for guidance. They were unsure, when John's call came, whether this compromise was what they should do.

A second phone call came while they were deliberating Cahill's offer. This time it was Aaron's mother, Mattie, calling from Parkersville. Her voice was shaking, an octave higher than usual. "Have you made plans for the week after Easter, Aaron?" Mattie asked.

Waiting to hear God's plans, he thought to himself. A silent prayer: *May God reveal His plan for me!* "No, Mom, we don't have anything special planned. Why? What's up?"

"I was hoping you would come down here for a few days. I do need to talk to you."

"Is something's wrong there? Any special reason you ask?" Aaron signaled Joan to get on the extension so she would be part of the conversation.

After a deep breath Mattie said, "Dad is on leave from the post office. I think he's seriously ill."

"Didn't you tell me you had seen Dr. Dunn in January and he told you Dad was okay?"

"Yes, but I know he's wrong. Dad is not okay. We have made an appointment to see a neurologist in Cleveland after Easter. I pray he'll be able to tell us more. I've asked Patty, and maybe Mark, to come along. I wish you could come after Easter so you can go too."

Joan laid down her phone extension to enter the study where Aaron was still on the phone with his mother. She waved her hand, signaling him that she wanted to talk to him.

"Mom, I'll call you back in a few minutes. I need to speak with Joan." Mattie agreed and Aaron hung up the receiver.

"I think I should go. I can even take the kids down before Easter if she wants us. You can come down right after the service," Joan said.

"No, I'll just tell Cahill that I won't reconsider staying and go down myself," Aaron argued.

"Do you think it's a good idea to add our upset here to whatever Mom is going through there?"

Aaron thought of his mother's voice on the phone, and her evident distress. Better not to mention the confrontation with the Board of Elders and their own uncertain future until he could see her face to face.

"You're right. I'll stay here the next week for the Church's sake and for Mom's. But you go down. It might make things easier here if you and the kids are out of town. I guess I'll accept the Session's offer to serve through Easter. Don't mention any of this to her."

"Do you think I would add this to her troubles? Don't you get carried away here and burn any more bridges," Joan said as she gave Aaron a warm hug. "Peace of God be with you, dear."

Aaron pulled Joan to his chest. "And also with you," he told her, adding under his breath, "and with Mom and Dad."

Aaron picked up the phone and called his mother. He told her Joan and the kids would be down there later in the week. He'd drive down after services on Easter, and stay for a while if he was needed.

"We'll have a lot to talk about when you come, dears. I'll be glad to see you all."

Joan joined the conversation. "Don't even think about making a fuss for Easter dinner, Mom. Patty and I will fix up something. Love you. Talk to you later."

When the conversation ended, Joan and Aaron sat down to talk. "Did you think Dad was confused while he was here in October?" Joan asked.

"I'm not sure. Yes, I guess his tone was much sharper with Mom than I've heard him use before. He seemed confused about how to repair our electrical outlet, and that would have been easy for him before. I had to call Mel to come and fix it later."

"At the zoo, he talked about your Uncle Josh and he remained silent a long time. I wondered what might be going on. I hope nothing is seriously wrong there. Our lives seem to be changing too quickly."

"I was so caught up in the excitement of the march, the inspiration of Dr. King's words. Then to face the shock of the murder, the long drive, the emotion of the memorial service and mass, and I come home to this challenge from people I loved and thought understood my preaching. If something is wrong with Dad…"

40

Mrs. Bates's School Program
SPRING 1965

When Mrs. Bates, fourth grade teacher at Parkersville Elementary School, planned a special program to showcase the various backgrounds of the children in her class, she assigned them to talk to grandparents or other older relatives and find out about something they treasured. The program was scheduled for April 14, 1965, the day before Easter vacation.

Brett Jones, Dar's nephew, a sturdy, dark-skinned boy with a sharp Afro, was the new boy in Mrs. Bates' class that year. He and his mother, Sophie, had moved to his grandmother's house in Parkersville, Ohio, the previous fall. He was not so sure about the assignment Mrs. Bates had given.

"Grandma," he called as he shuffled into the house, "Mrs. Bates wants us to bring something 'precious' to an older member of our family. I guess you don't have anything, huh?"

Brenda had to stop to think. What did she have that would fill the bill?

"I can go look in the shed or under the porch or anywhere else you might have something," Brett offered.

"Never mind, Brett. I'm sure I have the exact treasure you need. Let's go look in that old trunk under the hall stairs. I know we'll find something there."

They pulled out the trunk and lifted the pressed cardboard lid. It smelled of age, of must and of memories. Brenda lifted out some old quilts that were sewn together from scrap fabric and the pieces of old clothes that were not worn out. Moving aside a few baby things and some old letters, Brenda pulled out a stuffed chintz bear, now well worn. The bear was about twelve inches tall, with movable legs. It smelled of moth crystals, baby powder, and love.

The sight and smell of the old bear brought tears to her eyes. Brenda sighed. She hugged it to her chest. She recalled her first date with Brick Jones and the pride she felt in his skill and good manners. That was the day she first fell in love with Brett's grandfather.

—

When Brick Jones, tall and handsome, dark as the coal in the Ohio Coal Company mine where he had just been hired, walked into the Bethel AME church on a summer Sunday in 1930, all the young girls laid dibs on him.

"He's just up from Mississippi. Did you see those muscles? I hope he'll ask me out," Celia exclaimed.

"Not going to happen, girl. You're too eager," Marion said. "When he sees me strut my stuff, he'll fall all over himself asking me."

Brenda Johnson, a slender sixteen-year-old with skin like well-mixed coffee and cream, said nothing. She expected that Brick would take his time to get to know folks before he'd be ready to date anyone. To her delight, Brick did make a choice. Brenda was the one who got the prize.

"Will you go with me to the Washington County Fair this weekend, Miss Johnson?" Brick asked.

"With pleasure," Brenda replied.

—

At that time, perhaps seventy-five to a hundred Negros lived in Parkersville in small homes south of the railroad tracks, in the section of town known as Coaltown. As coal miners, factory workers, domestics, or small farmers, they had a defined place in the social fabric of the small town. For the most part they did nothing to upset the status quo. Race relations in 1930 in the Ohio community near the West Virginia border were placid enough for schools and community facilities to be open to blacks and whites, as long as the blacks "knew their place."

—

The Washington County fairground was awash with color: balloons, pennants, streamers, advertisements for the exotic food and entertainment, the holiday-making crowd decked out in their finest. The air was laden with the perfume of greasy fried foods, popcorn, and cotton candy—all the sweet, thick smells mixed with the odor of livestock and humans crowded together. Too-loud music, laughter, and the noise of the animals being shown for judging surrounded the young couple. They almost had to shout to carry on a conversation.

"What brings you to the mines here, Brick?" Brenda asked him as they wandered among the livestock barns.

"Cotton-picking machines are taking over in the Delta these days. One machine does the work of fifty pickers. Sharecropping as a way of living is on its way out."

"I guess jobs are scarce down there, aren't they?"

"The landowners aren't always honest with a field hand either. We buy our supplies from them and when it's time to get paid, they decide how much we have coming."

"It may be better up here, Brick, but it might not be," Brenda said as she took his arm. "I know the mine owners here are open to hiring because the Welshmen who used to work the mines here are striking."

"So I've heard, but a job's a job, and I need one."

———

Brick and Brenda spent the day gazing at livestock, admiring prize fruits and vegetables, cheering for contestants in relays, and enjoying talent shows. They watched the judging of pies and jellies. They ate barbecue pork on hamburger rolls, followed by drippy ice cream cones, laughing at everything and the pleasure of being there together. Finally they made their way to the area where sweating pitchmen were barking for the games of chance and skill they were touting.

"Step right up! Step right up! Try your skill. Win a prize."

One booth had piles of prizes to be won if the customer could shoot enough targets and moving ducks with the rifles provided. Business was slow, so the barker invited Brick to try his luck.

"Go ahead, Brick," Brenda urged. "Did you do any hunting in Mississippi?"

"Did I? I'm the best shot in the Delta," Brick replied. "Watch this."

Brick put down his nickel and took up the challenge. His first shot missed. Puzzled, he looked at the rifle in his hands. He noted that the barrel was ever-so-slightly curved. Brick made the mental adjustment needed. He fired again and hit the target, then the next target, and then the whole row of targets. He smiled at Brenda and politely asked the pitchman for his prize. Brenda noticed how deferential Brick was to the scruffy mustached white man.

The barker sneered, took the rifle out of his hands, and told him, "Take a hike."

Brick shrugged his shoulders. "Come on, Brenda. Let's go."

Incensed, Brenda dug in her heels. She was feeling confident and excited, as the day with Brick had been so lovely. "Mister Pitchman, we're not just off the farm. We expect to get the prize my boyfriend here just won." In truth, Brick was "just off the farm," but Brenda was not. She was a maid for the Hansons, who owned the funeral parlor and were one of Parkersville's most prominent families.

"Run along, girlie. You don't want no trouble. Your boyfriend had his turn and there's others waiting."

Brenda looked around. Most of the faces about her were white. She saw one black face, a friend from her church, sweeping the grounds across the way, but Granfield turned aside when he heard the raised voice of the barker. Several other folks, white fairgoers, stopped to see what was happening.

"We'll leave after you give Brick his prize," Brenda said.

A crowd started taking sides between the slight, cocoa-skinned girl and the sleazy-looking sideshow guy. Brenda reached across the counter and grabbed the chintz-covered bear on display. "Brick earned this and we're taking it with us." The pitchman grabbed for it and pulled it away, leaving Brenda holding the left leg, dripping sawdust onto the ground.

A few of the locals knew and respected Brenda's family, even if they were only Negroes. Several others had themselves been burned trying to hit the target with the faulty rifles, and they urged Brenda on. Many of the crowd, however, quickly sided with the man running the concession. A voice from the back of the crowd hollered, "What do these uppity niggers think, anyhow?"

Brick took Brenda's arm and steered her away. "Things might get bad if we stay to argue. Let's go get some cotton candy, Brenda," he said. He felt elated, boosted by the fact that Brenda had called him her boyfriend, when it was only their first date. He was determined not to make it their last. Sensing that this was another argument that her kind could not win, Brenda tossed her head, swirled around, and strode off with Brick.

As they walked away, Brick took Brenda's hand and squeezed it. "Sorry. I thought I'd win you a prize. But this doesn't look like a good time or place to argue about it."

"You're right, I guess. But I'm proud of how you shot the targets. I'm sorry the poor bear was hurt." Holding up the dismembered leg, she turned and smiled at Brick. "I'm glad we weren't, though."

That evening as the fair concessions packed up to move on to the next county fair, the carny tossed the disabled bear into the trash. Granfield, Brenda's friend, was helping clean up. He'd seen the fracas and when he saw the bear he picked it up and took it to her.

Brenda squealed with delight. "Thanks so much, Granfield. I'm so glad you were able to rescue this poor little bear. He'll have a good home here." She replaced the missing stuffing with some clean rags and carefully sewed the leg back on. She put the chintz bear on her bed, and each evening as she dreamed about Brick, she hugged it.

—

Such warm memories flooded Brenda as she gave the bear a small kiss and handed the treasure to Brett, smiling. "I can wash it up for you, child. Your momma and your uncle Dar played with this when they were little. By the time you came to live here you were too old to want or need a bear, and I almost forgot him. I think he might be quite the thing for your class project."

Brett took the toy, brushed it off a bit, and eyed it with curiosity. It was a funny thing to keep safe. It wasn't even very pretty.

"We hafta write up the reason that this is a precious thing. What can I say?"

"Your granddad won him shooting targets at the 1930 Washington County Fair. It was our first date. That's the important part of the story." Brenda took his hand and led him to the kitchen. "Let's go get some corn bread and milk. I'll tell you some more about your granddad. You remind me of him. He was a handsome, wonderful man, just like you."

—

So the morning of April 14, in Mrs. Bates's classroom, Brett set up his display with his grandmother's bear and an explanation of how much his grandmother loved the grandfather he never had met. Next to Brett's display, Annie set up the poster to accompany her grandmother's favorite possession, Great-Grandfather Jacob's Bible.

41

Mattie

The day of Mrs. Bates's program at school, I picked up my father's Bible to take for Annie's display. I took out the many bookmarks and treasures hidden in its pages. Once again I studied the letter from Mama that I had received when I was ten. I sat down in my rocker and unfolded the paper, noticing the wrinkles Aunt Susan must have smoothed out after I threw it down.

Mother couldn't have loved me if she could leave me so easily. What could have happened to her? And Joy? I wondered who was the lucky one: Joy, to go with Mama, or I? I had been so blessed. The surge of anger at Mama rose quickly, and as quickly started to fade.

April 14, 1965

I opened the Bible to a random page—it was the passage in Romans: *All things work together for good to those who love God.* Perfect. This was the passage I would have showing while the Bible was on display. It was the exact message that would give me the strength to carry on.

The afternoon at the school was a good break for me. Joan, Beth, and Grant were able to come to the school with me to see what the fourth graders had put together. We were all pleased to see the things the children had brought as treasures from their parents and grandparents: antique dishes, handmade quilts, well-crafted shelves, lace pieces, journals from trips abroad, dried flowers, a wreath made of woven human hair, a fan brought over from China, a book of poetry, even a coin collection with coins dating back into the 1800s. Each was displayed with an explanation written by the fourth grader who brought it. One of my former Cub Scouts was the father of Annie's friend Sarah, and I smiled as

I noted that Sarah had put on display a Popsicle-stick model of a cabin that once stood on the Ohio River near Parkersville. The model was crafted when Sarah's father was in my Cub Scout pack. I never suspected in those long-ago days that John Sheridan would become an architect, though as I looked again, all those years later, at the work he did as an eight-year-old, I realized that I should have expected it of him.

At the end of the program spring break began. The children rushed for the doors, free until school convened after Easter. *Just get through the holiday*, I thought. Soon I would have a better idea about what was wrong with Ron.

42

Easter Sunday
APRIL 18, 1965

Easter Sunday, 1965, was sunny and pleasant in Michigan. The sunrise service was delivered by the youth, who helped to plan the service with Aaron. The crowded 11:00 a.m. service had attendants who came once or twice a year, and the spirit was light and festive. Aaron knew it would be the last worship service he would lead there, though they would continue to live in the manse for a few more months. He missed Joan and the children's presence. He had already packed up the car so that he could make a quick getaway, but lingered at the door greeting and talking to the parishioners. Sheriff Otto Smedl stopped to wish Aaron a happy Easter. The meeting was awkward after what had passed between them a few weeks before. He told Ron about a local resident who had hit and killed a young bicyclist while driving in the morning fog yesterday. The driver was a seventy-year-old who was distracted and did not seem to know what he was doing when he was stopped by the sheriff's deputy down the street from the accident. After Otto told Aaron the tale, he asked about Aaron's folks.

"Is there a connection, Otto, between telling me about the accident and asking about my dad?"

"There might be, Reverend. We've been getting some bulletins about older drivers who shouldn't be driving any more. I was thinking back to last October and wondering; that's all."

"You could be right about my dad. I'm driving down to Parkersville after church today. I'm on my way to go with my mother and dad to see a brain specialist next week."

"Well, drive carefully, Reverend. I hope things are okay down there."

—

Easter Sunday services in Parkersville were also inspiring, though a misty, cold rain fell all morning. Mattie helped Ron button his shirt and tie his tie. After he struggled with his shoe laces for some time, she knelt down and tied them—like Jesus washing his disciples' feet, she thought.

In church Mattie's attention was tuned to Ron, rather than the message from the pulpit. She needed to prompt Ron when to stand, when to sit, when to bow his head. She noticed he seemed almost to cower when the strong alleluias of the choir and congregation rang out. Though she was concerned about Ron and what Dr. Martin's verdict would be, she mixed those thoughts with the glorious message of the resurrection. The Easter service was always the most boisterous service of the year, when the staid Presbyterians had permission to shout and sing like the Pentecostals celebrating the resurrection. *Celebrations should be more a part of our life, she thought. Wonder what Papa would think about how sober we are.*

The service ended with the choir, joined by members of the congregation singing the rousing Hallelujah Chorus from Handel's *Messiah*. Ron smiled and sang a bit of it. "He shall reign forever and ever." *So he shall, Mattie reflected. And we will get through this.*

—

Aaron must have exceeded a few speed limits. He arrived around ten that evening, and hugged his wife and mother. Ron and the children had already been sent off to bed, but Mattie had the coffee pot on, and they sat down to talk.

"How was church?" Joan asked.

"Big crowd. And exuberant. I think they catch the message of Easter better than any other sermon I preach all year."

Aaron reached for some brownies from the plate on the table. "When did you have time to bake, Mom?"

"Patty fixed Easter dinner at her house, so I made cookies and pies to take over. There is a slice of dried apple pie if you want it."

"No thanks, I'll eat it for breakfast if you'll let me. Tell me about Dad."

"We'll know more on Friday," Mattie replied. "He seems to not be able to come up with words. He is slower in his speech. I think I can often figure out what he is trying to say. It helps him if I just listen."

"I notice that he repeats questions quite a bit," Joan offered. "Does that bother you, Mom?"

"Not really. At first it made me a little angry to have to keep answering the same question. Now I realize that he can't retain recent memories. It's as if he never asked the question before, from his point of view. When he wears me out with questions, I try to give him something else to work on."

Mattie glanced up at the clock. "We'd better get some rest. Dad will be up early, and you'll want to spend some time with him. He's often better in the morning than later in the day."

43

~

Mattie

The message of Easter is one of joy and salvation, God loving us enough to die for us while we were yet sinners. And then Christ rose from the dead and promised us eternal life. That Easter of 1965, I had a hard time focusing on the message, for I was more and more concerned for Ron.

Easter Monday, April 19, 1965

Early Easter Monday Aaron awakened and went down to see if his dad was up. Ron wasn't in the kitchen, so Aaron retrieved the dried apple pie from the refrigerator and brewed himself some coffee.

As I came downstairs, I called from the stairwell, "Are you two having a good visit?"

"Dad's not here, Mom; I thought he was still upstairs with you."

I hurried into the kitchen, glancing outdoors to see if Ron might be in the yard. "Put on your coat and look around the neighborhood, Aaron. He's still in his pajamas. He shouldn't be out wandering." Aaron threw on his parka and rushed out. He jumped in his car and cruised the neighborhood streets in ever widening circles.

While Aaron was searching, I aroused Joan, who hurried to dress and search the neighborhood yards. I phoned Patty to ask her to hurry over. Then I decided to call Kathy. "You were right, Kathy. Ron is ill, and the dementia is getting worse. I wish you would come over here." At least the rain from yesterday had stopped.

After a frantic circling of several blocks, Aaron found his father on the steps of the Presbyterian Church, huddled in the corner. Aaron told me he exploded at his father, demanding to know what was going on. Ron, his pajamas damp from sitting on the wet steps, climbed into Aaron's car, with a vacant stare. "Going to church. It's Easter. We always go to church first thing on Easter."

"I'm sorry, Mom. I couldn't help yelling at him that yesterday was Easter. I caught myself, though, thinking that Dad lives in yesterdays," he told me when he brought his dad in.

—

When we saw Aaron drive up with Ron everyone breathed a sigh of relief. Patty went into the kitchen to call home and reassure them that Ron had been found. Joan took Bethie and Grant outside telling them to play by themselves for a while. She wasn't quite ready to answer their questions about what was happening with their grandfather.

When Ron came in the door he walked right past me and up to Kathy. He gave her a big hug and said, "I love you, dear."

Kathy had not been at our house since before Thanksgiving when she had come over to tell me she thought Ron was acting strange. I was stunned that he embraced Kathy and not me. For a second I couldn't catch my breath. "Ron? What's happening?" I asked. Then I looked at Kathy, who had shuffled back a step or two, almost stumbling. "What? What's going on?" I asked her. "What's going on with you and Ron?"

Aaron gave me a surprised look, then took his father by the hand and led him to our room to help him change out of his wet clothes.

Kathy and I were alone for the moment. I asked her again, "What is going on?"

"I'm as surprised as you are." Kathy blushed. "Ron's not himself now. That's the only explanation I can think of."

"Is there something I should have known about you two?" I asked. "Sometimes I wondered if Ron really loved you more than he did me."

"No, Mattie," Kathy replied as tears filled her eyes. "He has always loved you. I am quite sure of that."

"Do you have something going with Ron? Did you?"

"We shared some comfort for a while. It's been over for a long time. He helped me through the valley of despair when Josh was killed. But he always loved you. Before today he has never said 'I love you' to me, though I've wanted him to say it."

I sank onto the green easy chair as Kathy continued to speak. "Now, though, I think it's clear that he doesn't know what he's saying. He's out of touch with reality. You and Ron had a very special bond that I envied, especially when Josh didn't return."

Josh should have come home, I realized. Ron and I had promised to look after Kathy until he returned. And he never did. The war was almost over and the Japanese submarine should have been heading back to home waters, not sending its final torpedoes at Josh and his friends.

So sad. I was worried about losing Ron to this mind thing. Maybe I should have worried about losing him to Kathy. Now it seemed we had both lost him, as he had lost himself.

Patty came back into the room then. She looked at Kathy and me. She'd not seen Ron's hug or heard his words to Kathy. "Is Ron okay?" she asked us. "You two look so worried."

"Aaron took him upstairs to change," I told her. "He needed to get on some dry clothes." I'd take a while to process what I had just learned from Kathy. Was it worth a quarrel over the past when we couldn't change it? If we could rewrite history, she would be with Josh and Ron would never have felt the need to comfort her. But we can't rewrite it, we can only try to understand it.

Aaron came down then. He said Ron had decided to lie down after he got dressed.

I asked him, "What do you think, Aaron?"

"He's so unpredictable, Mom. How can you bear it?"

"It's hard, dear. But so many things are unpredictable in life."

44
~

Cleveland Clinic
APRIL 23, 1965

That Friday's appointment with the neurologist in Cleveland was at 1:00. Joan, Aaron, Patty, Ron and Mattie, and the five kids, from fourteen-year-old Roy down to eight-year-old Grant, piled into Patty's station wagon, with the youngest in the "way-back." The children looked forward to a visit to the Cleveland Museum of Natural History and ice cream at Isaly's. At the museum Roy would ride herd on Jake and Annie, and Beth would keep an eye on Grant. Not that much supervision was needed. All five of the children knew to ask directions from museum personnel or from a police officer and not to talk to strangers.

—

No one was sure what to expect from Dr. Martin. Ron asked over and over where they were going. Mattie and Patty and Joan each took a turn at answering the question, and Ron seemed satisfied with the answer. A few minutes later he asked again. When they walked into Dr. Martin's office, Ron seemed a bit agitated, but Mattie took his hand and led him to a seat. Joan and Aaron were shocked that Ron was so much less able to follow conversations than he had been in October.

When the pretty blond nurse in her crisp white uniform called Mattie and Ron into the examining room, Aaron went along to help his dad. Joan and Patty talked. "Your three kids are so grown-up all of a sudden," Joan said. "Sorry we're missing Mark on this visit."

Patty had been waiting for a chance to talk to Joan with no children present. "Mark might not be back at all. He's planning a move to a property near Oxbridge. He wants to start farming on some land he found available down there."

Joan frowned. She studied her sister-in-law and saw the tears forming. "Something's wrong besides Dad's strange behavior, isn't it? Tell me."

"I haven't said anything to Mom yet," she replied, "but Mark and I are having problems. I may need to get a lawyer soon to find out about a divorce."

Joan stared at her sister-in-law in disbelief. "You and Mark have been our role models for a happily married couple. You were so happy together when we visited during our engagement. Mark boasted about you and Roy from the beginning. I remember you were pregnant with Jake when Aaron and I married. Mark was as proud as a peacock of his growing family."

"Maybe so, but no longer. Mark met a girl down in Oxbridge when he went down to take a class, and he's having an affair with her. He pretends he's going down there to study, but my friend Meredith told me he isn't attending class. She's seen him going off with Julie. He would call me from Oxbridge to say he had to study late, or that the car had broken down or something."

"I'm so sorry, Patty. It seems so unlike the Mark I know."

"It has been on my mind since Meredith told me before spring break. Yesterday I confronted Mark and he confessed. He says he loves her. He wants to move down to her farm."

"What are you going to do?"

"I'm not sure what to do. Mark is my best friend, Joan, and has been for eighteen years. I don't want to let him go. But what can I do?"

Before Joan could answer, Mattie returned to ask her two daughters-in-law to join her and Aaron in the doctor's office while the nurse helped Ron dress.

Dr. Martin's office was richly furnished, befitting his position in the prestigious Cleveland Clinic. Since World War Two, the reputation of the Clinic had grown, as had the campus where it was located. Mattie was not comfortable in the setting, but Dr. Martin's compassion put her at ease.

Dr. Martin chose his words carefully. "Your husband is not well, but it is hard to say what's going on with him. Some forgetting is normal for any of us, perhaps more so as we age. However, Mr. Connors is not all that old, and his symptoms seem more severe. We call it hardening of the arteries or chronic brain decline. In 1904 a doctor named Alois Alzheimer described a patient with similar symptoms. There is a syndrome we call Alzheimer's after that doctor. Unfortunately there is no way to know if Mr. Connors has that."

Patty asked, "Do you think Dad has it? How would we know?"

"Dr. Alzheimer identified certain anomalies in his patient's brain, but he did so through an autopsy of the organ after she died."

"Well, that doesn't seem like much help," Joan murmured. "We certainly don't want to hurry Dad's death to find out. Could it be anything else?"

"Of course—it could be a brain tumor, or a vitamin or thyroid deficiency, or the results of a small stroke. We'll do a few tests to see if these can be ruled out. But from what I can see, it looks like your father has all the early signs of the dementia Dr. Alzheimer identified."

"Can Ron's brain be treated to get better again?" Mattie asked.

"Probably not, I'm sorry to say. The course of this disease, if it is Alzheimer's, always is downward and progressive. The patient can decline quickly or very slowly, but in the end it leads to total dependency, unless the patient dies sooner of some other cause. It's not a hopeful prognosis."

"Why haven't we heard about Alzheimer's before?" Aaron's question.

"The medical profession hasn't done many studies or published much about it. We just accept some loss of mental faculties as a person grows older. I think that's wrong, but that's the way it is. It's not even considered a disease. Many folks think it's normal."

"Well, Ron isn't normal, and I am not going to accept this without a fight," Mattie declared. "Will you talk to Ron about what you told us?"

"Mrs. Connors, your husband doesn't seem to be too worried about what is happening to him. I can see you are. It's not necessary to concern him with this. We think it's better not to tell patients about problems that can't be treated."

"Well, I will tell him," Mattie declared. Then, more thoughtfully, "At least, I think he should know."

"Suit yourself, but he may not even understand what you're talking about. Few places in the country are even looking at problems of aging. You'll be on your own."

Mattie was shaking as she stood up. "I am not on my own, Dr. Martin. I have God on my side."

Ron waited in the examining room for them, after the nurse had helped him to dress. "We have to meet the children and go out for our ice cream," Joan said to Ron. "Are you okay, Dad? Are you, Mom?"

"Where are we going?" Ron inquired.

45

~

Kathy
SPRING – SUMMER 1965

After Ron's Easter Monday outing, Kathy began to come on Wednesdays to sit with Ron. "Mattie, it's not much, but I can take Wednesdays off and you can go wherever, meetings at the church or coffee with friends, just get out. You need to refresh yourself."

Kathy and Ron listened to music or she read aloud. Ron would often fall asleep in his chair. As time passed, he interacted less and less with his surroundings. Kathy's mind wandered to her relationship with Roger. *What am I getting out of being with him? He won't even think of taking me out anywhere. He is too afraid some friend of his wife will see us and report back to her...I think I've given Roger enough of myself to have paid off the advance on my mortgage...He depends enough on me at the office, especially as he is setting his sights on a political career...He can very well raise my salary and I will quit being his mistress.*

Each week as she watched Ron slipping, she reaffirmed to herself the resolve not to accept the terms Roger had imposed on her. She considered options.

If I quit at the law firm altogether, I risk losing my house...I need some income to hold on there...Maybe I can find other work in town...No, with my education, the pay would probably be puny. As a last resort I could pack up and leave Parkersville to seek a better paying job...No, I can't do that! Mattie and Ron need me here.

By fall, she made up her mind to confront Roger. She met him at her front door one morning, dressed and ready to go to work.

"I don't want you coming here anymore. It's over, Roger. I'm through being your mistress. You'll need to find another sweetie pie. We're sticking strictly to business, from now on."

Roger's response surprised her. "But we're so good in bed! How could you even think of giving that up when it's so satisfying?"

"Do you mean that? I'm nothing to you but a receptacle of your passion. A woman wants and deserves more than 'Bam, bam, thank you, Ma'am,' and you've given me nothing but money. It's time for you to pay me a better wage for my work at the office, and to look elsewhere for your sexual drives."

"Now, wait, Kathy. That isn't true. You have always enjoyed our encounters as much as I have."

"No, Roger. I have not. A woman wants courtship and being cared for and being taken places and shown off. I've never myself had such a relationship, but I know it's possible and you've never shown the least interest in providing that for me. I'm not sure what your relationship is with Rhonda, but I could go and ask her. I can find another job, but I like this one. It's just the terms will have to change, or else."

"Give me some time to consider this. I thought things were fine."

"I'll give you a week to mull it over, but by the end of October I expect a raise or I'll take it up with Rhonda."

—

Kathy was surprised by Roger's "counteroffer." Leave it to a lawyer to look at a case from all the angles. "You want more? How about this. I need to travel to Detroit in December for some business, political business actually. Then next year I'll be making some regular trips out of town. Let's go together. You want to be wined and dined and treated to the high life. This would be our chance to travel as husband and wife, and you could get all dolled up and put on the dog. No one in those places would know the difference. It won't be like here in Parkersville where, you're right, we need to keep a low profile."

Negotiations were Roger's strong suit—not Kathy's. Though it wasn't what she had had in mind, she saw some value in such a trial. She could still fall back on her original plans if the Detroit trip did not bring her the pleasure Roger promised. So she accepted the offer and over the course of the next year she took many such trips, enjoying the status of a rich man's wife.

46

Mattie

*R*on's *illness was getting worse, but I thought I was coping pretty well with everything. Then the last week of the Parkersville school term, I asked the children about their summer plans and Annie started to cry. "Daddy's moving out, Grandma. He wants to live on a farm. He says our land isn't big enough for his plans."*

June 1965

I had missed Mark's presence for a while, but I was still surprised when Annie told me he planned to leave the family. I realized that Patty hadn't talked about their summer plans as she usually did.

"What? What are you saying?" I asked Annie.

Jake tried to hush his sister, but Annie continued. "I don't understand it. He seems so different now. I'm glad he's moving out if he won't stop being so mean!" She ran to me, nearly knocking me over with her embrace. Over her head, I raised an eyebrow to Jake, but he shrugged and walked out to the backyard.

"Ask your daddy to come see me, Annie. I think he and I need to talk."

Annie sniffled. "I hope he isn't mean to you. He yells at Mom a lot. But I'll tell him."

When Patty stopped to pick up the kids, she confirmed Annie's news, but she promised to tell Mark I wanted to see him. "I didn't want to add to your worries, Mom, but I think he is pretty determined to live at Julie Andrews's farm. He's been spending weekends there since Easter."

Mark avoided me for several days, but at last he stopped by.

"I can't stay long, Mom. I have a lot to do."

"You can stay long enough to hear this, Mark. Your dad is ill. He needs help more than he ever has before."

"I've heard that you think that, Mom. Are you sure you aren't blowing it all out of proportion? You tend to exaggerate."

"I'm not imagining it. Nor am I imagining what Patty told me about your recent wanderings."

"I don't know what your mean," Mark said, not meeting my eyes.

"With Julie Andrews," I said.

My bluntness took him aback. He glowered at me and said between clenched teeth, "You don't know anything, Mom. You're so wrapped up in trying to run everyone's lives that you don't know anything! Grandma Alice left you as a child and you've compensated by running everyone's life to suit you! Dad isn't sick. He's just shutting you out of his life because you're so interfering. You forced me to marry Patty when I wasn't ready. You pushed Aaron into entering the ministry when all he wanted was to study science. You always think you know best—I have news for you. You don't."

My jaw dropped. Where did that all come from? Had he been rehearsing it for all those days when he was avoiding me? Then the thought sunk in that maybe he was right. Was I a failure in all I ever wanted in life—to be a good wife and mother? I so wanted not to be like my mother.

Before I could put words to my thoughts, Mark walked out, slamming the door behind him. I sat for a minute, shaken by the confrontation. All of a sudden my tirade against my mother when I was a six-year-old came to my mind. Was I to blame for her leaving me? My heart was racing. I was breathing hard and I felt the heat rise in my cheeks.

Ron entered the room just then, and came over to give me a kiss. Mark's speech was burned into my subconscious.

"Are you all right?" Ron and I both began at once. I managed a smile. Yes, I was all right for the time being. Only time would tell with Ron.

47

Aaron and Mark
SUMMER 1965

Aaron had stayed several weeks in Parkersville helping with Ron. When he returned to Michigan he met with the church board members. Afterwards, he went home to talk everything over with Joan.

"They said we could stay rent-free until school is out for the kids. Once the semester ends, we could rent the manse from the church. They won't need it until they search for my replacement."

"Well, it would give you a chance to look around for another pastorate."

"I'm not thinking of looking for a church, Joan. I think I might go back to school, if we can swing it."

"What would you study? Where do you think you would go?"

"Answering your second question first: Ohio State University would put us closer to home and the folks. I think I want to teach young people, our future generation. The changes we need in this country will come from youth, I'm sure."

"I can go back to teaching for a while. The kids are old enough now. Let's do it. Sit down and write the application."

—

In mid-June Aaron went to Columbus for an interview at the University and then drove over to Parkersville to check on his parents. Mattie greeted him at the door with the news about Mark's leaving home. She did not report the scene she had had with him but said, "You need to talk some sense into him before he ruins his life…and Patty's and the children's."

Joan had already told Aaron what she had learned talking to Patty in April.

"It's a delicate situation, Mom," Aaron said. "I'll talk to him, but I'm not sure it will help."

———

Aaron called his brother at the emergency number Mark had left with Patty. "This is an emergency, Mark. Do I need to come down there to see you or will you come up here to talk? Mom is going to have her hands full in a short time."

Reluctantly, Mark agreed to ride his cycle over to Parkersville to talk to his brother. He sauntered onto the porch where Aaron waited for him. Before Aaron could even say hello, Mark tossed down his keys and jacket and started his tirade. "Don't lecture me, preacher man. Nothing is wrong with Dad except old age, and my life is not any business of yours."

"You are right on the second count, but Dad's fifty-four. Something is definitely wrong with him that is more than 'old age.' As for you and Patty, I know these days everyone says you can do anything you please. But that's not the way Mom raised us, and you know it." Aaron's tone was conciliatory, but Mark was not ready to listen.

"I love Julie! The single reason I married Patty was because I got her pregnant and Mom insisted on it to keep the whole town from talking about us. I have news for her. The whole town was talking anyway when Roy was born so soon after our wedding." Mark paced the floor, pouring out words he'd held back so long. "Mom made us marry, when we should have gone our separate ways long ago."

Not knowing which part of the argument he should tackle first, Aaron breathed a prayer for guidance. "I know you two were head over heels in love at the beginning. When Joan and I came down from college to tell Mom and Dad we were engaged, you two and Roy were our ideal for the kind of loving couple we wanted to be. Patty was already pregnant again with Jake at our wedding, and you were bragging to everyone who would listen how happy you were."

Mark paused to consider the happy occasion of Joan and Aaron's wedding, and six months later Jacob's birth. They *had been* happy then. What had gone wrong? It wasn't the strains of going to school, working, and having two kids to care for. Mattie had helped out with the children, providing constant child care and often serving meals for all of them, either at the house on Washington Street or preparing stuff in Mark and Patty's kitchen while she did some ironing for them or straightened up around their house. Even Annie's birth a year and a half later didn't generate the strain they might have expected. To be fair, he had loved Patty in those first years. People talk about the seven-year itch. Maybe finishing his education classes and getting the teaching job in junior high math was part of the problem. He didn't much care for teaching math. He would have preferred to teach more science courses, but they needed a math teacher and he qualified.

Aaron observed his brother deep in thought. That was an improvement over his ranting, so Aaron waited him out to see what he would say next. "I don't know, Aaron, where we went wrong. I'd like to blame it all on Mom, but I can't in all honesty. Do you think Dad is really getting senile?"

"Back in seminary Joan did a bit of substitute teaching. The little town we lived in didn't have a lot of folks trained in education, so she became sort of the 'regular' sub in the high school: whatever class needed a substitute they called her."

Mark listened intently, not sure where the story was going.

"She had no trouble with the English classes or the social studies classes or the science classes," Aaron continued. "She did fine in math and health and even mechanical drawing. But one day they wanted her to sub in band and orchestra. You know Joan. She isn't tone deaf, but the next thing to it. When she got home that day, she had a splitting headache. The kids figured out they could switch their instruments so the tuba player was doing the drums and the trombonist was playing a flute, and so on. Pretty soon it got so bad even Joan recognized they were way off key. She settled everyone down and gave them a study hall instead of practice. Then she declared she'd never do band and orchestra again." Aaron smiled, remembering Joan's description of the chaos.

"I've been thinking about Dad's brain problem as an orchestra where the players are messing up. If one player misses a note, it's hardly noticed as long as all the others are playing the score the right way. But if more and more players miss beats, or play the wrong instruments, soon it turns into chaos instead of music. Dad must feel pretty disoriented when he can't follow a conversation, or think of a word, or learn how to do something that's unfamiliar. Rather like a child learning, but with so much 'stuff' already in his brain he can't fit the new information in."

"Can't he take some kind of medicine? I don't understand why this is happening. I thought he was just reacting to Mom's overbearing ways."

"Dr. Martin said if the problem is hardening of the arteries, trying to keep the arteries clear might help. He talked about a recently discovered drug called propranolol that might help. Dad might need to go up to the Cleveland Clinic for visits. They don't expect it to change much, though."

"I could take him up sometimes, maybe. I should be able to get away from the farm if I know ahead of time when he needs to go."

"So the farm is a done deed for you? Is it Julie's farm?"

"Yeah. Her dad had about given up on it. Her brother has urged the dad to sell to the coal company, but she asked me to join her to keep him from selling.

You know I love farming on our acreage. I can make a success of this."

"So is it Julie you love or the farm?"

"Both. She's only seventeen, and she needs so much help. She thinks I'm wonderful because I can help her succeed with the farm."

"Let me see, Julie thinks you're wonderful and Patty knows your flaws. Is that the difference?"

"Preaching again, big brother. Can't get away from it, I guess."

"I'm trying to help you understand what you're hiding from yourself. I know the popular mantra right now is 'Do your own thing,' but keeping your commitments and doing the *right* thing are what Mom and Dad tried to teach us. Think it over."

"I'm thinking you're butting in where you don't belong, but I will help get them up to Cleveland if that's help they need and will accept."

"Thanks. I hope to be moving down to the Columbus area soon. I want to go back to school to take some graduate courses, possibly go into counseling or teaching. I've left my church, by mutual agreement."

There was a silence as each brother considered what he had heard. After a short pause, Mark asked, "Have you told Mom about your plans?"

"No, I didn't want to bother her until I was sure."

"Be careful how you tell her. I predict she'll go off the deep end when she hears it." Mark picked up his jacket. "I'll think about what you said. Tell Mom I'll help with the driving. I don't think I want to talk to her until I sort some things out." He bolted off as he heard his mother's footsteps approaching.

48

~

Mattie

I hate to tell you about what happened after Mark left that day. His offer to help should be an improvement, but I'm ashamed of how I reacted next.

June 1965

I came out with some lemonade just as Mark was leaving. Aaron told me of Mark's offer to help with the driving. I set the tray on the little table by the swing and sat down to drink.

"That's helpful, Aaron. I'm sorry he didn't stay to talk to me, but it sounds like you made some headway with him. Perhaps God will bring good out of this situation, as He has promised."

I noticed Aaron seemed to be a bit on edge, and I wondered if the conversation with Mark had been more stressful than he had admitted.

Finally, Aaron cleared his throat and said, "Mom, I want to tell you something else. Joan and I and the kids are thinking about moving closer to home."

I was thrilled. "That would be wonderful, Aaron. I heard about a vacant church over toward Wooster. Might you apply there?"

"Mom, I'm not looking at churches. I am leaving the pastorate to study counseling or education."

Aaron's words hit me like a bolt of lightning. *Leaving the ministry. What else could go wrong?* I jumped up, brushing Aaron aside, and blindly hurried inside. I rushed up the stairs to my bedroom and slammed the door as I dove for my bed. In a few minutes I was sobbing as I couldn't remember ever sobbing before. I put my fist to my mouth to try to quiet the sobs and buried my head in my pillow. Aaron came to the closed bedroom door and I heard his soft knock.

"Mom, are you okay?"

I took a breath and managed to get out a few broken words. "Go away! I'm fine, just go away."

A terrible lump rose to my throat. My chest hurt and I couldn't breathe. I felt forsaken and alone. The unfailing comfort of God's love, which had been with me through all my difficult times, suddenly abandoned me. What had seemed such a pleasant life—where my ambitions for myself and for family seemed to be so perfectly aligned with what I knew was God's plan for me—vanished. Did God not exist, after all? Was God not loving enough, or not powerful enough to protect his own obedient servants? Or was the fault mine? Had I not tried hard enough to follow God's commands? Were my devotions not sincere enough?

I thought of Papa's death, so sudden. I thought of the quick abandonment by Mama. I thought about Ida Sue, the daughter we so wanted, and the sorrow of losing her before we even knew her. I had felt God's presence through all of that. Now, however—

Now Aaron's words confirmed Mark's tirade. I *had* forced my children to become what they did not want. And Ron was dying the long, slow death of advancing senility. *God, why have you forsaken me?* Christ's words on the cross. He felt abandoned as I did. *I am a failure, after all.*

49

Aaron
JUNE 1965

Aaron waited outside his mother's door, not knowing whether to enter or follow her instructions to go away. She had been so stalwart through Dr. Martin's verdict, Mark's desertion of his family, and the struggles with Dad. Now his statement that he was leaving the ministry had sent her into a tailspin, and Aaron hadn't a clue why. Through the closed door he called in a loud voice, "Mom, it's not all bad. We'll be much closer to home. I can get over more often to help. Open the door. Talk to me."

Aaron heard her shuffling over from the bed. She opened the door, tears falling down her cheeks, and Aaron enfolded her in his arms as she buried her head in his shoulder. Neither spoke for a long time.

Mattie began to get herself under control. "All I ever wanted to be was a good wife and mother! I am a total failure at both."

Aaron was dumfounded. He helped his mother sit in the rocker and took his own seat on the edge of the bed. "Of course that's not so, Mom. Why would you say such a thing?"

Haltingly, Mattie was able to get the words out. "When I told Mark about Dad, he denied it all. He said I drove him to marry Patty and become a teacher when that was not at all what he wanted. He told me I was reacting to my own mother leaving me as a child. He said I drove you into the ministry when you didn't want to do it. He said I wasn't a good mother. I never wanted to be anything else. Was I so horrible to force you boys into paths you didn't want to choose?" Mattie sat shaking with her face in her hands, shoulders slumped.

Aaron wondered how long these feelings had been simmering below the surface of his perfectly controlled mother. How much had the failing cognition of his father added to the strain? And what could Aaron say about his brother's comments or his own change in goals for the future? How could he make her understand that these changes did not indicate her failure?

"Mom, you've given so much of your life to others, I'm not surprised you should feel like you're running on empty every once in a while. But God will soon be filling you up again. Trust him. Mark and Patty loved each other very much when they married, even though Mark seems to be forgetting that now. You rescued them and Roy from what would have been a terrible life if they hadn't married and made a family when they did. Mark knows that.

"As for me, I chose the ministry. I wasn't forced into it. You taught me to seek to serve God. I thought it would be through the pastorate, which was the right choice at the time. Right now, I think God's call has changed. I feel called to get a better education so I can work with college students—the future of this country—and help them see the God who loves them isn't confined to Sunday morning in a Presbyterian pulpit. I'm leaving the pastorate, not because I was forced to enter, by you or anyone, but because I feel God calling me now to a different mission."

"It's not just you, Aaron. I feel so abandoned. I thought I was past the hurt of Mama's leaving me. I'm not."

"Psalm 22 begins with a cry of despair, but it doesn't end that way," Aaron reminded her.

"I can't think past the words Jesus quoted on the cross, Aaron. What comes after?"

"Here's Grandpa Jake's Bible. Let's look it up."

Mattie turned to Psalm 22. She read the whole psalm, concentrating on the words.

> *Ye that fear the Lord, praise him...*
> *For he hath not despised nor abhorred the affliction of the afflicted;*
> *neither hath he hid his face from him;*
> *but when he cried unto him, he heard.*

"God does not hide his face but hears us. He really does," Mattie mused. "If anyone was hiding, it was me, not God. I realize now I have never forgiven Mama for her actions. I need to let go my resentment. I understand now how hard her life must have been. God forgive us both."

"You're on the right track now, Mom." Then Aaron added an afterthought. "I need to be more forgiving myself. Thanks for the example."

50

~

Dar and Black Power
JUNE – JULY 1966

The tall, dark man had just been released from his twenty-seventh time in jail. He spoke to the crowd that included Dar Jones from Parkersville.

> This is 1966 and it seems to me that it's "time out" for nice words. It's time black people got together. We have to say things nobody else in this country is willing to say and find the strength internally and from each other to say the things that need to be said. We have to understand the lies this country has spoken about black people and we have to set the record straight. No one else can do that but black people.

Stokely Carmichael was the leader of the Student Nonviolent Coordinating Committee (SNCC), the man who had arranged for Dar's 1964 "Freedom Summer" in Mississippi. Dar, listening to Carmichael's words, gave a shout of affirmation. "Right on! He's telling it like it is." He heard Stokely denounce the nonviolent tactics of Dr. Martin Luther King. King had failed to accomplish the goal of equality, and, further, that goal itself was not enough.

Dar Jones had completed his second year at Howard Law School, and chose to accompany Carmichael, King, and others in the 220-mile March Against Fear in June 1966. Attacks, beatings, and confrontations had led to many being arrested in Greenwood, Mississippi.

> We got so busy being white we forgot what it was to be black. The only thing we own in this country is the color of our skins and we are ashamed of that because they made us ashamed. We have to move this year…we are going to use the term "Black Power" and we are going to define it…We are going to

build a movement in this country based on the color of our skins that is going to free us from our oppressors and we have to do that ourselves.

Dar, rejuvenated by the adrenaline coursing through his body, called his sister Sophie, as soon as he could get to a phone. "Remember the words 'Black Power,' Soph," Dar told her. "Stokely says for us to define our own goals, lead our own organizations, and build community. That's what's been missing. We reject the values we've been hand-fed by whites."

"Dar, watch your words. That man's ideas will end in violence that can't be controlled." She lowered her voice to a whisper. "How can you be nonviolent and follow the path that man is preaching?"

"We'll change the name if we need to, Soph. We have been shackled too long."

"But Dr. King has urged and warned and inspired us to work within the system."

"He's wrong. How much longer can we ignore the hostility Whitey has used against us? You know about Watts last summer! Six days of rioting; one thousand people injured; thirty-four people killed; hundreds of fires; arrests; windows and cars shattered. Police were going crazy, clubbing and shooting, killing without thought of innocence or guilt. Over a thousand National Guard called in. Does that sound like nonviolence working?"

"Dar, what did it gain us but more hate?"

"You're right about that, Soph. The Dagos felt free to join the vigilantes and support police brutality. This is about more than eating at white lunch counters and being able to go to the library. It's about lost jobs and closed businesses, high crime rates and continuing poverty! Successful 'Uncle Toms' are moving out by becoming 'white'; it's left to the poor to fight for themselves. We'll tell the white liberals to act on changing Whitey's mind. We Blacks will use our power in numbers to make big changes."

51

Eddie and Kathy
CHRISTMAS 1966 – CHRISTMAS 1967

Eddie's training for the patrol craft fast deployment finished up as 1966 ended. Soon after arriving with his swift boat crew in the Gulf of Siam, he wrote his mother a Christmas letter.

Kathy had been getting regular letters from her son, once every other week or so. She wrote to him weekly as well. But the Christmas letter of 1966, which arrived mid-January of '67, disturbed her more than usual, for it reminded her of the later letters from Josh. What would Josh think about his son in danger? Danger Josh so foolishly welcomed for himself—and he ended up a wartime statistic! Why was this world so upside-down? Plenty of young men Eddie's age were being drafted to serve, and the army kept calling up more. She knew of others who had run off to Canada or were hiding in college classes avoiding service. Why was Eddie so gung-ho to be there? With these thoughts circus-leaping in her brain, she settled into the easy chair, welcomed Heather to settle in her lap, and read.

December 25, 1966

Dear Mom,

Merry Christmas—wish I could be with you, but Uncle Sam thought otherwise. I am here at the ▓▓▓▓▓▓▓▓▓▓▓▓▓▓ base (if you can call it that) at ▓▓▓▓▓. The USS Catamount brought our six swift boats and all our crews here in time for Christmas. For our Christmas dinner we ate C-rations. We ate it in haste so we could begin patrolling as soon as possible. We barely got our sea legs, but since the amenities here are old tents thrown up by the first couple PCF crews when they arrived earlier, we might as well get into action.

Don't worry though. The Secretary of the Navy has taken notice, waved his magic wand, and we should soon be getting the materials to put up some Quonset huts with some Seabees to help us out.

We'll patrol ~~the coast in the Second Coastal Zone and blockade the South Vietnam coastline against North Vietnamese gun-running trawlers.~~ These maneuver "innocently" out in the South China Sea, wait for the cover of darkness, and make high-speed runs to the South Vietnam coastline. Then they offload their cargoes to waiting Viet Cong or North Vietnamese forces. Our job is to stop them.

I'll just be here the year, and at least for now I'm not into the "counting down" that some of the grunts are doing. But I do look forward already to seeing you again. Hope Uncle Ron is feeling better.

Love to all of you.

Eddie

A second letter to his friend Dar was a bit more frank. To Dar he described his shipmates, especially the Vietnamese navy liaison, Ngoyen Thu. "He reminds me of you, Dar. Not physically. He is a thin, short man, not much older than a kid, but he's seen so much in his short lifetime. I'm tempted to ask Ngoyen's thoughts about the afterlife, for death is no stranger in this land."

Eddie's letter continued, "I volunteered for the swift boats because I hate taking orders. I want to be like my sailor father, or like heroes of cowboy movies and comic books. We patrol the coasts to assist our allies and troops. Unless the enemy is actually firing on us, we can't engage.

We play this game, speeding by the coast hoping to provoke the enemy to attack. If that works, we have a fight on our hands. Keeps us from getting bored.

We work with the VNN, the Vietnamese army, but it's pretty hard knowing the good guys from the bad. General Westmoreland wants us to win hearts and minds, but we don't find a lot of hearts and minds lying about waiting to be won. The big guy also wants a big body count from an encounter. We seem to be 'winning' if we kill more of them than they do of us.

We hear General Fine, who came here earlier in a CIA operation, even before the Gulf of Tonkin thing, believed U.S. intelligence about a bombing target that the Viet intel said was a leper colony. Turned out the Viets were right! We shelled the hospital. Now the VNN doesn't trust our intelligence, and we sure as hell aren't about to rely on theirs.

As advisors, the U.S. won't listen to their counterparts, but forge ahead with a 'Kill 'em all' mentality. We're like the British troops in 1776. The Vietnamese are the minutemen defending their turf to the death. 'Give me liberty or give me death' could be their motto. What are we doing here?

—

By the time Dar received Eddie's letter, he'd come to see the war as another example of the white power system trying to enforce its will on another country, a colored race. Black Americans, the ones who couldn't afford the college education that conferred draft deferment, fought in disproportionate numbers.

"This white boy is exhausting me with his complaints," Dar told his sister.

"Dar, he's not 'this white boy.' He's your buddy. He's your best friend."

"My best friends are black from now on. We're going to build a movement to smash everything Western civilization has created."

"Dar, you can't mean to cut Eddie off, after all you've been to each other."

"You can write to him, Sophie. Tell him the war is exploiting the Vietnamese and the soldiers. The Man talks about free elections over there but won't support free elections in Alabama, Mississippi, Georgia, Texas, Louisiana, South Carolina, or Washington, D.C. Eddie needs to get the hell out of there instead of playing Superman. He's a mercenary—all our fighting forces are."

—

Eddie' next letter ended the same as his previous one. "Here we were fighting to keep the world safe—from what? Can you tell me, buddy, what we're fighting for?"

Dar's reply shook Eddie's world further. "Don't bother to write me again, white boy." The words were like a slap in the face. "You're no longer a friend of mine. Dr. King was wrong. We were wrong to think that things will ever change without some action. Stokely is right. Black Power is the answer. From now on I reject your society and your values, your laws and your pretensions that you are better than I am because your skin is lighter and your hair straighter. From now on you are no longer part of my life."

Eddie wrote back as soon as he could, reminding Dar of their past ties. "I never thought of myself as any better than you. I know you're way beyond me in everything, friend. Let's talk some more."

The letter Eddie had hastily written to Dar reminding him of their friendship came back marked, "Refused, Return to Sender." Eddie stared at it, bewildered. *It doesn't make sense to cut me off. We've shared so much. He's rejecting me in
a way I never rejected him—and I never would.*

                        —

Eddie wanted to find a way to reach Dar, but he was stuck over eight thousand miles away. The war continued to escalate. The more it did, the more Eddie
could see reasons to oppose it. At least he was getting letters from Sophie, as
she expressed concern for the two young men and their lifelong friendship. In
her letters she told Eddie her brother was turning more radical, caught up in the
Black Power movement.

    "I'm worried that Dar is taking the wrong path," Sophie wrote. "All the
people I know are taking up sides. Dar's making the wrong choice—giving up on
Dr. King's dream and turning his back on nonviolence. "

    Eddie replied to Sophie's news with concern. "I hope you're wrong about
Dar, but it doesn't sound like it. Dr. King's dream has been his dream, too, since
we were seventh graders."

    Sophie's next letter laid out some of Dar's arguments, though she didn't
agree with what her brother had told her. "Dr. King and Stokely Carmichael
are following different dreams now. Dar takes Carmichael's position that white
people should be mending their own fences, working to change the Ku Klux Klan
members and white supremacists. Blacks should be working with blacks, *taking*
their rights instead of expecting whites to 'grant' them."

    Eddie wrote back to Sophie. "I'm sure seeing that the violence here isn't an
answer. I don't think we have any idea what we're doing here. But in the United
States, Dr. King's dream of white people and black people working together in
peace is making a difference. Dar must know that."

    Eddie tried again to reach Dar, with the message that Martin Luther King's
dream was worth holding on to. This letter, too, was returned unopened. On
the envelope Dar had scribbled, "We must decide our own terms without white
people's blessing."

    Eddie tried writing again, but Dar did not reply.

    When Eddie heard nothing from Dar, he wrote to Sophie, "I don't under-
stand how he can be so hostile to me when I've been in his life all these years."

    "Stokely has convinced Dar you're an oppressor just because you're white,"
Sophie replied.

    "Surely you don't agree with him, do you, Sophie? I've never seen the color of his skin, or yours, as anything special. We have too long a history between us."

The letters flying between Sophie and Eddie contained enough support for them to grow closer. Soon Eddie found himself courting Sophie much as his father had courted his mother through the letters he wrote to her. Increasingly, Sophie and Eddie seemed to be in tune with one another.

In one letter she shared with him the concern expressed by her twelve-year-old son Brett when a fatal fire on the launch pad killed all three members of the Apollo 1 crew. Brett was as dedicated to the NASA space program as Eddie had been to the U.S. Navy. Brett read everything he could get his hands on about the race to the moon. President Kennedy had promised to land a man on the moon by the end of the decade, and NASA was well on its way to meeting the goal when the Apollo 1 crew died. Eddie wrote to Brett to keep the faith, which Sophie was pleased to see reassured her son. She regretted even more the rift between the two friends.

⁓

Eddie, while arguing nonviolence to Dar, grew more skeptical about the military actions in Vietnam. He decided not to re-enlist when his tour was over. As he settled back into civilian life, he joined a growing number of Vietnam vets who opposed the war.

52

Joy Tannenbaum
THANKSGIVING 1967

Gene Wilson, Jr., packed up the letter Alice McEnroe Wilson had written to her daughter, Joy, after their mother's funeral, putting it with the sympathy cards which had come. Gene had no recent address for his stepsister. Delivering it was not a high priority under the circumstances. His life resumed, filled with the usual minutia of living, only occasionally thinking about Joy at all. Then in November of 1967, Joy came to visit in Lake City for Thanksgiving. She'd been out of touch for a long time.

She came alone to the house where she'd spent much of her growing up years. She was surprised when she found her mother wasn't there to greet her. Instead her stepbrother invited her in and poured them each a drink.

"Gene, why didn't you contact me when Mother was ill?" Joy asked.

"I didn't even know where you were. It's not like you ever made a point of calling or visiting." He refilled his glass, offering more to Joy.

She waved his hand away, sipping her whiskey slowly. "You're right, but I never felt welcome here, either as a child or after I left to seek my fortune in Hollywood. She threw my clothes out the door when I told her I was planning to leave. Told me not to ever come back. Did you ever hear Mother say she missed me or see her try to contact me over all these years?"

Gene thought that over. Joy was right about Alice's neglect as well.

"She kept to herself most of the time I knew her," Gene agreed. "More so after Dad died. As long as I knew her she and my dad fought like tigers. But, ya know, I always thought they enjoyed the fighting. Remember how they'd yell at one another so much that Hope and Faith would hide behind the table? You were the one to reassure the girls."

"It's true enough. Mom and Dad would always hug and make up, though.

Then they'd close themselves in the bedroom and—I think you and I both understood what went on in there."

Gene smiled. So his younger stepsister had figured that out. He had thought she was too young. "She never seemed cheerful again after Dad's death."

"Gene, I was sorry when I heard your dad had died. She wrote me that one letter, a heartbroken letter of grief. Did she ever get over the loss?"

"Not really. I think she loved Dad and didn't know what to do when she lost a second husband."

"She did, didn't she? A second husband. She never told me about my own dad. I just don't remember him."

A sudden thought struck Gene. He jumped up from the table and hurried out of the room. Joy wasn't sure what was going on, but he soon returned with the box of funeral cards. Quickly he pawed through them and produced the letter addressed to Joy. "I don't know how I forgot this. But here's the letter she wrote to you while she was ill. If I'd known where to send it, I would have...We should have kept in touch better. Both of us."

Joy nodded. She turned away, anxious to read what her mother had said in the letter. *Yes. Kept in touch,* she thought. *Too much has been left unsaid.* Yet, she was at a loss for words. Her mother had been dead for almost a year, and she knew nothing of it. She hoped the letter would help her understand more about her mother and the past.

As Joy read the letter her mother had left for her, Alice's bitterness at the end of her life was clear. Joy tried to recall any happy memories in her own childhood. She remembered nothing of the life before Texas. Reading her mother's words, she tried to conjure up an image of a place called Parkersville or a sister called Matilda. Nothing.

Joy's visit with her stepbrother and his family brought her mixed sorrow and comfort. It was good to see Gene as well as Faith and Hope, the two little half-sisters she had cared for. Their memories of Joy's mother were not happy either, but they were glad to see the sister who had been away so long. She thanked her brother and promised to stay in touch this time.

⁓

Joy returned to her palatial home in Wilmette, north of Chicago, for Christmas. She hardly knew what to say to her husband, Avrum Tannenbaum, but when he returned from his firm downtown, she showed him the letter. He read it twice, then, raising his eyebrows he asked, "Where's Parkersville? Did you know you had lived somewhere else before Texas?"

"I guess I knew, sort of," Joy said. "My stepbrother tormented me about not being a 'real Wilson' when I was a child, but no one would talk about it. I've no idea where Parkersville is."

"We'll look it up in the Rand McNally." Avrum took down the beautifully bound atlas and laid it on the mahogany desk. "There's a Parkersville in California, one in Indiana, one in Ohio, and one in New York. Parker sure got around, didn't he?"

"Avrum, get serious. I don't think my mother traveled all the way from California or New York to Texas. The Midwest sounds more likely. I never heard her talk about Jacob McEnroe ever."

"Well, we can hire a detective to follow up on this if you want," Avrum said, pushing his glasses further up his nose. "I can certainly have one of our lawyers arrange for one. What do you want me to do?"

"I'm not sure. Do I want to find a long-lost sister who is 'fussy, sassy, exhausting, and willful?"

"And stubborn, remember," Avrum added with a twinkle in his eye. "I'll do whatever you want. Just say the word."

"Let me think it over a while. I don't want Mother to upset our lives in her death as she always tried to do in her life." Joy folded up the letter and tucked it in her Gucci handbag. "For now, I think I want to leave well enough alone." Joy worried that were she to find her sister, Matilda might turn out to be vengeful and angry with her.

Avrum accepted Joy's decision for the time being, but he also considered how it might make his wife happy if he could bring about a reconciliation.

53

Kathy
1968

Kathy was enjoying the occasional week out of Parkersville with Roger when she could take on the social role of his wife. Rhonda knew nothing about the arrangements. Roger had told her the trips were strictly business. Like Cinderella at the ball, Kathy expected the midnight hour to turn her back into the ordinary secretary, but in the interim she would enjoy living the fairy tale.

Roger bought Kathy cocktail dresses and jewelry, even a fur stole. She wore them as they visited Detroit and Chicago and St. Louis every other month or so. The important Republican movers and shakers she met treated her as a VIP, though it was possible many of them knew the clandestine arrangement. Traveling with Roger gave her a status she thought she might come to enjoy if she allowed herself to do so.

Roger's goal, other than keeping Kathy happy, was to court influence and money that would help him win the election in 1968 for Representative Boyle's seat in Congress. Roger Gordon sought political favors wherever he could find them. When he was successful in garnering an endorsement or some cash for his campaign, he would be in a celebratory mood. Those weeks Kathy enjoyed dinners in fine restaurants—nights that included dancing and drinks with the newly recruited "friends."

—

In February 1968, Roger came dancing into their suite at the Palmer House in Chicago. "Avrum Tannenbaum has promised to pay my expenses to Miami Beach next August for the Republican National Convention, Kathy. That should put me on an inside track to RNC funds for my Congressional campaign.

Tannenbaum thinks I can help by using my contacts to elect a Republican to the White House this fall. Sky's the limit, Kathy. Go shop for a new outfit. We're meeting the Tannenbaums at the Palmer House for dinner to celebrate."

—

Joy and Avrum were perfect hosts; they spent lavish amounts, yet made their guests feel at home. Joy, fifty-three years old, looked like a woman in her early thirties. Her natural beauty shone because she ate right, exercised constantly, and took advantage of the cosmetic enhancements available to a well-to-do woman. She spent her time with charitable causes as befit the second wife of an important man. Avrum was a handsome, silver-haired, rather stout man who owned a couple investment companies and could afford to dress the picture of success.

Avrum knew Roger and his wife came from Parkersville, Ohio. He had invited them to dinner with an ulterior motive: to find out what he could about Joy's sister if this turned out to be the *right* Parkersville. In the course of the evening, after several rounds of drinks and a lavish dinner, Avrum brought up the fact that his wife had once lived in a town called Parkersville, but left as a small child. "She has recently discovered that part of her life through a letter her mother wrote on her deathbed. Are you acquainted with a woman named Matilda McEnroe?"

Kathy almost choked on her baked Alaska. She began to cough. Before she could speak she heard Roger say, "No. I think some people named McEnroe left Parkersville in the twenties. Father died of the flu, I think, and the mother moved away with her daughters."

Kathy stared at Roger. *What is he saying? He knows Mattie stayed in town, married Ron Connors. She's my sister-in-law.*

Roger gave Kathy a warning look, and suddenly glanced at his watch. "This dinner has been lovely, Avrum. It's a pleasure to have met you, Joy. I think I need to get Kathy back to the hotel room. She seems a bit under the weather."

With a hurried shuffle of his chair, Roger bowed to the company, grasped Kathy's arm, and led her out.

When they arrived at the room, Kathy exploded. "What was that all about? You know Mattie. Why did you deny it?"

"Think about it, Kathy. Do you want Tannenbaums coming to Parkersville and meeting Rhonda? I certainly don't. Better to steer them away with a little misdirection."

—

As the Tannenbaums drove their Cadillac Eldorado back to their home in Wilmette, Joy turned to Avrum with a bewildered look. "You knew they were from Parkersville and you didn't tell me. I thought we agreed that I wasn't going to look into that part of my past. At least not yet."

"That's what you said when you read your mother's letter last Christmas, but I think you do want to know what's happened to your sister. It's been weighing more on your mind than you want to admit." Avrum put his arm around his wife and pulled her across the seat to snuggle beside him as they drove home.

"Well, in any case, it didn't work out, did it? My sister left town not long after Mother and I did, apparently. You were right, though. I was curious and half-excited when you asked the question."

"Don't be so sure it was a dead end, Joy. Did you notice how Roger was so anxious to get his wife out of there once the topic came up? I have a feeling there's more there than they admitted."

"Whatever do you mean, Av? Do you think Kathy knows Matilda McEnroe and Roger wanted to keep her silent?"

"It's a stretch, I know. Maybe I read too many detective stories, but something doesn't seem quite right about the evening. Do you think I should follow up with Roger on the phone tomorrow?"

Joy considered for a moment. What if this turned out to be a simple way to learn about her past? Wouldn't it be better to take this opportunity? "I think I'm not sure—but I think asking Roger will get you nowhere. Kathy may know more. Do you have any way to reach her without going through her husband?"

"My friends in the Ohio Republican State Committee may be able to tell me more. I can check with them."

That night Joy sat up long after Avrum had retired, trying to imagine the sister she didn't remember. She had thought it better not to pry into a long-dead relationship. Her mother's letter hinted the abandoned little girl, the one left behind, had been unpleasant and rebellious. Now that Joy was settled into an affluent life, seeking out the sister might bring trouble.

The next evening Avrum came home, his eyes flashing with a mysterious gleam. "Today I learned that we have not yet met the real Mrs. Gordon," he told Joy.

"What do you mean? How did you learn that?"

"My friend, Max Thurber, informed me that Mrs. Roger Gordon is named Rhonda, not Kathy. Something fishy is going on here."

"Are they still around? Still staying at the Palmer House?"

"No, that's another strange thing. They checked out in a hurry this morning. I called the hotel after talking to Max. They had already gone."

"So, where does that leave my quest? Can we—should we—try to go to Parkersville after all? I'm a bit afraid of stirring up a hornet's nest, if my sister turns out to be vengeful."

"Whatever you think, sweetheart. Think it over and let me know if you want me to pursue the search."

54

Mattie

Have another brownie. This next part might seem boring, but I need to tell it. Months passed with little improvement in Ron's condition despite Kathy's prayers and Dr. Martin's medicine. Some days Ron seemed almost normal and I was encouraged, but those days were getting fewer and farther apart. He withdrew more often. Simple things, patterns, noises confused him. Ron seemed better on days when I didn't turn on the television at all.

I thanked God for the children's books I had read to Aaron, Mark, Ed, and to my grandchildren in turn. Ron liked looking at the pictures with the children, though I began to suspect he didn't remember their names.

I read him some of my Billy Bunny stories. The Wheeling Times-Leader had printed some as I sent them in with my column. I had even sent a few off to some children's magazines. When I read them to Ron, he nodded and smiled. Time dragged, and yet, it also flew by.

Christmas 1967 – Spring 1968

It was Christmas again. I set up the tree, placing the star myself. Kathy and Eddie came for Christmas dinner, but it was nothing like the festivities we used to have. Aaron, Joan and the kids, and Patty and her three came as well. Eddie had returned to Parkersville after mustering out of the navy and was looking for work. At the end of World War II, the nation treated returning vets as heroes. Not so for Eddie or other Vietnam veterans. He found work at C & D Construction Company. He began writing letters and flyers imploring government officials to end the war.

Kathy and I had been working at being friends again. It was an effort for both of us, I think, but worth it. Ron still seemed to be more relaxed when she was around. She was traveling with Roger on some of his political forays, sometimes for a couple weeks. Our conversations were awkward when I asked her about her travels, so I stopped asking. We avoided talk about politics, with another election year at hand.

With everyone there for Christmas dinner, it seemed to be a strain for Ron. Eddie talked about Sophie and Brett nonstop. I could see the topic made Kathy uncomfortable.

When Aaron changed the topic to events in Vietnam, Eddie jumped in to offer his views. He pounded the table and took a deep breath. His words tumbled out. "This war is a war where our country is trying to impose its will on the people in another part of the world. A lot of people are dying—our own service men and people over there in Vietnam—in some villages innocent people and children are being killed."

"Your father died in a war to preserve democracy," Kathy said. "I don't think you should take that lightly."

"Dr. King is convinced, and he has convinced me, the war in Vietnam is one of the most unjust wars that has ever been fought in the history of the world."

Kathy asked him, "How can you say that? I know Dr. King has been a huge force in stirring up racial issues. But is he an expert on war?"

"He says we are spending $500,000 to kill every Viet Cong soldier, while we spend a pitiful $53 a year on each person in this country characterized as poverty-stricken. Where are our priorities?

"Some of my comrades brought medicine and candy to orphans. I watched others destroying villages and murdering innocent women and children."

I recalled the commercial of the little girl with the daisy. "President John-son's 1964 ad scared people away from Senator Goldwater, saying he would begin a nuclear holocaust. Yet the situation seems to be leading there anyway."

"Well, at least this year some Democrats are opposing the war. President Johnson will have a fight on his hands if he wants to gain the nomination again," Aaron said. Our conversation was getting heated and suddenly Ron began to yell, responding to the raised voices. I took him over to the couch to lie down. The company made excuses to leave early.

—

Aaron was prophetic. On March 31, 1968, President Lyndon Johnson addressed the nation about Vietnam and the ongoing struggle. I sat watching our TV, the volume tuned low so it wouldn't bother Ron as he slept in his reclining chair. President Johnson spoke for a half hour about the lives lost and costs to the nation and the world. He proposed limiting American bombing and invited the North Vietnamese to come to talks to settle the conflict. Then he surprised everyone with these words:

> *With America's sons in the fields far away, with America's future under challenge right here at home, with our hopes and the world's hopes for peace in the balance every day, I do not believe that I should devote an hour or a day of my time to any personal partisan causes or to any duties other than the awesome duties of this office—the Presidency of your country. Accordingly, I shall not seek, and I will not accept, the nomination of my party for another term as your President.*

His words surprised me. I phoned Aaron. "What did you hear the president saying this evening?"

After some silence, Aaron said, "In this election year the Vietnam War is more unpopular than ever. Democratic candidates who want to end the war are entering the presidential race. Johnson just said he won't try for reelection, but will dedicate his time to ending the conflict in Southeast Asia."

"That's what I heard him say. I hope he can turn things around with that resolve. Eddie's doing all he can to tell people this war is evil."

55

Eddie, Sophie, and Kathy
SPRING 1968

As Eddie and Sophie grew closer they began to talk in earnest about the possibility of spending their lives together. Still, Sophie sensed that she was not welcome in Kathy's house, though her brother had been a frequent visitor there in the past. They had argued about his mother's attitude on several previous occasions, but it hadn't mattered when the bond between them was mere friendship. Now that Eddie was getting more serious about what their future might hold, Sophie was reluctant for him to say a word to Kathy.

"I know Mom is slow to accept, Soph, but she'll come around. She's hesitant to accept new ideas because of her upbringing. You know the old ways were meant to keep people apart, if they didn't share the same common background. Everyone in his 'own place.'"

"I know what you're saying, Eddie. Don't forget I've lived in Mississippi. But Parkersville has been a more accepting place in the past. Even so, I don't think they're ready to accept our marriage. Minds are pretty well set against such a thing. If we would be satisfied with carrying on a secret affair it might be more acceptable. But marriage between races...not so much."

"Mom will come around once she sees I'm determined to marry you."

"I'm not so sure. She's already lost your father, and now it looks like she's losing her lover. She won't want to lose you as well."

"Lover? What are you talking about? My mom doesn't have a lover."

"You're kidding, Eddie. Everyone knows that your uncle Ron has been her lover for years. Ever since your daddy died. They were discreet about it, but it got around the town nonetheless."

"Never! You're wrong, Sophie. They never—"

"Didn't your uncle Ron spend lots of his early mornings at your house when you were growing up? I used to watch him stop by around 5:00 a.m. when I was working with my mom for the Hansons—taking care of their kids. Kitchen lights would come on around six, after a little hanky-panky in the bedroom, I'm sure. Surely you wondered why Uncle Ron was always there for breakfast."

"I'm not going to listen to any more of this. You're just plain wrong, Sophie. I can't believe my mother and Uncle Ron were any more than friends."

"Well, I'll not argue with you. I could be wrong."

—

Eddie could not bring himself to believe Sophie's words. They didn't discuss her revelation again, but they spent many hours discussing the issue that had precipitated it: would Kathy accept Sophie as a daughter-in-law?

"It's the law of the land, you know, that we have the right to marry. The Supreme Court decided in *Loving v. Virginia* last year by a 9-0 vote. No one can be kept from marriage because two different races are involved."

"All that may be true, Mr. Lawyer Connors, but the Lovings were arrested and spent time in jail before the Supreme Court acted."

"You know Ohio law has never been like the laws in the Deep South in any case."

"People don't necessarily accept it, Eddie. And your mother certainly will not approve."

It was a running argument between them. Confusion about the war and about his romantic attachment to Sophie exhausted Eddie. His mind kept coming back to their recent conversation. *It can't be true that there was anything between Uncle Ron and my mom! It just can't. I know how these rumors start and won't die, but that can't be true. I'll just ask Mom about it. I don't want to say Sophie told me. That'll just make Mom more hostile to her.*

Eddie decided to take his mother on a drive out to lunch in Zanesville. She liked the Chinese restaurant there, so he suggested either her Wednesday afternoon off or Saturday.

—

Kathy had been mulling over her last trip with Roger. It had ended abruptly and on a sour note. They returned to Parkersville earlier than they had planned. The whole return trip had been made in silence. Once back in the office Roger tried to act as though nothing had changed, but in Kathy's mind everything had. She disdainfully refused Roger's offer of a "business trip" to Louisville. Kathy went about her office duties with her usual efficiency, but concentrated on business matters. She still pondered what she should do with the new knowledge that Mattie's sister was living in Chicago.

All this was on her mind when Eddie invited her to lunch in Zanesville. She wondered if she should ask Eddie what he thought she should do. She had also noticed Eddie's attraction to Sophie, but she had been hoping it would pass. Now she was actually beginning to think that maybe Sophie would be a good match for her son. She wondered if Eddie's invitation to lunch would reveal how serious the two young people were.

The next Saturday, February 24, sitting down to a savory bowl of egg drop soup in the Zanesville restaurant, Eddie deliberated what to say. As the meal progressed, Eddie's nerve steeled him to raise what was on his mind.

"Mom, I heard some conversation the other day in the barber shop. Those gossipy old geysers were talking about Uncle Ron's illness. One of the guys said something about you and Uncle Ron being more than friends."

Kathy almost choked on her egg foo yong. Then she smiled a mysterious smile. She sighed. "It's true, *Liebchen*. For a short while after your father died I took my comfort from Uncle Ron. It's a long story, dear, a complicated one."

Now it was Eddie's turn to choke. They continued eating in silence, Kathy in a pensive mood letting her thoughts wander to happier times with Ron, and Eddie concentrating on his meal. Furtively, he snuck a look. The Mona Lisa smile on his mother's face distressed him. They concluded what now seemed a tasteless lunch. Eddie hurried to pay the bill. He took Kathy's arm to lead her outside. As they came out into the sunshine, Eddie shook his head. He drove her home and entered her house, still saying nothing. Unsure of what he could or should say, he sank into her sofa, muttering, "I can't believe it, Mom. You and Uncle Ron?"

"You were so little and I was so lost. After we got the navy department telegram announcing your father's death, my world shattered. I had no idea where to turn. I did nothing but take to my bed, relying on others to take care of you. I left the phone off the hook. I wouldn't answer the door. After a time Uncle Ron came over and let himself into the apartment.

"I lay in bed, curled up, crying. I must have looked a mess. My eyes swollen red.

"I remember Ron said, 'I've lost a brother, too.'

"Josh and I had so much planned for the future. 'What am I to do?' I cried out to Ron. 'I feel as though there is no future for me now.'

"Uncle Ron started to reassure me. All of a sudden he was crying, too. I hadn't expected that. I'm sure he hadn't either. I stood up to guide him to my bed to sit. I thought I was almost out of tears, but they flowed again. I held onto Ron and he held onto me. We fell back on the bed, crying and trying to comfort each other."

Eddie shuffled his feet at the image. But Kathy's gaze was off in space as she relived that encounter.

"I had been denying the facts laid out in that telegram. Lying with Ron, I realized that denial was doing me no good. Uncle Ron must have known he too needed to give up the pain of Josh's death. We lay together for a long time. I relaxed at last, and fell into a deep sleep, a much-needed sleep. Ron's coming to see me was like lancing a boil, I think. The bitterness and anger were all bottled up, needing to be released. That day was the turning point for me.

"Later—how many hours later I have no way of knowing—I awoke. Ron was still beside me. His face reminded me of Josh. At first I thought it was Josh in bed with me. As I came to realize it was Josh's brother there, I sprang up. I rushed into the bathroom to check the mirror to be sure I was still Kathy. What was I to do?

"I showered, for the first time in a week or more. I dressed in my gray suit and madras blouse, the last thing I had worn before the telegram came. I was afraid to wake Ron. I went to the kitchen to put on some coffee. That was the last pot of coffee I ever made for myself. I wanted to get away from the Kathy who had been with Ron. I've drunk tea ever since. I called Mr. Gordon. I told him I would like to return to work."

Eddie was trying to take it all in. Uncle Ron was a beloved figure in his life. Sophie's comments had seemed so outrageous, but his mother's words confirmed everything.

"I didn't know what I would say to Ron. He was waiting for me, needing comfort himself and offering me support. He wanted to be in *our* lives—in our lives, yours and mine—as a father substitute. He'd done so much for you, the baby and toddler, for you had stayed with him and Aunt Mattie as I worked at the law firm. He promised to come to be there for you. Was that so wrong?"

Kathy's didn't expect an answer to the question. Eddie sat numb, saying nothing.

"We started out as friends, comrades with a single purpose, to provide for your needs growing up. Ron would bring you to the house from Mattie's when I got back from work. He'd sit for a cup of tea. We would talk about you and the world and life.

"Aunt Mattie's church and her causes kept her busy. She had Cub Scouts and hospital volunteering and Girl Scout day camp and vacation Bible school, though she continued to care for you every day while I worked. Ron and I grew closer. He would come by many mornings, before you woke up, and talk to me—and lie with me sometimes. I had needs, Eddie, physical needs, and Uncle Ron did, too. We found comfort in each other's bodies."

"Mom!" Eddie jumped up and paced a few steps, shaking his head to dislodge the uncomfortable image.

"I know you're shocked to think of your parents—old people—with physical needs, but we did have them. I had nothing except your uncle. For him, he had a quiet refuge from the busyness of his home—two teenage boys and a distracted wife."

"What did Aunt Mattie think about all this?"

"I'm not really sure. I never spoke to her about it until after Uncle Ron was obviously ill. On some level I think she knew for a while. At least she realized Ron was spending time with me. When she suspected it, I guess she considered her options. Would divorce be a solution? I don't think so. I knew I was just 'borrowing' his life when I was most vulnerable. Nothing permanent could change for me."

"Mom, I just can't believe what you're telling me. How long did this go on?"

"For a few years, I think. I can't tell you precisely when it ended. Before Ida Sue's birth. Mattie, the wife, claimed him in the end. He told me he had promised her we would not spend any more time together. But we drifted back into the old patterns. It took me until your father's navy friend, Butch Nelson, came around in 1960, to gain the courage to send Ron away altogether."

Kathy looked at her son with pity. *A lot to take in all at once,* she imagined. *Might as well finish the story.*

"And you will probably hear those old gossips in the barber shop talk about me with Mr. Gordon. That's true, too, but I am ready to end that right now. Roger is far too interested in his political career. I found that out on our trip to Chicago. Eddie, you'll never guess who I met there!"

Eddie looked at his mother in disbelief. He was still trying to take in the idea that she and Uncle Ron had been lovers. Now she was telling him she also had a relationship with Roger Gordon.

Kathy didn't seem to notice his shock. She continued in an excited voice, "I met Aunt Mattie's sister. Joy Tannenbaum, the wife of the Chicago investor we went to see, is Mattie's sister Joy. Joy didn't even know until a short time ago she had a sister in Parkersville. She was so little when her mother took her to Texas. Mattie's mother recently died, and just before she did she wrote to Joy about their beginnings in Ohio."

"Seriously, Mom? You aren't making this up?"

"Now why would I do that? I really did meet her. Only now I don't know what to say to Mattie about it."

Diverted by this new information, Eddie considered how his aunt might react to the news. "I think you should just tell her, Mom, and see what she wants to do next. Do you have Joy's phone number and address?"

"Roger would be livid. But, you know what? I don't care what Roger thinks now. Our affair is over in any case. And I would like to do something to bring some happiness to Mattie, after all she has been through."

—

Kathy's resolve prompted her to act at once. She called Avrum Tannenbaum's Chicago office on Monday morning and asked the secretary how she might get in touch with Joy. Avrum came to the phone and Kathy told him, "I have some information about your wife's sister. She does still live in Parkersville. She's married to my brother-in-law; they have two sons and five grandchildren."

"Your sister-in-law? Related to Roger?"

"No, I'm not married to Roger. That's all a sham. I'm a widow. I work as Roger's secretary in the law office. I was his mistress, but that's over. I know that Joy would love her sister. It would make Mattie so happy to know Joy is well. Can you come to Parkersville to meet Mattie?"

Avrum was delighted that he'd been right—Kathy did know more than she'd said at dinner. He arranged for Joy and himself to make a train trip to Parkersville the next week.

—

Kathy decided to be direct with Roger about the visit she'd arranged. "They know we aren't married, Roger. In fact, Avrum had already found out from one of his Republican cronies, but I don't think they'll make a fuss when they come. You can even introduce them to Rhonda if you wish, and they'll be discreet. They're so excited about finding and meeting Mattie. They might hold it against you that you tried to keep the sisters apart, but it doesn't matter. A happy reunion is about to take place."

56

⁓

Mattie

Mercy me. We've sat here all afternoon. Too much to tell you that has been unsaid so long. I am so thankful, Joy, that we did get together after all. I'm so glad you finally got the letter from Mama, and that you were looking for me as I had been looking for you.

March 24, 1968

Ron needed more and more help to cope with whatever was going on in his brain. I still wanted Ron to get out whenever we could arrange it. He seemed to have no sense of balance, so we transported him in a wheelchair. I still took him to church, where we sat in the back of the sanctuary. He enjoyed the music and the cadence of the pastor's voice. As for the sense of the words, it passed him by.

From one day to the next, Ron's memory was unpredictable, but anyone could see it continued to fail. I tried to keep up with the routines we had lived by, but it became harder each day. When old friends came to visit, Ron stared blankly as he sat in his own world. Each day I tried to start fresh.

Monday, March 24, 1968—I'll never forget that day. I went in to get Ron ready for company. Though Ron had not spoken for several days, I put on a bright smile and went into his room to help him up. "Good morning, darling. Did you sleep well?"

Ron's blank expression hurt me, but I continued to open the drapes and bustle about the room. "This morning we'll get ready for company. Kathy called and she's coming over to visit us. I don't quite know why."

Ron mumbled, "Kathy?" and I swirled to look at him. I was encouraged to hear his voice once again. Perhaps the long-ago memories were more accessible to Ron than what happened yesterday.

"Yes, dear. Kathy," I said. "You remember when Josh first brought her to Parkersville? Nearly thirty years ago."

"Kathy," Ron mumbled again as I helped him into dry clothes. I moved him to his chair and stripped the bed. Then I wheeled him into the kitchen to feed him his breakfast of scrambled eggs and toast. After I straightened up the kitchen I sat down at the typewriter to prepare my daily news submission. I wondered again why Kathy had been so excited when she called asking for a visit.

She came in, more animated than I had seen her for a long time. She'd barely removed her coat before she danced over to me.

"I have something important to tell you, Mattie. I've met your sister, Joy. She lives in Chicago, now, and she's looking for you."

"What? What are you saying? You've met Joy? How do you know it's her?"

Kathy began to explain what she had learned on her trip with Roger. "She didn't even remember she had had a life here. I'm sorry to tell you your mother is dead. She died of cancer last year. But before she died she wrote a letter to Joy telling her about you and Parkersville. Joy had never heard about you or her family here until she received that letter. She was trying to decide what she should do when Roger and I met her in Chicago."

"My mother dead?" I paused, trying to process all that Kathy was telling me. *I always knew Mama might be dead, but I still hoped she was alive and could tell me why she left me. If I'd only known she was ill. I could've gone to her.*

Kathy hurried on with her news. "I called Joy and her husband and told them you are here. They'll be coming down next week."

"Coming here? Really coming here? Oh, Kathy, I can't believe it. After all these years..." I hugged her. "I'm so sorry about Mother. But to reunite with Joy will be wonderful! To think I'll talk to her at last!"

—

The next Sunday evening you and Avrum took the night train to Parkersville, arriving Monday morning at 5:00 a.m. Kathy met you at the station and drove you to our house, where I was trying to be patient. I straightened the house once again. I set the dining room table with my best dishes.

"My sister's coming, Ron. Joy is coming. I never thought I'd see her again and now she's coming here. I wish you were able to talk to her so she could know you as you used to be."

"Yoo-hoo, Mattie. We're here," yelled Kathy. I turned to see her push open the door and escort you in. I was so excited I was ready to faint.

We embraced the instant we saw each other. No one ever told us as children that we looked alike, but your husband took one look at us together and commented, "Anyone could see you're sisters! The same nose, eyes, and mouth shape."

You with your platinum blonde hair and svelte figure looked years younger than I, I know, but I did see myself in certain ways you held your head and smiled.

You introduced Avrum. "He's responsible for pushing me to seek you out. Kathy, thank you again for bringing us together."

"And this is Ron," I said, introducing him to you. "He's retired now. You're too late to know him as he was." Ron smiled then, surprising me, for he seldom did it these days. I wonder if he thought, looking at you, he was seeing me as I had been. The expression was momentary, but I took it as a good sign.

"I'm so sorry to be this long in getting here. I didn't remember Parkersville at all. When I read Mother's letter, I tried hard to picture you, and I seemed to remember a big sister telling me stories. Bunnies that talked, I think."

I laughed in delight. "Billy Bunny! I've been making up those stories forever. I told them to my boys and my nephew and my grandchildren. I even sold a few to the papers and some children's magazines."

"Oh, Mattie. I wish Mother had told me years ago about you. I'd have found you. We could have done so many things together," you told me.

"When I was little Aunt Susan had me send Mother letters every year on my birthday. The single letter I ever got from Mother I received as a ten-year-old. After that I didn't send any more." I started crying as I remembered I had thrown away that letter. Luckily Aunt Susan found it and preserved it in Papa's Bible. "I was so sure she didn't love me. I couldn't understand it."

"Mother was convinced you were better off to have stayed behind. She even wished she had taken you and left me." You reached into your purse for Mother's letter to you. "She saved your letters, though. She included them in the letter she wrote me. You can read it for yourself."

For a while I sat and read what Mama had written. Years of wondering slipped away. I so wish she had written to me! We missed so much that we might have said to each other. She never met Ron or the boys or the grandchildren. It was her loss, but it was mine as well.

Remember, I told you about Ellen Nelson, how I thought she might be you. After our reunion I wrote her saying you were found at last. She wants to get together with you sometime.

I know you, too, were glad to find out about the family you are a part of. We were both talking at once, mixing tears and laughter.

I'm sorry about all those years we missed growing up together, years when we each were finding ourselves and becoming the women we are today. God's blessing in each of our lives has been apparent. In one sense, we found each other just in time—in time to share good times and bad together instead of apart.

57

Death
APRIL 5, 1968

The day after Dr. Martin Luther King, Jr., was assassinated in Memphis, Tennessee, angry riots filled the streets in cities around the country. Emotions erupted as fear and uncertainty gripped the nation. Mattie watched television coverage the next morning with the volume lowered so it wouldn't disturb Ron in his chair. She was startled by an image from a crowd scene, and she went to the phone to call Kathy.

"Kathy, I thought I saw Dar Jones on television in the news this morning."

"Dar? Was he rioting?"

"No, if it was him he was part of a Black Panther guard unit in Indianapolis where Senator Kennedy was speaking. Kennedy had to break the news of Dr. King's death to the crowd at his rally."

"Eddie told me Dar is a member of the Black Panthers now, so it could be him. Eddie gets his news through Sophie. I don't think Dar and Eddie are speaking right now."

"Senator Kennedy was urging his hearers to 'replace violence with an effort to understanding, compassion, and love...' It doesn't look like people are listening. The Black Panther guardsmen were trying to keep peace."

"Mattie, Eddie's trying to understand the Black Panthers and his friend Dar. Eddie told me they serve meals to children and work in a lot of community programs that alleviate poverty and improve health for Negroes."

A small groan escaped Ron's lips. Mattie looked over at him. His face and arm suddenly went limp. He slumped over in the chair. "Kathy, I'm hanging up. I have to call Dr. Dunn. Something's wrong with Ron."

Dr. Dunn arrived within ten minutes. Ron had suffered a fatal stroke. With a sad shake of his head, Dr. Dunn turned to Mattie.

"I'm so sorry, Mattie. There's nothing to be done for him."

"No, not for a long time," Mattie acknowledged. "He's been dying by inches."

—

April 7 was declared a national day of mourning for Dr. King. President Johnson spoke to the nation on the television, urging people to stay calm. Prayers and tears nationwide did not stop the rioting until it ran its course. Eddie, as he listened to the news, worried again about Dar's part in the violence.

—

While the rest of the country mourned Dr. King, Parkersville's focus was on the funeral of Ronald Connors, former letter carrier, former Scoutmaster, former city councilman. The evening before, Mark decided he could not bring himself to attend the funeral or the visitation. Late that evening he called Mr. Hanson to ask to sit with his father's body for a while. He wanted to say goodbye to his dad. Sitting beside Ron's coffin, Mark poured out his thoughts, seeking to justify himself, hoping his father's spirit would absolve him of his guilt.

"I'm sorry, Dad. I know I got carried away when I first met Frank Andrews and went out to their farm. I met Julie, who was totally impressed by all the things I knew. She had an ailing father, a ne'er-do-well brother, and a farm that needed help. I thought I would help her and her family out. She called my idea, and me, 'cool.'

"We listened to a lot of Beatles songs and Bob Dylan and just hung out. It seemed like we were soul mates. It was time for me to take my life into my own hands, not do whatever Mom or Patty told me to do. I didn't much give a damn what anyone else thought about me." Mark glanced at his father, but Ron still lay quietly.

"Julie's brother Frank was a stupid jackass. Frank talked his dad into signing with the coal company. When Frank collected the down payment, he went out to Vegas to try to make a stake. He didn't, but he thought he would stay out there, so Julie, her dad, and I were left on the farm, with orders to move out before the next spring when Ohio Coal would be ready to mine."

Mark paused, gathering his thoughts. "Julie blew the whole thing off. 'So what,' she said. 'Why should we stick around here anyway? Let's pack a bag and head out to the coast. That's where things are happening.' About then I sobered up. Julie was going off the deep end, hanging with a bunch of younger hippies, and didn't seem to remember what we had started on with the organic farm idea. She told me I was too straight for even thinking along those lines. She was headed west, with or without me. When her friends came by with their tricked-out van, I could've gone. I almost did. Oddly, her dad said he'd join up with them. 'You can come, or not,' she told me. 'You're too middle class. Loosen up. We can have a blast in California.'"

Mark's gaze went out the window as he pictured the psychedelic van and Julie waving goodbye. "I thought about Patty and the kids. I even thought about you and Mom. I wondered if maybe Mom was onto something with her middle-class ideas. She wouldn't get anywhere fighting the coal company, but maybe there was a chance to get some serious reclamation of the land when they were done looting it for the coal. I could even be a part of that. I wonder if Patty would ever take me back?"

—

The next day many friends swelled the crowd of mourners at Ron's funeral. Mattie and Kathy sat together at the church, celebrating the Resurrection of Jesus and the life of His servant, Ron. Patty and her children, Joan and Aaron and their children, accepted the condolences of friends and neighbors. Mayor Reed gave a eulogy about Ron's service to the community. Joy and Avrum Tannenbaum came, for with Joy's reunion with her long-lost sister she sought to extend comfort as she had not been able to do over the years. Roger Gordon came with his wife Rhonda, but stayed only for the church service and then left by the side door. He avoided seeing the Tannenbaums. The Jones family, Brenda, Sophie, and Brett, attended the service with Eddie, but Dar was absent. Eddie told Sophie about how his friendship with Dar started. Eddie was picturing his uncle walking the streets of gold and indulging in "good things to eat." "I know his memory and his body are restored now, as he enjoys God's presence. My dad, and yours, Sophie, are there in the welcoming throng. There's peace there, though we still struggle here."

58

—

Mattie

A few days after Ron's funeral, Mark called me. He had asked Patty to consider taking him back. She told him to make peace with me and with the children. Only then would she think it over.

April 10, 1968

That evening Mark sat down with me in the kitchen where I poured him some coffee. For a while we sat without speaking, each wrapped in thought.

I finally broke the silence. "Mark, you know my mother, your grandmother Alice, left me with Aunt Susan and Uncle Bob and took Joy off to Texas when I was only six—after Grampa Jake died." My eyes filled with tears, but I managed to keep them from overflowing. I dabbed my eyes with my handkerchief. The catch in my voice kept me from going on.

Mark looked at me with tears in his eyes as well. "I knew that. But until now, I hadn't thought about the feelings of abandonment you must have faced then. You must think of me as one more person who abandoned you."

I could see Mark had done a lot of soul-searching over the last little while.

"Mom, I'm sorry about what I said to you. You've been a wonderful mother, but I've been a terrible son."

It was my turn to try to explain. "When my mother left me, I knew it was because I was a terrible daughter. But I see I was wrong. My reunion with Joy has helped me understand. It was just too hard on Mama to carry on with her life and raise two daughters as a single woman alone in the world. Aunt Susan convinced her that Uncle Bob and she could raise me better that Mama would have been able to.

"As I grew up, I swore I would never leave my children, no matter the circumstances. Perhaps I didn't let you make your own mistakes. I guess when you left Patty, you were, at least in part, trying to show me that you were grown up and *could* make choices, even if I didn't approve—maybe *because* I didn't approve."

Mark looked at me. He shook his head. "I don't think that's so, Mom, but I'll think about what you've said. I was foolish, and I made a foolish choice. Julie had me thinking I was better than I was, more appreciated than I had ever been. That's all over, no matter what Patty decides about taking me back. I made a mistake to leave Patty. I'll work the rest of my life to make it up to her and the kids. I want to make it up to you, too. Please forgive me."

"I learned a lesson, too, Mark, over the past few years. I know I can't control circumstance in my own life, let alone in the lives of those around me. I don't know what the future will bring for any of us. I do know that it's all in God's hands, though. Like Paul, I'm content. If there's anything to forgive about your outburst to me, I do forgive you. I love you. I hope you and Patty can figure out what is right for you both."

Mark rose and came around the table. He knelt by my chair. He put his head in my lap like he used to as a little boy.

"I truly blew it, Mom. I'll try to make it up to all of you."

"You need to know things won't be the same as before. We can hope that in some new way they'll be right again. The Gospel of John tells us that Jesus told his disciples, 'In the world you have tribulation; but be of good cheer, I have overcome the world.' "

Mark looked up at me beaming. He embraced me, almost squeezing the breath out of me. He left whistling "We Shall Overcome." I smiled and breathed a prayer of thanks.

59

May 1968

Patty arranged for Mark to talk to the children one at a time. Roy and Jake were able to see their father's actions as something in the past they could forgive, if not forget. Annie, who empathized with her mother's and her grandmother's hurt, was less ready to accept Mark back into her life. At thirteen, an age where her friends' opinions were so important, she called her best friend, Sarah, to plan what she might say when her father approached her.

"What should I say to Dad, Sarah? When I told Gram Dad was leaving, she about had a fit. She had to sit down to catch her breath. At first she didn't believe me. You know my grandmother! She's always trying so hard to help everyone have sympathy for other people's points of view."

"I know she's like that. My mom says your grandmother would make excuses for the Devil. What did she say?"

Annie put on her best grandmother face, raised her voice an octave, pinched her lips, and said, " 'Your father has had some difficult times in his life, Annie. He didn't get the educational opportunities your uncle Aaron had. He had to go to work to support your mom and little Roy. He had to take his classes at night.' I know Gram didn't approve of his choice any more than I did, or Mom did, but there she was making excuses for him. She said someday Dad would change his mind. Now that he has, I'm not so sure that this is a good thing."

"You and your brothers and your mom are getting on all right without him. But between having a father there and not having one—I know what I would choose. What are you going to do?"

"Well, I asked Mom what she thinks I should do. She took a long time to answer me, and I don't blame her for that. She said Dad is 'repenting,' like the Bible says. She wants to give him the chance to show he has changed. I guess if

Mom's willing to give him another chance, I should be, too."

"I hope it'll help make your grandmother happy. She never even bakes cookies any more. Maybe we should bake some cookies at my house to take to your grandmother. Wouldn't she be surprised?"

Giggling, relieved that there was some action she could take, Annie went with Sarah to bake some peanut butter cookies. The two girls were rewarded by the broad smile on Mattie's face when she was presented with their love offering.

—

When Patty had talked to the children, she told Mark he was still on trial. He moved to an apartment in Parkersville, and he went to work over at the reclamation site where the Ohio Coal Company had finished mining. It was a good role for him, for it used his skills and engaged his interest. The hard, yet satisfying work made him feel useful again. When he wasn't working, he was courting Patty harder than ever. In due time Patty saw the changes in him, and Mark convinced all concerned—even Annie—to give him a second chance to be a good father, husband, and son.

—

Eddie, as he was growing closer to Sophie and her son, wanted to share some of the things he loved with them. He told them of the stories his aunt Mattie had made up, and he searched out the old fairy tale book his mother had read to him as a child. Brett came to love the stories as well.

Late in May Eddie was taking Sophie and Brett out for a spin in his mother's car—the Magic Carriage, they called it. Eddie thought it might be interesting to drive his uncle's old mail route to show them the sights. Brett was delighted with the rolling hills, so Eddie stepped on the gas. "It's like a roller coaster ride, but this is more fun," Brett exclaimed. "Grampa Ron must have loved doing this every day."

Soon they came to Egypt Valley and saw the Giant Earth Mover, the coal company's GEM, taller than a ten-story building, working to lift the tops of the hills off the coal veins.

"Wow!" Brett shouted with excitement. "That's a real giant. Imagine a tailor taking that monster on!"

Eddie laughed as he recalled the fairy tale they had read the previous day of the giant and the tailor. "You're right there! A couple of pickup trucks could fit inside that bucket with room to spare. It could truly rip up a 'whole forest at once, with one stroke. The whole forest, young and old, with all that is there, both rough and smooth.' "

"It's a monster, for sure," Sophie said, realizing Brett had no sense of the devastation to the land it represented.

60

1968

More trouble was still to come in 1968 for the rest of the country. Robert Kennedy was himself murdered. Civil rights conflicts were constant.

The Republican Party met in Miami Beach on August 8 and nominated Richard Milhous Nixon and Spiro Agnew to run for the White House. On August 25, the Democratic Party Convention in Chicago nominated Hubert Humphrey and Edmund Muskie. Bloody confrontations between police and demonstrators broke out in the streets of Chicago. Some 10,000 protestors, who were objecting to U.S. military involvement in Southeast Asia, attended a "Festival of Life" in Grant and Lincoln Parks with rock concerts, marijuana smoking, beach nude-ins, and draft-card burning. In all, 16,000 Chicago police, 4,000 state police, 7,500 army troops, and 4,000 national guardsmen brutally subdued the crowd. Governor George Wallace of Alabama ran as a third party candidate, declaring "segregation forever." In the election on November 5, Wallace took 13.5 percent of the popular vote, Humphrey 42.7 percent. Nixon, with 43.4 percent, won the Electoral College and became the thirty-seventh president of the United States. Roger Gordon was not elected to Congress, but defeated by his Democratic rival.

That fall the 1968 Summer Olympics in Mexico City saw two medal winners for the men's 200-meter race raise their black-gloved hands in a Black Power salute as they stood ready to receive their medals. The International Olympic Committee banned Tommie Smith and John Carlos from the Olympic Games for life.

One positive note for the year was that NASA was about to make good its mission to reach the moon and return safely before the end of the decade.

To accomplish this would be a powerful affirmation of America's strength—and after a divisive decade, perhaps a way to bring people together.

Excitement over the upcoming moon shot was filling the schools. Eddie had always encouraged Brett in his dream of becoming an astronaut. Brett and Annie's eighth-grade class had built a life-size model of the capsule that would land on the moon the next summer and, at least in Parkersville, a girl and a black boy could take the role the nation had so far assigned only to white males.

61

Mattie

1968 *had been a very difficult year. But it was the year I finally found you, Joy, and whatever else happened, that was the most important thing in my world. That and Mark returning. And Annie and Sarah bringing me cookies. And Aaron being close and enjoying his schooling, and, and, and. It was even more delightful when I was able to help with the wedding.*

Christmas 1968

Throughout 1968 Eddie had been courting Sophie, trying to convince both her and his mother they could form a cohesive family unit with Brett. By Thanksgiving Eddie's sales pitch closed the deal. Sophie Jones and Edmond Connors celebrated a small but joyous ceremony in my living room with Annie and Brett serving as attendants, and both their mothers, Brenda and Kathy, embracing the couple. Sophie looked stunning in her colorful minidress, blocks of bright red, green, blue, and yellow in a Mondrian pattern. Her lovely long legs in white boots to the knee completed the look. Annie wore a red knit mini and flats. Eddie and Brett wore patterned shirts with bell bottom trousers. We enjoyed seeing the couple against the background of poinsettia flowers I had placed by my fireplace. I served a simple supper of tea sandwiches followed by the wedding cake I baked.

As the couple left the house for a brief honeymoon, Kathy sat with Brenda and me. We were all sitting in silence until Brenda ventured, "Wouldn't Brick be surprised to see his daughter's new husband?"

"If he could see how happy they are, he would be pleased," I said.

"Josh would approve, I'm sure," said Kathy. "He was so much more used to the beautiful varieties of people in the world than me. I'm sorry, Brenda, that I missed so many opportunities to be the friend I could have been."

"I'm sorry, too," Brenda said. "Now we're united by the marriage of our children. I hope we can get to know each other better."

"I wish Dar were here to witness this," I said.

Brenda nodded. "Both Sophie and Eddie wrote inviting him. He's still working out who he is. I hope he'll come to recognize how the world is changing. He thinks Black Power will speed up the change, but I'm not sure."

Kathy leaned over to hug Brenda once again. "I think Sophie and Brett will add true joy to Eddie's life. I worry about Dar and the Black Power movement. But when I consider how my own thoughts have changed over the years, I take comfort in that. I think Dar's good sense will win out in the end. There'll be a peaceful reconciliation between the two young men and across the nation. It might not happen for a while. For too long people have clung to old prejudices. I was one of them, but I missed out on so much by being closed minded. Dar will see that, too, I hope."

Brenda looked over at Brett and Annie, who were gobbling up more sandwiches as they went through the motions of clearing the table. "I see in those two young people a growing friendship without as many barriers as Eddie and Dar faced. I'm glad for them."

"Dar will remember who he is and how important he is to this newly formed family," I said. "I'm sure God has Dar safely in his care."

The next morning I sent the wedding announcement to the *Times Leader* and the *New Pittsburgh Constitution*.

July 21, 1969

So I've told you about what happened here over those years you've been absent. I kept thinking about you, only to discover that for so many years you didn't even know about me or Papa or life here in Parkersville. I'm so glad God brought us together. When you left with Mama, the only thing I thought about was how Papa would no longer be with me. Losing you and Mama was nothing in my mind compared to losing him. But through the years I realized that though Papa wouldn't return in this life, you were somewhere out there. We've come full circle, Joy. I longed to see you again, and now you're here.

Acknowledgements

Many thanks to many people are in order. John Miller, Norman Kolenbrander, Jaci Ray, and Robin Martin read early drafts and made many useful suggestions.

Margaret Winfield Sullivan has been a source of inspiration ever since we were freshman year roommates at The College of Wooster.

Kathryn Daugherty has been my writing partner for the past two years, as we each struggled to write our novels.

My housemate, Barb Ashton, an amazing photographer and documentarian, provided the photos for the cover and encouragement throughout the entire writing process.

Instructors at the University of Iowa Summer Writing Festival over the past four years inspired and critiqued my development: Hugh Ferrer, Sandra Scofield, Charles Holdefer, Eric Goodman, Susan Chehak, and Sharelle Moranville

My writing group, Marion County Writers Workshop in Knoxville, Iowa, was helpful at many points.

I received lots of ideas from posts on the Internet, especially Storyfix.com by Larry Brooks.

Hannah Crawford, my editor at the Write Place, brought just the right look and sound to the final manuscript. Alexis Thomas, from the Write Place, designed the cover and interior of the book.

For all my family and friends who encouraged me to keep going on the project and filled in for me at other tasks I should have been doing, myriads of thanks.

I hope all of you enjoy reading about these adventures.

CPSIA information can be obtained at www.ICGtesting.com
Printed in the USA
LVOW101418010713

340892LV00002B/13/P